THE RAKE & THE MAID

Lotte R. James

ISBN-13: 978-1793489746
ISBN-10: 1793489742

To all the villains I have loved, and to the man with the green eyes. I am writing again. But most importantly, to my mother, BB.

.

I.

Harcourt Sinclair was not a man accustomed to such difficulties when it came to the long-practiced art of seduction. It was meant to be a simple affair, quick, and delicate. Certainly nothing as complex and tedious as it had so far proven to be.

Harcourt gazed out of the window of his study, a scowl on his face that gave him the air of some infernal wraith hiding in the shadows. Which wasn't entirely far from the truth.

How was it that his oh-so-perfect plans, twenty years in the making, were now being thwarted by the very unexpected resolve and shrewdness of little Lady Lydia Mowbray?

It was his own fault really, he had underestimated the little thing. Petite, angelic blonde, with crystal blue eyes, delicate features and curves, a delightfully full, shapely mouth, she definitely looked like an easy target. *Easy prey...*

Only so far, she had been anything but, carefully countering his attempts, crafting her own enticements to ensure his continued interest. As if he could ever lose interest.

Little did she know she was only the small cog in a much grander scheme... Her ruin was not debatable; only how quickly he could manage it was.

Any doubts he had, needed to be squashed, and this messy affair concluded. Loathe as he was to admit it, it didn't help the matter that he actually *liked* the little creature.

Desired her, and wanted her in his bed. And every time she refused him only made his need greater. *Careful not to seem desperate...*

Raking his fingers through his unfashionably long dark curls, he sighed, hoping to find perhaps some divine inspiration among the throngs now ambling around Green Park, and the hordes of workers and gardeners milling about the new landscape therein. Desperation, or any hint thereof, was sure to scare her off. No, delicacy, always. *And jealousy...*

Why had he not thought of that before? Perhaps because he could think of no other, little Lady Lydia seemed to be invading his every thought... *Pull yourself together, damn you!*

Yes, his own disinterest was sure to peak her own he decided. The illusion of his disenchantment of her bountiful charms was sure to coax her straight into his arms. *Yes, perfect...*

Only now, he needed to find the bait, and set the trap. He couldn't just use anyone, either. *Delicacy, always.* Couldn't very well be another of the *ton*, that would take weeks to organize properly, and then there would be expectant families to wield off...

Out of the question.

Neither could it be one of his many acquaintances of the *demi-monde*, who were much too well known to even the most innocent debutantes. A common whore might suit, but then, to find a clean one, who did not instantly and with a sharp, perfunctory glance, give away her profession... That would be tricky. Not impossible, but tiresome.

Much like this entire business seemed to be becoming. *Tiresome.* He would certainly not refrain from using Lady Lydia well once he ensnared her, he was being put through far too much trouble for it to go unpunished.

And punishment would begin with his choice of bait. *Genius...*

Someone plain, simple, unremarkable in every possible way, to truly whet Lydia's jealousy. He could almost hear her now. *You would choose that wretched drab thing over me?*

Oh, yes. That would do. *Very nicely indeed.*

'Rawlings,' he bellowed towards the door. 'Rawlings!'

There was the sound of a scramble on the stairs, and in the

corridor, a few shouts and expletives, before his footman, Rawlings, threw open the door and rushed in, attempting to regain some manner of composure whilst red-faced and out of breath.

It was almost amusing; he had the look of mole on the verge of heart collapse.

Harcourt would have laughed if he had any attention to spare, but he had a mission.

'Yes, sir,' Rawlings squeaked, smoothing the few hirsute strands of grey hair on his head. 'What may I do for you, sir?'

'That housemaid,' Harcourt said gruffly. 'The plain one.'

'Which, sir?'

'Gods, it's not my job to remember them all,' Harcourt growled, waving his hands, trying to find the words to describe the unremarkable thing he had seen lurking about occasionally. 'The young one.'

'Miss Fortescue?'

'Good God, is that the creature's name? Most interesting thing about her.'

'What about her, sir,' Rawlings asked hesitantly, bringing Harcourt back to the room.

'Bring her here. I must speak with her.'

'Sir, if there are any concerns -'

'Did I stutter, Rawlings? Bring. Her. Here. Now.'

'Yes, sir,' Rawlings said, rushing back out to find the housemaid in question.

Harcourt knew it was irregular, and that he should have more patience with his servants, particularly Rawlings who had served him well for the past five years, but he needed to conclude his business without delay.

Delicacy would not prevent them all from their below-stairs gossip anyways.

Besides, it would not be the worst, nor the most notable happening to occur in this household. They may not approve of his rakish behaviour, but their wild tongues did enjoy telling the tales of it.

And there would be plenty of fodder for their gossip once he had finished with Miss Fortescue.

And for that matter, Lady Lydia Mowbray.

II.

Effy was making her way downstairs with a bundle of sheets from the master's bedroom when she was intercepted by Rawlings. She groaned internally, any meeting with Rawlings was a disagreeable one, weaselly little rat that he was.

'There you are girl,' he panted, blocking her way down the narrow servants' stairs. 'Master wants to see you.'

'Me,' Effy snorted, surprised. In her three years working for Harcourt Sinclair, not once had he spoken a word to her. She was entirely sure to him she didn't exist. Which suited her very well. 'What does the Master want with me?'

'I was going to ask you that, missy,' Rawlings hissed, pulling himself upstairs by the balustrade, getting once again too close. *Thank God for the laundry...* 'What trouble did you manage to get yourself into now?'

'I have not the slightest idea, Rawlings,' she said flatly, her eyes warning him to keep a safe distance, reminding him silently what happened last time he had tried to touch her. 'Why don't we go find out?'

Rawlings' eyes narrowed, and his lips pursed.

In other circumstances, Effy knew he might try to make her pay for her insolence, but as it appeared the Master should not be kept waiting, he relented, turning on his heels and making his way back downstairs.

She would have to be on her guard tonight, and for a while thereafter, he would surely find a way to make her suffer at some point...

Wretch. Effy had never liked him. There was an aura of dishonesty and conniving around the man, his beady eyes full of greed, and his hands far too presuming in their wanderings. He had tried to pinch her bottom once, her first day here, but she had flattened him with an uppercut. Since then, she had carefully avoided any further scrapes, though Rawlings seemed to be constantly lurking, ready to pounce should she forget to watch herself.

Little did Rawlings know she *never* forgot to watch herself. She had before, and that had cost her everything.

Besides, her care was not only for herself; she couldn't afford to lose this position. And if she crossed the line with Rawlings, and the *loyal* footman went on to report to the master, that is precisely what would happen.

Rawlings glared at her as he knocked on the door to the master's study, and she smiled with overt sarcasm and feigned innocence. *Snake...*

'Come in,' came Mr. Sinclair's booming voice; deep, sharp, and unmistakable.

Careful not to come too close to Rawlings, Effy slid into the master's study, realizing only then that she still carried the bundle of sheets.

Very few times had she been in this room, Mr. Sinclair only rarely asked for the servants to tidy here, and then it was typically Mrs. Jenkins, the housekeeper, who took charge of it herself.

Never before, had she been here with the master present.

She stood there like a ninny, frozen in half-shock, half-embarrassment, staring at him, a bundle of sheets in her arms. Had he always been this tall and imposing?

I think?

His figure was even more intimidating now, backlit and framed by the window. His mane of dark brown curls looked like a strange halo, and she could feel his black eyes boring into her own.

Only too late did she remind herself to at least avert her gaze from his own, less she be thought insolent. Instead, she let it wander over the rest of his honed and handsome features. The thick, dark brows which were now joined in a scowl. The strong, faintly hooked nose that had been broken many times before. The chiselled and well-defined cheekbones and jaw, darkened by a morning shadow, and the lips. The straight, but generous lips that were currently curling into a less than reassuring snarl.

Effy swallowed, trying to calm her nerves, readying herself for whatever *this* was, and trying to stop herself staring. She had forgotten how handsome he was; over the years she had only caught glimpses here and there, and every time she had it made her heart race.

Though that could also be attributed to the fact she lived in fear of being noticed, and subsequently, thrown out of the household…

'Miss Fortescue,' Rawlings announced in his most grating, ob-sequious tone.

'Why is she holding those,' Harcourt asked with disgust, eye-ing the sheets.

'Sorry, sir,' Effy said, coming back to her senses, and careful to use her most inconspicuous voice. 'Rawlings,' she checked her-self when Harcourt raised an eyebrow. 'Mr. Rawlings caught me when I was on my way to the laundry. Sir.'

'Take those and leave us,' he told Rawlings.

Effy couldn't help but smirk as she bestowed her load onto Rawlings, and he slithered out of the room. *Ha!*

Turning her attention back to Mr. Sinclair, she was alarmed to noticed he had somehow managed to fly across the room sound-lessly, was now standing shockingly close to her, and was exam-ining her like some dedicated scientist.

Or like she was chattel.

It sent a shiver down her spine; no matter what the man had done for her, she would never suffer that sort of treatment again.

Perfect, Harcourt thought as he examined the creature before him. *Plain, and unremarkable, but useable. Dear God, she's per-*

fect... Dark copper hair, pleasant enough though it was mostly well-concealed under the appalling cotton cap, save for a few strands escaping around the nape and temples. Deep dark brown eyes, cold and surprisingly *vif* and intelligent, but guarded. Tiny delicate nose, sweet, and entirely kissable lips.

Her features were not entirely unpleasing, when examined individually, but somehow her face was altogether unremarkable, her cheeks round and undefined, giving her the look of an unkempt country lass.

As for the rest of her, the word sturdy came to mind. Her pear-shaped figure added to the picture, generous hips and thighs, smaller bust; not unappealing nor absent, simply, unproportioned, and not to his taste. She was tall too, taller than most women; her eyes came nearly level with his own.

Not *ugly*, but certainly nothing compared to Lady Lydia Mowbray.

If he was honest, he was expecting far worse when he had called for her, but this, he could work with. She even had spectacularly clear skin, a nice warm pale.

Yes, you'll do very nicely...

Besides, a few hours with Madame. Chanteclair, and she would look every bit the part of an alluring, tantalisingly rich rival to Lady Lydia.

One sure to have her crawling back to him without restraint.

'Yes, you'll do,' he whispered, running his finger lightly along her jawline.

∞

For a moment, when she had first seen him, his unmistakable beauty had made Effy forget precisely how dangerous a man Harcourt Sinclair was. But now, as he stood so close, his finger drawing the line of her jaw, his twinkling black eyes bearing down into hers, she realized he was just as much of the devil as everyone said.

It wasn't that she had ever been unaware of his reputation, she had heard the stories same as everyone else; and witnessed much more so having lived under the same roof as him for the past three years. *Rake. Gambler. Seducer. Duellist. Murderer.*

To be fair, the last one, true a claim it might be, she could never fault him for.

In truth, she had heard it all. Not until now, however, had she been close enough to feel the raw power and danger emanating from him.

She felt herself shiver again as he took her chin between his thumb and forefinger, and for a second, she had the absurd notion he was about to kiss her.

'Sir,' she asked faintly.

What on Earth is he doing? This behaviour was shocking, sudden, not to mention highly inappropriate no matter her rank. *Is this why he refused to hire young women in his household?*

What was even more shocking was that her body seemed completely in tune, and drawn to his. And he smelled delectable. *Spices. Musk. Hint of brandy. Lavender.*

Harcourt seemed to return from whatever reverie he had been engrossed in; she saw his eyes refocus, and his lips curl into a rather terrifying smile.

'Don't be afraid, pet,' he said softly. 'I won't harm you.'

'I'm not your pet,' Effy spat before she could stop herself. Harcourt cocked his head slightly, surprised at her harshness and impudence. So, she added, 'Sir.'

'Well, you've got spirit underneath it all it seems,' he admired.

Lazily, he removed his hand, and took a very exaggerated step back away. All the tension in Effy's body seemed to vanish, and she took a deep breath.

Careful, mind yourself Effy…

'Why am I here, sir,' she asked, resuming her role of servant with as much dignity and composure as she could muster.

'What's your name?'

'Fortescue.'

'Christian name?'

'Euphemia, sir. Though everyone calls me Effy.'

'I need your help, Effy,' he said in his most infallibly charming way.

'*My* help, sir,' Effy asked, careful not to give in and laugh in his face. *What in God's name?* 'What do you need my help for?'

'A private, discreet matter. Do you think you might be up the task, Effy,' he asked challengingly.

The master was enjoying himself, she could tell, and it angered her.

He was being condescending, inappropriate, and manipulative, and he thought he could get away with it because she was only a dull, drab, plain, servant.

No matter what she owed him; what she'd been forced to endure and become, she would not suffer *this*.

'Perhaps if I knew what the task was, *sir*, I might be able to pass judgement.'

Harcourt whistled, impressed.

He couldn't help but smile, and had to give it to the tall creature before him, she was quicker and had more bite than she looked. He was used to people's disdain and disgust of him, but this, this was different. It was almost as if she was trying to remind *him* of his place.

This whole affair might be rather fun and not so tedious after all.

'I need your assistance with a lady,' he said, waiting for her retort.

'I highly doubt that, sir.' *Quiet, Effy!*

'Under normal circumstances, you would be quite right,' Harcourt conceded with a slight incline of his head. 'However, in this instance, you are mistaken. I do need you.'

'To do what,' Effy asked, her eyes narrowing.

What is the man playing at?

'How much do I pay you, Effy?'

'Sixteen pounds a year. Sir.'

'What if I said I would give you twice that for two days' work with me?'

Effy stared at him incredulously.

That was a fortune for someone in her position, and meant that what he was asking was either scandalous, questionable in legality, dangerous, or all the above.

Not that it would make a difference. He could ask her to follow him to the depths of Hell and back and she would do it. But he didn't know that. And she certainly wasn't going to let him even suspect it. She may have sworn her life to him; but that was her business, and hers alone.

Just as it was her business, and hers alone that she had enough of a fortune already without his meagre thirty-two pounds.

Mindful to make him suffer and doubt, and work for her acquiescence, she crossed her arms and straightened herself proudly. *That should do it...*

'What would I have to do,' she asked, peppering her voice with a little quake.

'Come shopping with me, wear a pretty new dress, and go for a drive in the park.'

'You can dispense with the reassuring and coddling tone, sir,' she sighed. 'Truth.'

'Very well, Miss Fortescue,' he said, his voice cold enough to freeze any man's heart. Effy smiled, half because she knew it would annoy him. 'I need you to get tarted up and be seen in my company to make another woman jealous.'

'That doesn't seem like a lot, for thirty-two pounds, sir.'

'Discretion is costly.'

'And?'

'And, I may have to, touch you,' he sighed, relenting. And he had thought she would be easy to convince... *Blasted women, all the same.* 'Make it seem as though we are on intimate terms.'

'Very well,' Effy said flatly. She could have tried to negotiate the price, but she could sense she was already pushing her luck. 'I'll do what you ask,' she said, holding out her hand.

Harcourt stared at it, shock barely keeping him from laughing in her face. Instead, collecting himself, he took her hand and shook it, noticing the strength and delicacy of it beneath the callouses.

'Sir.'

'Miss Fortescue?'

'Anything else you'll be needing, sir?'

'No, thank you Miss Fortescue. I will speak to Mrs. Jenkins, you will be relieved of your duties for the next two days.'

'Very well, sir.'

'You may dispose, Miss Fortescue.'

With a hurried curtsey, Effy let herself out.

Not until she was safely hidden from any eyes in the darkened corner of the empty drawing room did she allow herself to take a deep breath, and steady herself against the wall.

What had gotten into her? She had nearly cost herself everything by acting like such an impudent brat. Why couldn't she just say yes to whatever he asked or demanded? Play the fool as she did so very well?

Because you don't want him to see you like a fool... For the first time in three years, the man she had pledged her entire being to, had noticed her. Needed *her.* And she couldn't bring herself to just turn into another weak and pliable wallflower, bending without force to his will.

Lord... What have you gotten yourself into this time Effy? Trouble, that's what...

Harcourt was still staring bemusedly at the spot where only minutes ago Effy had been standing.

She had definitely given him a run for his money, and had veered to the side of impudence at moments. Any other master would have fired her on the spot. Then again, any other master wouldn't have been making such an outrageous proposal to the girl in the first place...

Never mind Effy Fortescue. She had agreed to do his bidding.

Now, it was time to make all the arrangements, to ensure the delightfully doomed Lady Lydia fell into his perfectly laid trap.

Delicacy, always...

III.

In other circumstances, Effy may have been able to appreciate the beauty of the park, sat in the most fashionable, and comfortable of barouches, beside the most handsome of men. Not today. Nothing of the illusion was real, and perhaps in another life she might have been able to convince herself it was. Not so in this life, when she had long forgotten how to dream.

Instead, she sat there, stiff-backed and rigid, fiddling with her gloves and re-adjusting her bonnet. It was a perfect day for a ride; a warm, spring day, the sun just at the perfect low height to illuminate without blinding, the heat of the day well dissipated.

Birds chirped, echoes of laughter and conversations hung on the air. Even the horses' hooves on the path were rhythmic and hypnotising.

Effy couldn't focus her mind enough to notice any of it.

'Stop fidgeting, Fortescue,' Harcourt snapped. 'A lady does not fidget.'

'I am not a lady. Sir.'

'Today you are,' he challenged, raising an eyebrow.

Effy sighed, and attempted to calm her nerves.

He was right. Today she was a lady. *Again*. It wasn't as if she didn't know precisely how to comport herself.

She glanced over at him, confident that he had returned his gaze to the path ahead as he waited for his quarry to appear.

He sat languidly beside her, one arm draped over the side of the carriage, the other was behind her, ready to draw her in when it was time; his legs were crossed, lazily spread out before him. Indeed, he seemed almost bored.

But beneath the crisp, immaculate linen shirt, dark grey brocade waistcoat, perfectly tailored black wool coat, and buckskin breeches, there was unmistakable tension. Beneath the cool, perfect, and controlled veneer, there was a wildfire.

Not five minutes ago, he had discarded the hat and gloves, tossing them to the seat across from them, and now, he was scowling again, his black eyes darting around and ahead as the wind whipped his dark curls across the sharp planes of his face. The hawk surveying the land for its prey.

If she had thought he looked the Devil everyone said before, the image was even more complete now. If Effy had ever been asked to picture the fallen favoured son of God, she would have pictured Harcourt Sinclair in all his dark beauty.

He seemed to sense her gaze, turning away from his surveillance to survey her again instead. She saw his eyes wander from head to toe, ensuring yet again that Madame Chanteclair had done her best.

As if anything had changed since he had checked that in the shop earlier this afternoon, when she stood before him in the agreed upon style.

When they had been in his study, and he had examined her, she had felt like chattel. When he had examined her when Madame had finished her work, she had felt much more an actual woman.

If he had expected to be disappointed with Madame's work, particularly since she had only taken an hour to tend to the maid when they had visited her shop for a first fitting yesterday, he found himself then, for the first time in a very long time, pleasantly surprised.

The blue, semi-opaque muslin and silk dress she had chosen suited the girl perfectly, rendering her generous curves somewhat appealing.

The lace trim on the bodice and sleeves dissimulated and enhanced. The bonnet, of the same shade as the dress, with a bunch of cornflowers and yellow ribbon, suited the girl's complexion and rested perfectly on the now perfect copper curls. There was only the slightest hint of rouge on her lips and cheeks, brightening her complexion without seeming garish.

All in all, the girl had exceeded his expectations.

Though she might not be able to hold a candle to Lady Lydia Mowbray's beauty, Harcourt couldn't deny she had a certain charm, and elegance which he hadn't expected. He hadn't even needed to redress her, give her any hints regarding comportment or posture, though he had set aside some time to do just that. She carried herself as a lady, without any instruction, and he had wondered for a moment where such a lowly creature had learned such manners. Been imbued with such a distinguished air.

No matter.

The time he would have spent on schooling her yesterday afternoon had been better spent attending to other affairs, which he had been forced to set aside whilst he dealt with Mowbray.

The girl had instead returned to her duties, and this afternoon when they returned to the shop, it had been very a very quick visit indeed.

All in all, he could not fault the creature.

Though now, she was grating on his nerves.

'Stop fidgeting,' he repeated gruffly. 'You'll drive me to insanity. You've behaved yourself until now, whatever has gotten into you?'

'Sorry, sir,' Effy said, forcing her hands to stay placidly on her lap. 'It's just the waiting, sir.'

'Well, you have the air of a lamb going to slaughter, Fortescue. I'm not going to hurt you,' he sighed, reminding himself that yelling at the creature wouldn't make her any more amenable. Already yesterday, despite her fire, he hadn't missed the slight shivers when he had gotten too close to her. 'I will try to make it pleasant, no need to fear. It's not as daunting a thing as everyone makes it out to be.' Effy snorted. He thought this was about the kiss? *He would think that.* Who would deign to kiss a plain, lowly housemaid like her? 'Please, do tell what I have done to amuse you. I shall continue to do it, for you seem to have finally relaxed.'

'It's nothing, sir,' Effy said graciously. 'I thank you for your kind reassurances.'

Harcourt eyed her for a moment, and was about to say something, when a rise of high-pitched laughter reached his ears.

He turned towards its origin and spotted precisely what they had been waiting for.

Lady Lydia Mowbray was looking every bit the bright angel amongst the drabs she was promenading with, a delicate lace parasol twirling innocently over her shoulder.

Harcourt felt, more than saw, her crystal blue eyes fix themselves on him, and he slid his arm around Effy's shoulders, pulling her close to him.

'Relax, for the love of God, Fortescue,' he hissed. 'Your bonnet is poking my cheek.'

'Sorry, sir,'

Effy took a deep breath and readjusted herself against Harcourt, snuggling perfectly into the crook of his shoulder, the length of her body against his, trying not to think too hard about how delicious he smelled, somewhere between Christmas morning and extreme masculinity.

'Better,' Harcourt said approvingly, actually enjoying the feel of her. She was quite the pleasant armful after all. 'Do you think you could manage a longing gaze in my direction?'

'Yes, sir.'

Shifting slightly, she turned her face up to him and put on her most longing and forlorn expression.

Not that it was that difficult to muster with Harcourt. She let her eyes roam over the sharp lines of his face, perfectly countered by the sweet curls of silky brown hair draping around them. She watched as his lips tightened, jaw clenching almost imperceptibly as his eyes watched the approaching party, dark and calculating.

For the briefest moment, Effy felt safe; for the first time in nearly ten years. She felt as if she were precisely where she was supposed to be; as if all the rest of her terrible life had simply led her to this.

She chastised herself silently, and reminded herself that though she may belong at Harcourt's side; it was never to be in this manner.

'I'm going to kiss you now, Fortescue,' he announced gravely, turning his attention to her. 'Excellent gazing by the way.'

'Yes, Sir. Thank you, sir,' she said, barely suppressing a smile when she saw the laughter in his eyes.

Timing was everything.

Lady Lydia needed to be close enough to see what they were about; but far enough to endure the spectacle for a lengthy, tortuous amount of time. *Delicacy, always...*

There they were, just a few feet away from the horses. Their driver had been instructed to keep the pace nearly untenably slow, and it seemed the party of gaggling women itself was walking at just the languid pace he had hoped for. *Perfect...*

A chaste kiss was what he had promised the girl. Illusion, nothing more; even a chaste peck on the cheek would have sufficed to scandalize.

To his own surprise, however, when his lips touched the creature's, all his promises seemed to disappear. She did not stiffen, did not keep her lips tightly closed against his, but instead parted them just enough for their mouths to fit together gently.

Her lips were soft, and deceptively generous and inviting. He couldn't resist exploring her limits, slowly, coaxing her to open beneath him. Again, he was surprised to find that not only was she yielding, she herself was inviting *him* to open himself to her.

Miss Fortescue, how unexpected, he thought to himself, grinning. *Very well, then...*

There was no reason not to enjoy this, he determined, and so he explored her mouth, nibbling, coaxing, testing, his tongue slowly finding its way to hers. She responded in kind, deepening the search, her hand sliding behind his back to better steady herself, and draw him in.

How delightfully surprising Miss Fortescue, he mused, enjoying her taste.

There was definitely more to her than he had expected. She tasted of deliciously dark sin, rich and deep, with notes of sweetness. But she was much more of a rich claret than a sweet fruit, and her touch and explorations were languorous and experienced. The world melted away; he forgot for a moment all about Lady Lydia Mowbray, altogether more intrigued by the creature in his arms.

Then, the laughter faded, and the carriage lurched ahead. The driver had been told what to expect, and what to do.

Harcourt pulled away sharply, checked they had indeed passed Lady Lydia's party, and settled back into his seat. He wiped the corners of his mouth, running his tongue over his lips to wash away the last of the creature's taste, then straightened his coat, and resumed his initial position.

He felt Effy straighten and pull away beside him, but decided against indulging the girl with any semblance of interest.

A delightful surprise she may have been, a pleasant interlude, but he could not afford to indulge himself, or her, with thoughts of anything more.

Though he had been glad of her presence, for she had served his purpose, and well at that, there was a reason he was careful not to employ young ladies in his household. Temptation was not something he needed in his house.

Thinking on it now, he wondered how she had managed to gain employ to begin with. *A question for another day. Now, it is time to return home, and wait for Lady Lydia...*

Revenge may be unpleasant to some, but Harcourt Sinclair was thoroughly enjoying himself.

∞

18

When Effy heard the front door slam below, and spied Harcourt striding down the street, she knew precisely where, or rather to whom, he was going. Not even a full day after their ride in the park, and he was off to meet Lady Lydia Mowbray. His plan had worked to perfection, and though she was glad of it, she also felt an unexpected pang.

Silly, silly, woman, she thought, shaking her head, and returning her attention to the polishing set before her. Their brief interlude, the brief pause in her life, was over. Now, it was time to return to the tedious simplicity of her duties, which most of the time she actually enjoyed.

There was beauty and calm in such menial, repetitive duties. She usually found solace and soothing in household tasks; their normalcy was a stark contrast to her previous lives.

Not today.

Today, there was only frustration.

Annoyance as she briskly made her way through the pile of pots and silver, which was larger than usual thanks to Rawlings. *Worm.*

Try as she may, she hadn't been able to shake off the feelings which had emerged during their ride, during their *kiss*, yesterday.

A chaste kiss. That is what he had promised. That is far from what it had been, despite her resolve to ensure she remained tight-lipped and as rigid as a severe spinster.

Then, his lips had touched hers, and her resolve had melted away as she had let herself melt under his embrace.

It was the only time he would ever kiss her, so she might as well enjoy it.

She had felt his surprise as she had offered herself to him, and deciding that if she was going to give in, she might as well make the most of it, she had let her boldness take hold, exploring his mouth as much as he did hers.

She could still feel the tingle of her lips, as though it had only been moments since they had parted. *Silly, silly, woman.*

In her defence, she had not expected the rush of feeling when his surprisingly soft, gentle lips had touch hers. She hadn't expected his testing and teasing, and what woman in her right mind wouldn't rise to such an occasion? His lips and tongue had known precisely how to excite and entice, and he had tasted as delicious as he smelled and looked.

Dark, sensual, full of spice, and notes of coffee, and *him.* Who wouldn't, with such a delectable meal before them, indulge in it?

And then, just like that, her purpose had been fulfilled, and he had broken away, leaving her cold, and staring like a complete fool into nothingness.

Lucky that he had paid her no attention after that; she had time to recompose herself. One glimpse of her and he would have known just how much she had felt in that moment, and if he had, she would have been out of his house in less time than if she had indulged her fantasy and thrown Rawlings down the length and breadth of the main staircase.

And then where would she be?

Skulking like a shadow to follow him around and fulfil her own purpose. *Damned fool, Euphemia, that's what you are...*

Sighing, she looked at the collection of silver before her and realized she had managed to finish it all in half the time, frustrated and distracted as she was.

Ha! Small consolation as it was, if she continued at this rate, she would manage to finish her chores with time to spare, and then perhaps Mrs. Jenkins would allow her part of the day to herself.

Even an hour, to herself, to read, as she hadn't had a chance to in months, that would be paradise.

And the perfect distraction from the dangerous waters her mind was straying to.

Effy tidied the room, gathered her polishing materials and anything else she could carry and that needed to be returned to Mrs. Jenkins. She made her way downstairs and left her load in Mrs. Jenkins' office, though she herself was nowhere to be found.

Effy's ears perked up as she left the housekeeper's office.

Hushed voices, from down the corridor. The hackles on her neck raised. Somehow, Effy knew that whoever it was, they were trying to remain unheard, and unseen.

Quietly, she made her way towards the servants' entrance, heart beating madly. She didn't quite know why; it was more of a gut instinct. That the business being conducted was secret, and that she had to know what it was.

And where was everybody? Normally the servants' quarters were never quiet. At this precise moment, it seemed the entire floor had been deserted; she couldn't even hear anything coming from the kitchen, which was highly unusual.

The hushed voices were louder now; someone was definitely at the servants' entrance.

Effy froze, tucking herself against the wall at the corner by the door. She recognized one voice. *Rawlings, you cockroach... Should have guessed.*

'You'll get the rest when he's dead,' growled another voice. A stranger's, definitely a man, and not too well educated from the sound of it. 'And he ain't dead yet.'

'But I told you everything else, that's what I was being paid for,' Rawlings snivelled.

'Then you don't need to worry then, do ya? He'll be dead before lunch, and you'll have your money by tea.'

There was a cold cruel laugh, and footsteps.

Effy pulled herself together, and ran, as quietly as she could back the way she came, all the way back to her room. Her retreat was covered by the other servants, who seemed to have suddenly returned from wherever they had been.

A few gave her inquisitive looks, but none tried to stop her.

Only once she was safely in her quarters, door locked tightly behind her, did she will herself to breathe again, her mind racing.

He'll be dead before lunch... There was no doubt of whom they spoke, and Effy's blood ran could. She knew Harcourt had gone to meet Lydia Mowbray, and she also knew that something much, much worse was waiting for him there.

Did he know? Did he suspect?

Doubtful. She knew he was much too blinded by the prize he thought to be within his grasp at last to clearly see anything else.

What the Hell can I do? What could I do? He may not know there was a trap waiting for him, but Harcourt Sinclair could more than handle himself in a fight. He was just as dangerous, if not more so, than anyone who would be sent to kill him. Even if she knew where he was, what purpose could she serve?

Other than get in the way or distract him. She may know how to defend herself, but going up against an unknown number of deadly assailants was not something she had tremendous experience of.

If she did know where he was, she could try to warn him. But there was no assurance she could even arrive in time. *He'll be fine...*

Yet even as she thought it, her stomach fell. That feeling of dread and foreboding returned to the pit of her stomach. She didn't know why, but she knew she had to do something.

First, she would have to find out where he had gone. Easy enough. *His study.* He had received a note from Lady Lydia.

And then? *Improvise...*

God, if you still have any grace left for me, use it to keep him safe...

Effy repeated her prayer as she crept out of the townhouse, careful to remain unseen lest she waste time having to answer questions, and conjure up lies.

She repeated her prayer as she rushed down the streets towards Covent Garden, reassured by the feel of the blade in her boot, and the touch of the cold hard steel as her hand clutched tightly around the pistol in her pocket.

And if you could make it so I don't have to use this thing. In broad daylight, in the middle of the city...

IV.

As he wandered down from his club towards the discreet little tea house Lady Lydia Mowbray had designated as the place for their rendezvous, Harcourt wondered if anyone watching him would notice the literal spring in his step.

Everything was going perfectly, just according to his plan. He wasn't even so upset with the little chit for the delay she had caused with her reticence. It would only make the conquest all the sweeter.

By the time the day was over, she would be his, and by the morning, the Duke of Mowbray would be defeated. Mostly. *And then there would be three…*

Harcourt had stopped quickly at his club before attending to Lady Lydia, needing to pass the time before he was due to call on her. He had felt like a caged animal in the townhouse, and decided that the club was the perfect solution.

If he was a few minutes late, all the better. It would make her fret, and whet her appetite even more.

It had been an unexpected pleasure to run into Viscount Percival Egerton, who, though he knew none of the details of *why*, knew of his pursuit of the delightful Lady Lydia Mowbray.

And apparently, news of his little carriage ride yesterday had travelled fast.

'Dear God, Sinclair,' Percy said, settling himself at Harcourt's table, looking fresher than could be expected. Percy spent his nights in the gambling hells and other assorted establishments of ill-repute. Still, even at an hour when most gentlemen with similar hobbies would be nursing themselves in bed, Percy showed no signs of his lifestyle. His bright hazel eyes were as lively as ever, studying Harcourt with amusement. 'I thought you were pursuing the Mowbray girl? What's this I hear about you and some other woman *kissing* in the middle of Hyde Park? Who is this new mystery woman? Finally found yourself another mistress?'

'Percy, you really shouldn't pay any attention to the gossips,' Harcourt drawled, grinning like the Devil. 'That was nothing more than a bit of theatrics designed to draw Lady Lydia out.'

'Well, you've managed quite the scandal,' Percy said, raking his fingers playfully through his golden locks. 'Hope you know what you're doing.'

'I always know what I'm doing.'

'Who was she?'

'What? The girl in the park? One of my servants. Nothing to fear from her, if there is a scandal, no one will know who to name, and she has no reputation to uphold in Society.'

'Very clever,' Percy conceded. 'And Lady Lydia, then...?'

'Ripe for the plucking,' Harcourt smiled. 'Meeting her, well, in the next half hour.'

'Mind yourself,' Percy warned, lounging in his chair, disdainfully watching the few comings and goings of the club. 'Her father has great plans for her, and he has not taken the news of your sniffing around her well. He will settle for a title worthy of his own, nothing less.'

'You mean not a *cit*, like me,' Harcourt corrected. Percy raised his eyebrows; neither could deny the truth of it. A fortune may open doors, and insure he had friends, but it did not change his frowned upon position in Society. 'We shall see, Percy.'

Harcourt was careful not to mention the fact that he had no intention of marrying the girl.

No matter how loyal a friend Percy had proven to be over the years; his honour would demand intervention should he learn of Harcourt's plans.

Any of them.

'I suppose we shall... I don't underestimate you Sinclair, once was mistake enough for me.'

'Wise man.'

Percy laughed heartily.

The two shared a coffee and a few minutes of more polite conversation before Harcourt excused himself. Lady Lydia Mowbray was waiting.

Harcourt rounded the corner and turned onto Short's Gardens. He had to admit, the girl was clever, and knew how to pick a discreet spot for an illicit *rendezvous* almost as well as himself. He wondered for a moment how precisely she had managed to extricate herself from chaperones and family.

But he shook the thoughts away, caring not for the how, only for the fact that she had managed it. He stopped before the cafe she had designated in her note.

Not a place for young ladies of the ton, he admitted.

It was a miniscule teahouse, popular and unpolished, with darkened windows and alcoves which would suit their purpose to perfection.

He checked himself in what little reflection there was, pushing away a few curls and straightening his necktie.

But just as he made to move for the door, a strong hand appeared on his shoulder, and he felt the distinctive cold point of a knife at his back.

Oh Lydia, you traitorous little snipe...

He'd been foolish. Blind. And walked himself straight into a trap.

He sighed heavily. His gloriously perfect day was rapidly turning into a tedious, dangerously annoying one.

'Morning Mr. Sinclair,' growled the voice behind him. 'What say you we go for a little walk?'

'As flattering as your attentions are,' Harcourt said lazily. 'I must admit you're not exactly my type.'

'Come quietly, now Mr. Sinclair,' the voice advised.

Harcourt's eyes flicked back to the reflection.

Though he couldn't make out the man's face, he could make

out his bulky figure looming behind his own. And the figures of three other men nearby. *Damn.* Four to one.

Not impossible odds, but not favourable ones either. And if the hand on his shoulder was anything to go by, the man behind him was a formidable brute. The others would not be so different if he knew anything, and Harcourt knew much.

Whatever fight was coming, it would not be an easy one. *This is my favourite shirt...*

'Lead on, my good man,' Harcourt sighed, giving an outward show of defeat.

A tightening of the man's hand on his shoulder indicated they should proceed towards the left.

Harcourt did as he was bid, using whatever time he had to calculate his odds, take stock of his assets, and make a plan.

The blade up his sleeve, and the one in his boot. His walking stick. The bag of coins in his pocket. Weapons enough to give him a fighting chance.

He would need to be quick, strike fast and hard, and depending on the terrain where they were leading him, find a way to ensure he faced them one by one. He had faced worse odds before.

Still, that didn't stop him feeling that somehow, this time was different.

Oh Lydia, you gutless traitor. I will make you regret this too...

∞

Effy felt like her heart might explode, and she could barely breathe by the time she arrived outside the little teashop that had been named in Lydia Mowbray's note. She knew she should have hired a hack, rather than run here, but she was afraid to lose one precious second.

Peering through the windows, she saw no trace of either Harcourt nor Lydia Mowbray. *God, I'm too late...* Or maybe Harcourt had already realized it was a trap, and escaped, and was even now safe back at the townhouse.

No... Something is not right... Think, Effy, think!

This was a quiet street, but still travelled. If anyone was going to do harm to someone like Harcourt Sinclair, for all intents and purposes, a *gentleman*, they would need to find somewhere they would not be interrupted. But this entire area was full of alleyways and passages, and private gardens.

Soho was a stone's throw away, and the perfect sort of place to conduct sordid business. And there was nothing to guarantee he hadn't simply been thrown into the back of a carriage, and driven away to the docks or some abandoned building... *God, help me!*

There was nothing to do but conduct as quick and thorough a search of the nearby area as she could muster. Cutting through Neal's Yard, Effy made her way north-west, making for the general direction of Soho via any alleyway or desolate passage she could find.

Nothing.

No trace, no sound, nothing.

Her heart was beating fast, and she was drenched in sweat. Her feet were beyond tired, and she could barely think straight. People were looking at her askew, and she knew she must be presenting quite the frightful sight. It didn't matter. Nothing other than finding Harcourt mattered.

Cutting across Shaftesbury Avenue, she made for St. Giles' passage. Shouts, grunts, and the unmistakable sounds of a fight.

God, thank you...

She ran towards the gardens ahead, but slowed when she arrived at the entrance.

Surprise and stealth would be everything if she was to make it out alive against whatever lay ahead.

If they were both to make it out alive.

The sounds of the struggle were becoming louder. She edged her way in, staying well concealed behind the trees and beds of wildflowers. Along the path she nearly screamed as she came across a body, a ruffian with a bloody line across his neck.

Harcourt would not go quietly...

But how many more are there? Effy knew that if Harcourt was killing men, she would most likely not be able to afford leaving the pistol in her pocket.

A shot, however, would bring the watch, and onlookers. Which in other circumstances may be useful, but not today when there was a dead body to be found. *Dead bodies*, she corrected, coming across another bruiser who had suffered a similar fate as the first.

Ripping off her coat she bunched it up, then extracted the pistol and cocked it. Hopefully, her coat would be enough to muffle the sound, while still causing enough harm. Untested, but then this whole situation was very new territory...

Effy tucked her skirt up and shoved it into the belt of her apron, hoping to clear her path to the knife in her boot.

There were more grunts, a shout, and the distinct sound of something large hitting the ground.

Peering out from behind a tree, she finally saw what was waiting for her.

And it was not pretty.

In fact, it was utterly desperate.

Harcourt was the one who had fallen. He was sprawled out on the ground, and unconscious from what Effy could tell.

A towering, giant brute, and another more weaselly little fellow were currently showering him with kicks. If he wasn't dead already, he would be soon. *God, give me strength...*

Effy took aim from her vantage, and decided on the smaller of the two bruisers, as he was closest, and she was unsure how far the bullet would actually manage to travel. *Far enough it seems...*

The man went down in slow motion, hand clutched to his chest, blood pouring out from beneath his fingers. The shot had hit its mark, and her theory had worked; the sound had been muffled just enough.

But Effy didn't have time to gloat. The other man was already on his way to find her; luckily Harcourt was out of danger, for now.

Whirling around, back under cover, she dropped the coat and

pistol and took out her dagger. She edged through the plants, hoping to make it out, and be able to come back around behind him.

She chanced a glance at Harcourt, who looked even worse than she first thought. Her stomach rose to her throat, and she felt sick.

Sick and angry. *And tired…*

The run here, and the search, had exhausted her. If she didn't finish this soon, she wouldn't be able to put up any fight whatsoever. Lucky for her, it seemed the brute wasn't very clever. He had stopped to rifle through her coat. Without a moment's hesitation, she crept up behind him. He must have heard something, because just as she was about to make her move, he whirled around.

Effy saw the confusion when he saw what she was, then the rage, and the bloodlust. He snarled, his lips curling over his black stumps that were once teeth. Bald, his thick cheeks, neck, broad shoulders, and enormous chest gave him the look of a terrifying ogre. But even the greatest monsters have their weaknesses.

He lunged out for her, but she sidestepped and as he passed her, she kicked out, her foot hitting his knee and forcing him to the ground with a howl of pain.

'Bitch,' he snarled, making to get up and lunge for her again.

Despite her tiredness, however, Effy was quicker.

She whirled around, and planted her blade masterfully in the side of his neck. His hand reached up and the shock and disgust on his face were enough to force a satisfied smile from Effy.

She watched proudly as the blood poured from the wound, and the giant fell to the ground. She spat on him, then, sure his life had ended, she retrieved her blade, wiped it, and returned it to her boot.

Oh God, oh God, no, please… Effy knelt down beside Harcourt, flipping him over onto his back. It was far, far worse than she expected, and if he wasn't tended to urgently, there was a very strong chance he would be dead. His pulse was already dangerously slow, and she could barely feel his breathing.

God, please... His face was a mess, beaten to a literal pulp. One of his hands had been smashed, by a boot in all likelihood, and she didn't want to even think about the state his ribs were in. There were cuts and bruises everywhere, his clothes were torn and bloodied; this was very serious indeed.

Harcourt needed a physician. And she needed to get them both out of here before someone found them. She knew there was another exit, closer, and then she could head onto Stacey Street, find a boy or someone to get a physician. And a carriage.

And then?

She couldn't very well bring him home. Rawlings would certainly call whoever had paid him to begin with, and lock her up in the root cellar while they finished the job. *Think, woman!*

Get out of here, find a doctor, deal with the rest later... She ran to the entrance she had come into, and closed the gate. She couldn't lock it, but she could discourage people from entering.

She found her coat, threw it back on, then stashed the pistol back in her pocket. Harcourt's walking stick was by his body, as was the blade she guessed he used to kill the first two men.

The blade she pocketed, the stick, she disposed of in some bushes; there was nothing extraordinary about it that could lead to his identification.

With the last of her strength, she slid her arms under his, and dragged him out of the gardens, shutting that gate as well.

'God, Harcourt,' she moaned, venting her frustration on him while she could. 'Why did you have to be so tall and made all of muscle. You bloody heavy lump!'

Effy propped him up against the wall at the end of Filcourt Street, grateful that they had yet to encounter anyone.

The street itself was dim, dark, and untravelled, and so she hoped it would remain long enough for her to find help. She pocketed his coin purse, signet, and watch, lest anyone be tempted, and she would need coin to hire a carriage and a physician.

Then, steadying herself, trying to restore some semblance of normality to her appearance, she left him there, and went in search of assistance.

Don't let him die, not now, please God. I swore my life to him, you can't take him from me.

V.

The sound of chickens, and the crow of a rooster pierced through the blackness and brought Harcourt back from the nothingness that he had been lost in for... Well, for how long, he didn't know. What he did know, was that there were no chickens or roosters in Green Park.

His eyes flew open with panic as his last memories flooded back to him. *Lydia. The teahouse. The trap. Four men.* He had killed two of them, quick and soundless, like a viper. He remembered the shouts, the blows. Reaching for one, being caught at the neck by another. He had fought hard, but then, he had lost consciousness.

There had been voices. Faces by candlelight. A man. Spectacles.

A mane of red hair.

Was he dreaming? Then, the feel of a carriage. Horses' hooves.

But again, was any of it real? He thought he remembered a soft, reassuring voice, calling to him in the darkness, and cool wetness, on his lips and cheeks. *An angel...*

Oh dear Lord... He shouldn't have opened his eyes. His head felt as if it had been put through a sieve, and he could barely organize his thoughts through the powerful throbbing.

The blinding, warm light that filled whatever room he was in pierced like daggers through the fog. He blinked, trying to use his other senses as he adjusted to the daylight.

Bed. A comfortable bed, with a thick, warm duvet. But not his bed. He shifted slightly, realizing he was in a light cotton night-

32

shirt. And that his entire body hurt. His right hand, that was the worst. He couldn't move it.

But he could raise his arm. He glimpsed thick bandages, and a splint encasing it. The little weasel had stomped on it. That he remembered.

There was a window before him, above a dresser at the end of the bed. He couldn't see out, not unless he shifted higher to sit.

Groaning, he only just managed it, though he had to take a moment, close his eyes, and breathe deeply as dizziness and pain washed over him, sending chills through his otherwise warm body.

Green, rolling hills. Pastures. Trees. *Definitely not London.*

How had he gotten here? Wherever here was?

A cottage. Tiny. The bed was against the wall, beneath another window. Beside him, a small table, with a basin of water and cloths, his watch and signet ring.

Beyond it, a wardrobe, and a privacy curtain. All simple, pastoral furniture. Nothing personal, nothing that could help him identify whose house he was in. Panic began to rise.

Just because whoever had brought him here had tended to him, didn't mean they meant him no harm. It simply meant they needed something from him before he passed to the other world.

Beyond the curtain he glimpsed a large oak slab table, four chairs, a hearth, and other indicators that it was a kitchen.

A one-room cottage somewhere in the countryside.

The questions multiplied, and Harcourt knew he needed answers, and quickly.

Slowly, carefully, pushing past the pain, he managed to pull himself out of bed. He greedily swallowed the contents of a glass of water that had been set on the table beside him.

Unsteady, dizzy, he made it to his feet, and after a moment, he managed to begin shuffling across the room towards the kitchen, and the door.

It smelled delicious, he noted, bacon, eggs, and coffee. A fire was roaring in the hearth to his right, and it warmed the very cockles of his heart. This place was simple, unadorned, but it felt, *real*… Homely.

Later. He could investigate for food and sustenance, later. Now, he had to find whoever it was that brought him here.

Voices. From outside. *Cooing?*

The rush of light and fresh air forced him to sway backwards when he opened the sturdy oak door. He lifted a hand to shade his eyes, and blinked furiously, trying to make out something in the landscape ahead.

A chicken coop.

A small pen with two pigs.

And a tall figure fussing over them.

A woman.

Feeling his gaze, she turned, and shot him a familiar smile.

He blinked again. It couldn't be. Could it?

Fortescue?

∞

Effy felt his gaze, the hairs on the back of her neck prickling, and she turned to find Harcourt standing at the cottage door, clad only in the nightshirt, swaying slightly. It was a humbling image, a very stark contrast to the strong, dangerous face he typically presented.

Though he was no less handsome, that was undeniable. His beard had grown, she hadn't dared tend to it lest she worsen the cuts beneath it. His hair was loose and dishevelled, the nightshirt was clinging to his honed body with the whip of the wind, and despite looking every bit the ailing patient, he was no less captivating.

Effy couldn't help but smile. She saw the confusion on his face, and it was worth a sack of gold. That she could surprise him, if only a little, amused her.

Adding fuel to the fire, she waved to him congenially, before slowly making her way to him, dropping the last of the food in the pen, and bidding her animals good day.

'Fortescue,' he croaked, his throat dry and unused for too long. 'What the…?'

'Good morning, Mr. Sinclair,' she said brightly, coming to stand before him. He would survive. *Thank you God.* Worn, tired, bruised, and pale, but he would survive. 'It's good to see you have returned to the land of the living.'

'Fortescue it is you,' he exclaimed, only just accepting it was her. 'What is this? Where am I? How long -'

'Perhaps we should return inside,' she advised. 'You're still not fully recovered, and you look as though you might topple over at any second.'

Effy made a move to usher him inside, but he stood strong, refusing to move until his questions had been answered.

He saw her smile faintly when he steadied himself with a hand on the doorframe.

'Very well, Mr. Sinclair. Ask your questions and I shall answer them.'

'What the Devil happened,' he hissed, recovering more with every second, his need for answers adding to his fire.

'You walked straight into a trap. When I found you, you were close to death. I dragged you out of those forsaken gardens, found a boy, who in turn found a carriage and a particularly discreet doctor. Then, I brought you here for your recovery.'

'There were four men,' he said hesitantly. The fact that he'd blacked out with two left was one of the few things he recalled properly. 'I killed two. The others?'

'I killed the two others.'

Again, his surprise was supremely entertaining.

'You…? How did you even know,' he asked, making to try and grab her, but failing as he could barely keep straight himself. 'Are you part of this?'

'Oh for Heavens' sake of course not you bloody fool. I overheard Rawlings. He was talking to one of the men hired to kill you.'

'What?'

'Yes, the men were sent to kill you,' she said slowly, patiently, though her patience was actually wearing thin. 'And Rawlings betrayed you. And I saved you. I know it's a lot to take in, but there you go.'

It was the truth, and Harcourt knew it.

It was too far-fetched and incredible to be anything but. Yet, no matter how he looked at the facts, and then at the creature before him, he couldn't seem to bring himself to believe it.

He, Harcourt Sinclair, deadly rogue, had been saved by his *housemaid.*

Effy could see the thoughts flashing through his black eyes, cold as steel even in the warmth of the spring sun. She saw the confusion and surprise turn into resolve. She had known it wouldn't be easy to convince him of what she'd done. But that didn't mean she wasn't allowed to be slightly annoyed.

A week she had sat by his bedside and nursed him. A week she had barely slept herself, praying, tending to him, talking to him in the hope she might call him back from whatever darkness he had fallen into.

A week of soothing him through the nightmares, of hearing his screams and moans for hours on end. A week she had felt as if her heart was on the verge of breaking, as fear, despair and anguish coursed through her at the thought he might not make it.

And now he was here, alive, and looking down at her as if she were nothing. *Well, what did you expect?*

'Where are we, exactly,' he managed finally, his eyes returning to hers, watching her closely, trying to find sense of her in her eyes. 'And whose nightshirt am I wearing?'

'Sussex. And technically, my brother's cottage. And his nightshirt,' Effy said flatly.

'And where, pray, is your brother?'

'Oh, I don't have a brother. This is all mine. The clothes are here to maintain the appearance. I have a local woman who comes by daily when I'm away, so...'

'So, you...?'

'Forged papers, yes. Oh, don't look at me like that, I know for a fact *you've* done, far far worse.'

'But you're...' Effy raised an eyebrow and he stopped himself. 'Why did you bring me here?'

'Safest place I could think of. Couldn't bring you home, lest Rawlings call back whoever paid him to finish you, and me, off. London, they would have found you eventually. This place, no one knows it exists. It was risky, to transport you, but it's all I could think of. Oh,' Effy added, remembering. 'I did send a note, while the doctor was tending to you. To your friend, Viscount Egerton. I advised him of the general situation, but without too many details. I asked him to deal with Rawlings, and cover for your absence in Society for as long as possible. I imagine it wasn't too hard, what with the tales of our park ride already swirling through every salon.'

Effy's annoyance washed away as she saw Harcourt's jaw drop.

She smiled again, her heart full once more. He was alive. And she could still surprise him.

It was the small things, really.

'What species of creature are you,' he breathed, in a voice so tempting Effy felt the heat rise to her cheeks.

'A very rare species,' she replied, allowing her tone to match his.

'Why did you help me?'

'That, Mr. Sinclair, is a question which is only answered with a tale. Come, let us have some breakfast, and I shall tell it to you.'

Harcourt nodded, and moved just enough for Effy to pass him by.

His eyes would not leave her. *Plain, unremarkable.* Those had been his first impressions. But now?

So different she seemed. Stronger. Bolder. Beautiful almost. Like a wild thing, sprung from the ground to meet the spring. He watched her as she moved around the kitchen, confidently, spritely almost, fixing them breakfast.

Watched her intently as she helped him into a chair, and served him coffee before placing a blanket over his shoulders. She was warmth itself, and she smelled of fresh, new life. *You're losing your mind, man, it's only the circumstances...*

Yet each time he found her eyes, he saw nothing of the creature he had first disparaged. Nothing was left of his housemaid, the mask she had worn, had disappeared.

The creature before him, was the same that had melted into his kiss in the park. Who had teased, and experimented, and tempted *him*. And who apparently, had saved his life, and killed two men.

Effy served him breakfast, delicious looking eggs, ham, and fried toast, and settled down beside him.

'Can you manage,' she asked, gesturing towards his hand. He had almost forgotten.

'I think so,' he said, tucking into his food hungrily. 'Thank you.'

Effy smiled, and nodded.

She knew it wasn't just a *thank you* for offering to help him with his breakfast. It was a *thank you* for everything she had done. And it would be the only one she would get. She didn't mind. It was enough.

He was enough.

'It is broken,' she added. 'Though not too badly. Physician said it would be about a month. You have cuts and bruises a bit of everywhere, but no broken ribs, as you surmised.'

Harcourt nodded graciously, and set about cleaning his plate.

Once they had both finished eating, Effy topped up their coffees, and set herself back down. Taking a deep breath, she readied herself to tell the tale she had prayed she would never have to.

Circumstances, however, had changed, and the past week she had made a decision.

Trust Harcourt. Tell him the truth. Offer him help.

'I always feared one day you might ask how I had come to work in your household,' she said, her voice now wistful, and full of sadness. 'I was not unaware of your rules against young women. But it seemed, my plain and un-tempting appearance was enough to avoid your notice of me. Do you know how long I have worked for you, Mr. Sinclair?'

'I admit, I don't,' he said, wondering what this had to do with anything. But her eyes were now as dark and full of shadows as his own, and he knew whatever she was about to reveal would cost her. 'A few years?'

'Three, to be exact,' she smiled. 'I came to work in your household not long after you fought a duel. Against Lord Almsbury.' There was a flash of understanding in his eyes, and Effy nodded. 'A month, it took, for him to die. For the poison in his blood to take his life. Not bloody long enough,' she spat.

'How long were you in his service,' Harcourt asked, his voice unsteady, anger rising at the thought of what had happened to her.

'Four years,' she managed, before the lump in her throat choked her. But she wouldn't cry. Wouldn't show weakness. Not to him. 'The day he died, is the day I pledged my life to the man who had ended him. To you, Mr. Sinclair. I know you can understand now, why I would have done such a thing. Most of London knew of what happened beneath Lord Almsbury's roof. Though never once did anyone do anything to stop it.'

Silence invaded the room.

Disgust filled Harcourt's heart. All of London did. Though he had ended Almsbury's life for a different reason; the reason had not been so removed from the truth of her experience he posited.

Four years... Four years of torture, and degradation, and... He looked back to Effy, but she showed no emotion. She was as still and unflinching as a statue. He understood her too well in that instant, what had been taken, what she had endured, and how she had survived. Closing herself off to everything, avoiding the pain and memory of it all.

He wished he could kill Almsbury all over again, make him endure what she had.

'You weren't afraid? Pledging your life to me, of all people?'

'Your reputation may be fierce, Mr. Sinclair, but truth be told I would have sworn myself to the Devil himself had he been the one to end my torment.'

'Perhaps you did,' Harcourt mused. Effy smiled faintly and nodded.

'You are tiring, Mr. Sinclair,' Effy said, rising. 'You should rest a while. We still have much to discuss. And you have, I think, quite a lot to make sense of as it is.'

'I think you're right,' Harcourt admitted, somehow unafraid to show weakness to her.

'Come then, back to bed.'

Effy helped him settle back in the bed, ensuring the blankets were tight and snug, and that the glass was once again filled with water.

She really does look like an angel from this vantage…

It had been a very long time indeed since he had been tucked into bed like a sick boy, with such tenderness and care. It had been a very long time indeed, since he had felt safe, unburdened of troubles and worries.

Which was a wonder considering how he had gotten here to begin with.

And what lay ahead.

Effy's face, her sweet smile, were the final images in his mind as he drifted back to sleep.

Revenge could wait until tomorrow at least.

VI.

T he relief that had washed over her when Harcourt had awakened, was quickly replaced with dread. Dread that he might guess the underlying truth of her feelings, a truth which she had only just realized when she had seen him on the ground of the gardens, and which she had had no time to make peace with and conceal.

It really was no wonder that she had managed to fall in love with him. He was wickedly attractive, his eyes and body holding promises of passion any woman would dream of. And of course, she owed him her own life.

Hardly surprising.

And yet, it was because of the very reasons she had no choice but to fall in love with him, that he could never know the truth of it.

Any power she might have now, any chance of success in what she was about to propose, depended on the caveat that he see her as an equal. A capable and useful woman; not some forlorn, ruined creature. And the knowledge, or at least, the rumours of what had happened to her, were enough to ensure he could never look at her with anything other than disgust and pity.

She was a broken, ruined, thing.

Not some beautiful heiress or passionately beautiful mystery.

If she could have avoided telling him, she would have, but that had not been an option. She needed his trust. His understanding, no matter the cost.

No, he would never know the depths to which she had fallen.

Either in her other life, or in her feelings towards him.

She was glad of the respite, the chance to steel herself and prepare for what lie ahead as he slept through the next two days. The time was enough to further prepare what she had to say, and properly conceal her emotions.

Effy went about her chores, enjoying her time in the country as she had seldom had the chance to since she had bought the cottage three years ago. Here, she found peace, solace, and meaning, even in the most menial tasks, such as feeding the chickens, or tending to the horses.

Someday soon, she hoped, this would be her entire life, not just stolen moments here and there.

Soon... Once you have concluded your business, and seen to it that he has concluded his own...

Only when he lay fast asleep, in the dark of night, did Effy chance to feel what she did. She would watch him, his dark eyelashes resting peacefully on his cheeks, the slow, rhythmic rise and fall of his chest, the peaceful beauty he exuded calling out to her heart like a siren. She slept little in those two days, snatching hours here and there in the stiff kitchen chair by the fire.

Harcourt woke on the morning of the third day. Still aching, he felt somewhat human again, and rose with less difficulty. His hand was still the worst of it. He stretched out, feeling more refreshed and at ease than by rights he should.

Chancing a glance at the kitchen, he noticed Effy sleeping on the table, head buried in her arms. So he hadn't dreamt *that*.

Sitting on the edge of the bed, he swallowed down the glass of water she had left, and wet one of the cloths to run across his face. He flinched; apparently there were more bruises and cuts there than he had expected.

He ran through everything Effy had said when he had last woken.

There had been no dissembling, of that much he was certain.

Though he still could not fathom how the creature had managed everything she had.

Most women would have gone into a fit of nerves at the very mention of a life in danger. She had killed two men, dragged him out of danger, and seen to even the smallest details, such as Percy, to ensure his continued safety. *Clever, resourceful, with unimaginable strength.*

Yet there was something still missing in her tale. She was no housemaid, that he knew for certain. His impressions when he had seen her in Madame Chanteclair's shop would not fade away.

Nor the insolence she had shown before then.

And he had not missed the fact that not once she had called him *sir*, preferring instead *Mr. Sinclair*. There was something more to her. And he would find out what it was.

First, he needed to get dressed. Cleaned. *Shave*, he thought, touching his jaw, and realizing he must have been here for over a week by the feel of it.

Fortescue had said the nightshirt was her imaginary brother's. *Also, forged papers?!* There seemed to be no end to her surprises. In any case, that surely meant there would be clothes too.

Quietly, he rose, and went to the wardrobe. Sure enough. Old fashioned, and rustic, but they would do. He set out undergarments, stockings, long breeches, a shirt, and waistcoat. They seemed old and worn, and slightly bigger than his own size, but the cotton and wool were sturdy and well-crafted. Boots, a necktie, and a coat were added to the pile on the bed.

Before long, he also managed to procure a looking glass, and shaving implements. He hadn't thought she would be so foolish as to forget to place those items here to add to her deception. *Clever girl…*

Harcourt barely recognized himself in the glass. He saw his eyes widen in shock, but the rest seemed foreign.

Everything seemed to be of varying shades of black, blue, green and red. His nose had been broken and reset. There was a deep slash in his left eyebrow; bruises and cuts covering everything else which wasn't hidden by his growing beard. His hair was more of a matted mane than its usual self.

There was a thick black line across his throat, where the little one had strangled him. He knew his body would be covered in more such markings. *Lucky indeed...*

The realization that he might have indeed died; that the men had meant to kill and not simply discourage, even though he had already had an inkling of it, hit him hard.

He might have died, his purpose unfulfilled, had it not been for the most unexpected creature imaginable. He felt himself shudder at the thought. *Pull yourself together, man...*

Staring down at the shaving implements before him, he realized this might be a more complex operation than originally expected, with one hand, his dominant, out of commission.

'Damn,' he muttered.

'Let me,' came Effy's voice. She strode over to him with a smile, and planted herself beside him. 'I didn't dare while the cuts were still so fresh, but if you are determined, I will take care of this. And then I shall prepare you a bath, I see you've already found the clothes.'

'Thank you,' Harcourt said, settling in the chair.

Effy masterfully prepared him; warm cloth on his face, another around his neck. She then delicately spread the shaving soap on his face and set herself to the task.

It may have been many years since she had done this, but Harcourt never would have guessed. She swept away the beard swiftly and with barely any feeling, slowing only when she approached his wounds.

He watched her carefully again, she was so close it was hard not to. She frowned in concentration, her eyes soft and focused. Her hair had been swept to one side, but not pulled back in any manner, just hung there, rich copper waves splayed across one shoulder. She smelled just as fresh and enticing, with a hint of richness, of the earth, about her. He felt something stirring in his abdomen, and checked himself.

This was most certainly not the time for that sort of business.

'There,' she said, hands on her hips, proudly examining her work.

'Thank you,' Harcourt mumbled, running his hands over the smooth surface, wincing slightly as he hit the injuries.

That was enough to cool his ardour.

'I'll prepare you a bath, then you can get dressed, and we can have some lunch,' she said, heading out to the yard. 'Then, we can talk.'

Effy hoped she sounded as nonchalant as she had tried to, though the nearness of him had definitely troubled her.

Shaving another was such an intimate gesture; it had taken all she had not to falter and nick him. The cool spring air brought her back to her senses, and she set about her tasks. *No distractions.*

She was no untested woman. She was not inexperienced.

She knew herself, and the ways of the world all too well.

She was better than letting foolish notions of love cloud her thoughts and actions. Once had been enough.

Once, had cost her far too much to let it happen all over again.

∞

It did not go unnoticed that Fortescue kept her distance from him after that, preparing and setting the bath before the hearth, then scuttling away to do *chores*. He wondered if she had also sensed the danger in their closeness. Not that he was complaining. He needed to be alone, to have time to restore himself to the man he was without distraction.

With his bath, during which he did indeed find his body as battered as his face, though luckily not as broken, he had washed away everything. Doubt, fear, even the fleeting longing he had felt for Effy.

She had saved his life. She was a woman. She kissed very well.

It was natural he should feel some reaction to her presence.

Bathed, fresh as a new-born, hair combed, and clothed in another man's clothes, he felt himself again. Strong. Fearless. Vengeful. Even more so now that someone had thought it a good idea to come for his life. *Was it Mowbray*, he wondered.

Percy had warned him that the Duke was not taking kindly to his attentions for his daughter. *Bit extreme nonetheless...* He may not be a respected peer, still, he had standing in Society, and a fortune. His death would not be unnoticed. Whoever it was, he would find them, and pay them the same respect they had shown him.

They had eaten in silence, save for enquiries of his injuries, and the sounds of her livestock outside. Neither had glanced at the other, content in directing their attentions to the rather sumptuous mutton stew and dark bread with fresh butter.

Not until after they had finished, and sat again with coffee before them, did they look at each other again.

'I should return to London,' Harcourt began. She had said they should talk, but in his mind, there was nothing more to speak of. He had to return to London as soon as possible and finish this. 'Do you have a horse I could perhaps borrow?'

'Indeed,' Effy said with the faintest smile. She was studying his eyes, and he found it somehow deeply troubling. 'You are welcome to borrow one, ride to the nearest village and join the mail coach back to London whenever you wish.'

'But?' He could sense there was more.

'But, I would not think it to be wise,' Effy advised.

'And what would you know of such matters,' he snapped, harsher than he meant. She did not flinch, only cocked her head slightly. 'I must return to London and deal with those who have attempted to take my life.'

'Indeed, you must.'

Her complacency was grating.

'Good God, woman, if you have something to say, please, do!'

'What happened, in truth you only really have yourself to blame,' she said calmly, baiting him. She saw his jaw clench, and continued. 'You grasped too tightly. You were desperate, and blindsided.'

'I ask again, what do you know of such matters,' he growled, leaning in close, hoping to intimidate.

Again, she didn't flinch, only met his gaze squarely. There was a circle of black around the brown of her eyes, he noticed. Coupled with the black of her irises, it seemed almost that her eyes matched his own.

'I know,' she whispered. 'About your quest for revenge. I do not know the particulars of why, but I know. Almsbury. Mowbray. Bolton. Campbell. Russell.' She saw his eyes widen, and knew she had his attention. *Now, to keep it.* 'You have worked your entire life to build a fortune great enough to give you the means to exact it. To gain you entry into their world. But the truth is, you are still not welcome. You thought they would bend the rules for your fortune, and so some have. But not the rest. You are lost in a world you do not know how to play in, and the fact of the matter is Mr. Sinclair, without playing by at least some of the rules, without help, you will never win.'

'How do you know about them,' he asked, even closer now, their noses nearly touching.

'I have worked in your home for three years, Mr. Sinclair,' she said simply, smiling again. 'I made it my business to know who you were. And what you wanted.'

'What do you want, hm,' he asked roughly, his fingers now curled around her throat, tightening ever so slightly. 'Who are *you*, Miss Fortescue?'

'You need not use such methods to root out *my* secrets, Mr. Sinclair,' she said with the slightest trace of disappointment. Not fear; disappointment. 'I have suffered far worse, and such actions have little power to intimidate me anymore.' Harcourt felt a pang, hating himself for raising a hand to one who had suffered so much already. He relaxed his grip, though he left his fingers on her skin, gently caressing the place they had taken hold, as if to wipe away the pain of the action. 'I want to help you. And I want my own revenge. I can, help, if you accept it. As for my own, I need, to my own dismay, the assistance of a dangerous man to manage it.'

'And what help could you possibly offer me,' he teased,

47

tempted to make her forget his previous action with a kiss. She did look rather scrumptious in the light of the late afternoon, breeze fluttering her hair ever so slightly as it flew in through the open windows. 'Why should I need *your* help?'

'I was not always, diminished, as I am now. Once, another lifetime ago, I was one of them. A baron's daughter. I know their ways, their rules. I can help you. Help you infiltrate their world better than you could ever have dreamed.'

'A baron's daughter? There is a story there.'

'Not one for today,' Effy said, conscious to keep her eyes fixed on his, and her mind away from the touch of his fingers on her skin. His apology, which was giving rise to much, much more. 'If you accept my proposal, we will have plenty of time for my tales of woe, later.'

'And your revenge, then, tell me,' Harcourt asked, genuinely curious. Her eyes were darkening, and not from the woe she spoke of. Rather, he mused, from his touch. It was pleasant, igniting his own desire to watch hers rise. 'Who do you seek to revenge yourself upon? I would not have thought it a ladies' business?'

'I did tell you once, I am not a lady,' she challenged. 'There are more responsible for my downfall than Lord Almsbury alone.'

'Your, proposal, then?'

'The Season has only just begun. Wait a while before returning to London. A month or so. Remain here, with me, and we shall prepare a new plan for your revenge. And one for mine. Your friend, Viscount Egerton has already, I am sure, put it about that you have retired to the country for a sojourn with your mistress. It will allow you to preserve what is left of your reputation, and give us time to find those responsible for the attack on your person.'

'A month? You wish for me to remain here for a month? And then what?'

'More or less, yes. And then, we return to London, with me as your spinster cousin perhaps, and we set about our business.'

'Aren't you afraid? That someone should recognize you? From

your former life. *Lives.*'

'People see what we tell them to see,' Effy whispered.

And he knew she was also referring to him.

'You are a strange sort of creature, Fortescue. Very rare in-deed...'

Effy saw his gaze fall to her lips as his fingers found the hollow at the base of her neck. She saw the desire in his eyes, the consideration of what he could do.

What she might allow him to do. But he was using his powers of seduction to control, to disarm, and that, she would not, could not allow.

'So you accept then,' she asked, colder, without hint of flirtation, signalling that their little game was over.

For now.

'I accept your proposal Fortescue,' he agreed, slowly, languidly removing his fingers, and settling back into his chair. 'Though I reserve the right to return to my original plan should I wish.'

'Naturally,' Effy acceded, with a tilt of her head and an overt show of graciousness.

'Shall we begin, then,' Harcourt asked, eyes twinkling dangerously.

Oh Lord, Effy... You got what you wanted...

Only now, she realized just how terrifying a prospect it was.

∞

Some fifty miles away, in the drawing room of a Mayfair townhouse once the paragon of opulence and fashion, now faded and dusty, cobwebs and grime covering what was left of the meagre furniture, sat a rather anxious brute, who decidedly did not belong in such a place, no matter the state of disrepair.

'You assured me, sir, that the matter would be handled,' his employer sneered, the voice clear and sharp as ice despite age and circumstance. 'Yet here we are, a week later, and Harcourt Sinclair is still alive, and more galling, nowhere to be found.'

'I sent me best boys,' the brute said, trying not to let the fierce grey eyes discomfort him. 'Dead, all of them, I don't know -'

'Enough of your excuses, I want him found, and dead. Rumour says he has taken to the country with his mistress, but we both know that is not the case. He will return to London, and soon, I venture. I want him watched, and dead. But you will let me know of your plans *before* you enact them, we cannot risk more failure. Nor can I risk it being known *I* am here. I had enough difficulty discovering that Mowbray girl's involvement without my own being known.'

'Yes, of course -'

'That will be all,' the man's employer drawled, waving a hand in dismissal.

The brute might be a reputed terror of the East End, but that did not mean he did not know he should fear his employer with every bone in his body.

He scurried away, unheard and unseen, back to his safe and comfortable lair, to await Harcourt Sinclair's return.

Soon, Mr. Sinclair... Soon I shall make you pay for your sins...

Everything had been taken away since Harcourt Sinclair had appeared. And before long, the debt would be repaid.

You can run, hide, and lick your wounds, but I was at this game long before you were born.

VII.

The relief on Effy's face must have shown more than she hoped when she glimpsed Harcourt ride over the horizon back towards the cottage. Backlit by the breathtaking sunset and rising mists he looked like a mighty knight springing forth from an age-old tale. A knight, in very rustic armour, which still somehow did nothing to conceal his looks.

It must have shown, for when he rode up to meet her, he shot her a wolfishly satisfied grin, and a tug on his cap.

To be fair, he had set off at sunrise, and had been gone all day. Effy couldn't help but wonder if he had decided to leave, return to London after all. He owed her nothing.

Not even his life, for surely he could argue he had saved hers and now they were even. Yet here he was. He had returned. *To me.*

Their accord stood fast, and yes, she was relieved.

Harcourt slid of his horse carefully, silently cursing as he hit the ground.

It hadn't been wise to ride so far, and it had taken him longer than expected, his bruised ribs and useless right hand making his progress slow.

How he had longed for a good gallop across the lush countryside of the South Downs, to truly clear his mind and restore his soul.

But no. He had confined to a slow, pleasurable, but tediously slow walk.

It had felt oddly heart-warming, riding up over the hill to see

Fortescue waiting, *for him*, a fire-lit angel, a vision of a simple life, there before the little cottage, her plain and rustic cotton dress blowing in the wind.

In another life, a vision such as that might have been enough to slake his thirst. Not in this one.

Though, he couldn't deny the unexpected jolt of pleasure he had felt when he had seen Fortescue's relief. Determined, clever, stubborn, she may be, but still, he was sure, she must have doubts about allying herself with him.

What woman wouldn't? Particularly one who claimed to know him so well? And yet, she had been relieved, *glad* almost, to see him.

'I didn't mean to worry you,' he said, leading the horse to the tiny stable, Fortescue at his heels, expectant. *Though not of an apology judging by her face...* 'It took me longer than expected. I'm not quite as recovered as I imagined...'

'Oh,' she said, her eyes full of concern as they swept over his body. 'Leave Sam, I'll tend to him. There's a bath ready, I was going to have one, and then you appeared... You're welcome to it.'

'Are you sure? I can -'

'Nonsense. Off you go.'

Harcourt nodded graciously, and left her too it.

A bath would in fact be most welcome, though he felt bad taking hers.

He had barely held his tongue, and nearly offered her to share it. He chuckled to himself as he settled into the soothing hot water. He would have at least enjoyed her reaction; been curious to see how she would answer.

Effy Fortescue was not immune to him, that much was clear. And he was finding himself less and less immune with every hour. She was confident, sure of herself, and prettier every day. She had been an eager enough participant in their kiss, so why was he now sure she would not respond so favourably to any advances?

Almsbury, you fool! He had almost allowed himself to forget her past. To her credit, whatever she had suffered, she had learned how to hide it well.

But whatever she had suffered must have had some effect on the way she dealt with men. So many unanswered questions...

Perhaps it was the mystery of her he found enticing. *Must be,* he told himself, washing off as quickly as he could so she could still have the chance of a warm bath, no matter that his own muscles longed only to sit in the warmth forever. *Or better yet...*

Effy gave him time enough to have a proper soak, his muscles would need it. She gave herself time enough to focus and regain composure, tending to Sam, and the other animals, settling them in for the night.

When she was quite sure he must have finished, she knocked on the door, and entered.

It smelt gorgeous. Roasted meat, and lavender. *Lavender?*

Harcourt was busying himself over the hearth, *cooking?* She touched the water in the bath; she had hoped she might have just enough warmth for herself, and nearly jumped.

It was almost boiling hot.

'I felt terrible, taking your bath,' he said, stirring whatever he was cooking. There was a delectable smell of onions and beef rising from the pot. 'And I got us dinner in the village.'

'I... I... Thank you,' Effy managed through the sheer shock of the scene before her.

'It's nice to see I can still render a woman speechless. Hurry now, or the bath will be cold.' Effy froze. She hadn't thought this through. Too close. Not enough room. He would *see.* Sensing her reluctance, he turned, and smiled gently. 'I won't look, though it's hardly anything I haven't seen before. And we can talk.'

Quickly, sure he was staring at his creation, Effy dropped her dress, and climbed into the bath with her chemise.

It wouldn't conceal much, not once the thin linen was wet, but enough, hopefully, in case he did chance a glance.

'Did you get everything done,' she asked, relaxing slightly, letting the warm water, and extra lavender oil he had added to it work its magic. 'In the village?'

'Yes. I sent word to Percy that I intended to remain here. I asked him to reorganize my household, and ask for whatever new housekeeper he hired to see a few of my things brought here.'

'You told him where to find you,' Effy exclaimed, and Harcourt turned out of habit. He immediately knew his mistake, and returned to his food. 'Can you trust him?'

'Percy is the only one I can still trust, Fortescue. And I have known him for far longer than I have you... He may not know the particulars of my business, but he will see that what I have asked, is done. And will not disclose our location to anyone.' He heard her slide back down into the water, and tried to chase the image of the transparent linen clinging to her ample and inviting breasts. 'I also ordered some gowns for you, cousin. I peeked at the wardrobe; not suitable I think.'

'Excellent idea, thank you. I shall repay you, of course.'

'No need, Fortescue.'

'If we are to be partners, we must be partners in all things,' she said firmly. 'I will not be indebted to you more than I already am.'

'Very well. Though I believe a life has been paid for with a life.'

Harcourt could understand her pride, and her reluctance. Her need for independence.

But he also had *wanted* to pay for the gowns. It was, in his own small way, a treat.

A gift of thanks for what she had done, and was offering to do.

'By the way, perhaps we should discuss the matter of our living arrangements, Fortescue.'

'I fear there aren't many solutions, Mr. Sinclair.'

'Indeed. We can't have you sleeping in a chair for a month, and chivalrous as I wish I could be, I'm afraid neither can I.'

'We can share the bed, unless you have any objections. There is enough room for us both, and would avoid trying to build a paillasse or purchase another bed.'

'No objections, Fortescue. I just thought, we should make sure we were all on the same terms.'

'Indeed, Mr. Sinclair.'

There was a mumbled curse, and a splash from behind him. It took all the will he had not to turn.

'Fortescue? All well?'

'Towel.'

'God, yes, of course, apologies,' he said. Careful to keep his eyes averted, he felt for the towel he knew he had left close by. Once he'd found it, he held it in proximity to the bath. 'I'm afraid I've not prepared a bath for anyone before.'

'Well, thank you,' Effy said, grabbing the towel and wrapping herself in it before retreating quickly towards the bedroom. 'It was perfect!'

Harcourt grinned, pleased that he had managed to perform such a simple act.

She might not want his gift of gowns and treasures, but if he could please her with such simple domestic tasks, so he would.

Why? Why did he feel the need to please the creature?

God knows... Returning his attention to his meal, he could not help but revel in the domesticity of it all, if only for a short while.

It saved him from examining these new feelings and desires any closer, at the very least.

∞

Never before had a simple roast beef, onions and carrots ever tasted so delectable. Perhaps it was the fact that she hadn't had to cook it herself. Or perhaps, Harcourt was in fact, a rather talented cook. Effy wasn't sure why it should surprise her so, but it was likely due to her imagining he had always been the spoiled, served-upon rake whose desires were command. An image, which was quickly dissolving, and leaving her on very shaky and unstable ground indeed.

Neither of them had spoken much again, both too tired and hungry to care for anything but the meal he had prepared with such care.

Both their bowls had been quite nearly licked clean, and now, Effy felt a warm, comfortable glow as they both sat by the fire, glasses of the French brandy she had stashed in the wardrobe in their hands.

'So,' Effy said quietly, watching the shadows dance on Harcourt's face. He too seemed content, satisfied, and it pleased her to see him somewhat unburdened. The harshness of his manner, his coldness had dissipated, and she felt privileged to see this other side of him. 'Perhaps we should discuss your original plans. Then we can see how to proceed?'

'Indeed. And you should tell me more of your own plans, I think,' he countered, raising an eyebrow, his coal black eyes meeting hers. They were inviting, hypnotising, and searching. 'I imagine you guessed about Mowbray?'

'You sought to ruin his daughter.'

Harcourt nodded.

'Bolton and Campbell will be easy enough,' he said. 'They are business partners.'

'Shipping, as I recall? Same as you?'

'You've done your homework, Fortescue,' Harcourt said appreciatively. 'The wheels of their demise are already in motion. Within a few months, their business, and they themselves by extension, will be ruined. They are counting on a large account, which will very soon be mine.'

'And Russell?'

'Degenerate gambler.'

'I see. Though, if I might suggest, one of the lesser gambling hells? Say, Camden, or Whitechapel perhaps' Effy said with a faint smile. 'You would not need to play him yourself, and unpaid debts in those establishments suffer quite a more significant punishment.'

'An interesting idea. The scandal wouldn't be as potent,' Harcourt conceded. 'But the punishment would befit the crime much better.'

'And what is the crime, Mr. Sinclair?'

'I have no great knowledge of those places I fear,' he said, ignoring the question.

'Good thing then that I do.'

Effy had his full attention then, though why she had let herself divulge that tidbit, she did not know.

She had promised herself she would not let him see the depths of her own demise and depravity, and yet here she was, flaunting it before his eyes. *Because it will serve him. Because you want him to leave you be...*

Harcourt looked over at her, and he knew the surprise and wonder must have been apparent. But he didn't care. Her eyes glittered in the firelight, and a smile danced on her lips as she sipped her brandy teasingly.

Never before had a woman been able to continue surprising him, and look so damned charming and dangerous doing it.

'Another story, I sense, you will not tell me?'

'Indeed. Suffice it to say, I am known to such places, and can easily play there. You'll need to find a way to get him there, of course.'

'Of course,' he said, inclining his head to the master she was.

'As for Mowbray, your intent was clever, but you shouldn't have tried to finish the business yourself.'

'You mean hire someone?'

'Of course not. But I am sure Lady Lydia has a first love somewhere, that could be fetched and thrown back into her way.'

'How can you be so sure,' Harcourt asked, leaning in.

'There always is,' Effy assured him.

'Another tale you shall not tell?'

'It's not my turn yet,' she teased.

God the woman was driving him mad.

She knew how to play the game as well as he did. And he knew her to be just as deadly. How could he have not seen it before?

How could he have missed his own reflection in her soul?

'So, we find out Lady Lydia's first love, entice him to ruin her. And how might we do that?'

'Why, your cousin of course! I feel that she will be well accepted into Society, and make great friends with Lady Lydia and

Lady Lydia's bosom friends.'

'That will not be enough,' Harcourt warned.

'Well, what had you planned for him then, once *you* had ruined her?'

'Ah, I must keep some secrets, Fortescue,' Harcourt teased, smiling. 'Your turn. What of your vengeance then?'

'My tale of woe, then...' Effy took a rather large gulp of brandy, and let it do its worst. Unlocking all the barriers in her heart, freeing her tongue. 'I was nineteen when I ran from home. I was about to make my own debut in the Season, having delayed it for a year after my mother passed. My father, as it happens, had already arranged a marriage for me. An earl, ageing and cruel. I refused, and pleaded for him to wait, to allow me to find my own match during my Season, but he would hear none of it. He wanted a good title, and to join his lands with the earl's adjoining ones. So, I ran. I survived on my wits and the jewels and money I had taken, for a while at least. Then, I realized I would need to seek employment if I was to avoid the gutter. I found a good position, in the household of a childhood friend. Widowed, she had moved away from where we had been raised, and so I thought I might be safe. She welcomed me with open arms, and though we could never be friends as before, I was grateful for what she had given me.' Effy paused, drawing a breath, and finished the brandy. She was very much aware of Harcourt's eyes on her, but she could not bear to meet his gaze. 'My first love. His name was Daniel. A friend of the family. But as it happens, my friend, Sarah, had designs on him. When she found out about us, she sent me away. Though I did not know the reason at the time, she pleaded that her circumstances were changing, and she had arranged for a new position...'

'In Lord Almsbury's household,' Harcourt said quietly. *Women and jealousy...*

'Indeed,' Effy said as lightly as she could muster, pushing back the tears and the lump in her throat. *Why does their betrayal hurt more than anything Almsbury did?* 'It didn't take long for me to understand what Sarah had done, and why. I thought, for a while, that Daniel would come for me...'

'But he didn't,' Harcourt guessed.

Wrongly.

Effy shook her head, and finally met his gaze. He saw the tears welling up, and wanted to reach out, touch, her reassure her, but he was afraid to spook her. That she would withdraw, and never open to him again.

Why am I so interested?

'Oh, he did,' she whispered. 'He came, and we managed to meet in secret. And I gave myself to him. And in the morning, he sent me back.'

'Why?'

'He said that I was already spoiled goods, and that he had only finished the job. No use letting what little I had left go to waste.'

'Why did you go back,' Harcourt asked.

Though he knew the answer.

'He would have found me, and then, it would have been worse.' Effy said, her voice returned to its, flat, almost normal tone, the tears swallowed back. But Harcourt knew the man's words had cut more deeply than any wound she had suffered. 'At least, I knew what to expect, I knew how to survive it. There were rules. He never... He never touched me, not in that way. The wounds of the flesh are, easily enough healed.'

'Daniel, and Sarah? They are your business, yes?'

'Yes. The Marquess de Beaumont and his wife.'

'What happened, to you,' Harcourt asked tentatively after a moment.

It was a terrible question; one he did not expect her to answer. But he needed to know.

To know *her*.

Indeed, when she smiled faintly, and rose, placing her glass on the table between them, he thought she simply meant to walk away.

Instead, she turned her back to him, and unbuttoned her dress. Her breathing was shallow, rapid, but there was no hesitation in her movements. She held it against her chest, tightly, pulling her arms out of the sleeves, then unlacing the front of her chemise until she could slide both from her torso.

Why was she doing this? Why was she letting him see?

Because she wanted him to see. Perhaps then, he would leave her in peace, cease his kindness and flirtations.

Besides, it would only be a matter of time, living as they would be. Only a matter of time before he glimpsed her by accident, and then, it would be far worse...

Now, emboldened by the brandy, and by him, by those eyes, full of concern, and almost a cold, scientific interest, she could not stop herself. He would see. He would know.

And then perhaps, he would leave her in peace. *There...*

Effy heard the sharp intake of breath behind her as the dress and chemise dropped to hang on her hips.

She closed her eyes, and forced herself to breath, while she waited.

'God, Fortescue,' he whispered, sounding almost hurt.

Hundreds of scars shone brightly in the firelight across her back. Tiny ones, long ones that stretched across her entire back, wove together in a sickening pattern telling the tale of their twisted and sordid origin. Barely an inch of skin had been left unmarked.

Harcourt was hurting. He was nauseous, and disgusted, and angry.

He rose, quietly, and ran his fingers across them, gently, softly as he could, but Effy shivered nonetheless.

'There, now you know,' she said, her voice as cold as the blood in her veins. 'Spoiled goods.'

'Fortescue -'

'Don't, please. I know the look in your eyes without even having to turn,' she said grimly. 'Disgust, and pity. I have seen it too many times before. But you asked, and now you know.'

'I will not deny I am disgusted,' Harcourt said, placing his hand on her shoulder. 'But not with you. With the monster who did this. Look at me,' he ordered. Effy obliged, turning, steeling herself, his hand strangely comforting and grounding. 'See, there is no pity. I only wish I had the power to wash them all away.'

Effy searched his eyes, desperately hoping to find the pity she expected there.

But there was none. *Earnestness, care.* That is all she found. *Openness. Recognition.* Things which made he seem even more beautiful, even more perfect in the firelight.

His power and danger a shield for her, against the world.

'I would never see them washed away,' she said, swallowing her desire, and redressing herself. 'For those scars made me what I am.'

'And who is that, I wonder,' he asked softly, sincerely curious to discover who Effy Fortescue truly was.

'Someone strong, master of her own fate. Someone not to be trifled with.'

Was that a warning?

'That was not the first time you took a life, was it?'

'What answer would suit the picture you wish to paint of me Mr. Sinclair?'

'Harcourt, please. And I do not wish to paint a picture. I wish only for the truth.'

'No,' she said with a wan smile. 'It was not. My life has forced me to do many things I never believed myself capable of.'

'As it does to many.'

Harcourt nodded sadly, and watched the creature return to her normal self before him.

He could almost see the layers of the disguise; of the walls she had built around herself being rebuilt after his short glimpse beyond them.

How could anyone be disgusted by her? Those scars made her unique, incredible. She had survived, thrived beyond all odds. His warrior goddess of death and destruction.

His?

How could he have thought what he had about her? This creature was magnificent, beautiful, deadly, and fierce. His double, his twin soul.

Even now, as he watched her resume the character she presented to the world, he knew she was doing it to protect him, to protect them both. Such closeness as he now understood he truly desired, would jeopardize everything.

Desire was dangerous; they both knew it.

And they both had greater purposes which needed to be fulfilled.

'Thank you, for trusting me, Fortescue,' he said as they sat back down, and she poured them another brandy.

'We will need to trust each other if we are both to succeed,' she said simply. 'Perhaps, someday soon, you will learn to trust me.'

Harcourt nodded, and raised his glass.

They toasted, and settled back into a companionable silence.

He did not tell her that he did trust her, more than anyone he ever had.

He simply sat there, drank his brandy, and returned to his plans for vengeance.

VIII.

A week later, in the donkey-drawn cart alongside Effy's order of supplies, came a trunk of Harcourt's things, and a note from Percy. It was the most interesting and exciting thing to happen all week, and both Harcourt and Effy were relieved to have a distraction.

Their week had been studious, and tedious. Long hours had been spent discussing the details of their plans, the alternatives should something go awry, and the arrangements which needed to be made before, and once they had returned to London.

Effy began her schooling of Harcourt in the rules and necessities of Society, and they discussed their *family history*, as well as their relationship as cousins.

In the evenings, they played cards. Both were formidable opponents for the other, and both saw an improvement in their own skills, and tricks, though Effy only lost when she decided to be kind on Harcourt's ego, something he was not unaware of. *Kind little minx...*

In that time, they had settled into a cold sort of companionship, a meeting of minds. They both behaved as if they were simply two professionals in the game of revenge, who had joined together to ensure each other's success.

No further mention was made of Effy's tale, and no further questions were imparted upon Harcourt as to the reasons behind his own vengeance.

There were no further close encounters, both seemed to have been cured of their momentary lapse in judgement, and indeed, if there was any attraction which remained between them, it remained unexplored, and unmentioned.

Both were careful to never retire nor rise at the same time, and to remain at an acceptable distance from the other whilst in bed.

And so, it was a welcome relief to have a break in their monotony with Mr. Brown.

Mr. Brown, who along with his wife took care of the cottage when Effy or her *brother* were not in residence, found nothing out of the ordinary to comment on other than the tremendous and unexpected pleasure it was indeed to finally meet Mr. Fortescue.

To his credit, Harcourt did nothing to dispel the notion, simply chuckled at the appellation, and indulged Mr. Brown in a light conversation about the weather before moving his trunk indoors.

Effy spent a while longer with him, unloading her order, enquiring about his wife and children and grandchildren, deftly distracting him from any questions he might try to ask about her brother and their mutual unexpected arrival.

An hour later, the cart fully unloaded, and Mr. Brown happily on his way after several cups of tea, Effy peeked into the bedroom where Harcourt was busy perusing the contents of his trunk, Percy's letter open on the bed.

He nonchalantly threw a jacket over the pile he had just been rifling through before turning to her, but Effy was anything but fooled.

He was hiding something from her, and though she might hate herself, she knew she would have to do some riffling of her own in due time. It annoyed her, that despite her sharing so many of her secrets, he still seemed unable to fully trust her.

She understood, but after what she had shown him, it hurt nonetheless.

'What does the Viscount say? Anything interesting,' she asked, gesturing to it.

'Few things,' Harcourt said, straightening, a frown on his face. 'Oh dear.'

'Yes, it seems that Lady Lydia is engaged.'

'Disappointing, but not an insurmountable problem.' Effy sighed.

'My thoughts precisely,' Harcourt said, the frown disappearing. Effy's lack of concern was somehow entirely reassuring. 'Percy writes that Rawlings has been dismissed, and advised never to return to London. A new household awaits us, just in case. He was most curious about my *cousin's* arrival, and hopes in the meantime I'm having a splendid time with my mistress.'

'Excellent,' Effy said with a sly grin. 'Any news of...?'

'The bodies we left in the gardens? Yes... Four dead, known and convicted criminals were found, though enquiries are not progressing as to the culprits, and it seems no one is very enthusiastic about the task either. There were no witnesses, and for now the supposition seems to be that it was a gang territory affair. We are safe, for now at least.'

'Good. Another murder trial wouldn't be the best for you.' The one Harcourt had already faced, for Almsbury's murder, had been quite enough to tarnish his reputation, though the judges had of course been lenient as it had been a matter of honour, despite the fact it was a peer who had died. 'He didn't, ask?'

'No. And he has engaged a Runner to make enquiries of his own regarding whose employ the men might have been in.'

'I didn't realize you had asked him to do so,' Effy said, raising an eyebrow. 'You trust him with much it seems.'

'Percy is not unaware of the shadows I live my life in, for his own life is not so very different. I've been thinking, actually,' Harcourt said, eyeing Effy, waiting for her imminent disapproval. 'About how to get Russell into one of your suggested establishments. Percy, as you may be aware, has quite a large circle of friends. Including some dandies, with a taste for cards, and who, it is said, Russell has a taste *for*.'

Effy sighed, crossing her arms, and biting her bottom lip.

It was an interesting thought, and more than they had had so far. She had heard rumours of Russell's particular proclivities, and this might be just the thing to lure, with an unseen and untraceable hand.

'It's a good idea.'

'And more than we had.'

'Indeed, but you would need to tell Percy a bit about what he's getting into.'

'Why,' Harcourt asked, crossing his arms now, suddenly defensive.

'Because, if we succeed, his reputation might suffer. He will have had a hand in Russell's demise,' Effy said flatly. 'And he needs to agree with knowledge of the potential consequences.'

'So now you're starting to have a conscience,' he snapped, his voice cold steel.

'I may not have much left in the way of morals,' Effy said bitterly, his judgement somehow worse than any other she had faced. 'But that does not mean I am devoid of them altogether. He is your friend. You trust him, or have so far. I'm not asking you to divulge your grand scheme or secrets behind it, Hell, you haven't even shared that much with me, and we're supposed to be partners. But you can't ask him to go in blindly. Besides, all he needs to do is start asking questions, and we're finished.'

Harcourt stared at her, surprised at her sudden vehemence and bitterness.

Did she not understand how dangerous trust could be? Percy may be his friend, for the most part, and both men recognized in each other the same darkness, the same danger, but that was precisely why trust was out of the question.

Twenty years he had managed to stay the course, alone, secretly, and now he had joined forces with his *housemaid*, and she wanted yet another brought into their confidence.

Yet, despite his surprise, and annoyance, he did see the sense in her words, as much as it cost him to admit it. Effy raised an eyebrow, waiting for him to come to the conclusion she knew he would.

Harcourt shook his head, relaxing slightly then, amused by the realization that he knew she was right, and she knew that he knew, and was simply waiting for him to concede.

Infuriating creature.

'Very well,' Harcourt drawled with an eye roll, making sure his annoyance was well marked.

'And since you've already hired a Runner, perhaps you could set him next upon finding something useful for me?'

'I shall do so at once when we've returned to London,' Harcourt said with a conciliatory smile.

Despite her attempts over the years, and his own research into the peers of London, neither seemed to have so far been able to acquire anything of use against the Marquess and Marchioness de Beaumont.

'Thank you,' Effy said softly.

It was hardly surprising that after a week of having been cooped up together, spending long hours working, they should begin to feel slightly claustrophobic.

Besides, keeping her emotions in check was proving more exhausting, and daunting than she would have imagined, and so it was only natural that their tempers should begin to show.

If they were to survive the rest of the month, however, they would both need to remain clear-headed and detached.

That is what she had decreed.

'Perhaps we should take the rest of the day,' Harcourt suggested. 'We can resume our work tomorrow.'

'Yes, I think perhaps we should,' Effy nodded. 'I might go for a ride.'

'I can prepare dinner, if you wish?'

'That would be… Yes, thank you.'

'Very well, then. Enjoy your ride.'

With a nod, Effy disappeared, and minutes later he heard her ride off.

Bareback, with no riding habit, and astride like the wild creature she is…

∞

If Effy had hoped her ride would clear her head, and her heart, she was sorely mistaken. Instead, it had only stirred her blood, re-igniting the fire within her. It had taken her longer than usual, or needed, to tend to Sam and the animals that evening; longer than usual to push her emotions back into the depths of her heart.

They had supped in silence again, neither it seemed able to meet the other's gaze. Effy made only to compliment Harcourt's cooking again, indeed his rabbit stew was mouth-watering and delightful, to which she received only a grunt in response. After that, both decided there were too tired for an after-dinner drink or game of cards.

Harcourt insisted on cleaning up, Effy sensed he needed as much an excuse to be away from her as she did to be away from him, though she purported for very different reasons.

She hoped at least he wasn't planning to run back to London without her; it did not fail her notice that he had not taken kindly to her insistence on bringing Percy further into their confidence.

Harcourt was still an unknown quantity, and though she had trusted him more than anyone else, she still had to tread carefully. She had no doubt that Harcourt felt no loyalty towards her, and would abandon her as soon as she had outlived her usefulness.

Or annoyed him.

Yet, as she changed into her nightshirt and robe, she couldn't stop her eyes wandering towards his open trunk beside the wardrobe. She could still hear him clattering in the kitchen.

It was risky, he would not take kindly to her snooping, and could very well pack up and leave should he find her, but then, she couldn't abide him hiding things.

Besides, she too felt the need to discover the man beneath the mask.

Carefully, quietly, she made her way to the side of the trunk he had so nonchalantly covered with his jacket. Attentive to how things were arranged, she slid her hand around, feeling for anything which felt as though it did not belong. Her fingers stopped on a cold, metal surface, and feeling around the edges, she realized it was quite small; the size of a travel looking glass. Yet she knew there would be no reason to pack such a thing.

Lifting it out, she realized it was a delicately gilded silver frame. Within it, was a watercolour portrait of a young woman, not so much older than herself, with the same dark curls, eyes, and sharp features as Harcourt.

'My mother,' came Harcourt's voice.

Effy detected a note of sadness and disappointment.

'I'm sorry,' I shouldn't have,' she said, not daring to meet his eyes as she hastily replaced the frame, and rose. 'I don't know what came over me.'

Harcourt said nothing as Effy retreated to bed, her cheeks burning with shame.

She could feel his cold hard stare watching her every move, and chastised herself at having been so foolishly tempted. She had glimpsed something very personal, and Harcourt would not forgive her for it.

Once Effy was settled, Harcourt changed into his own nightshirt. He felt oddly betrayed, particularly since he had already decided to tell her the truth of it anyways.

All day, he had gone over and over her words, until finally he had realized her anger had sprung from the fact that *she* had trusted him with her most painful truth, and he had yet to trust her.

If only she had waited, instead of rifling through his things like a thief in the night. And yet, he had to admit, he would have done exactly the same. *Had she not had the courage I lacked to share her wounds...*

He settled into bed himself, and blew out the candle.

He could tell Effy was frightened beside him, her breathing rather too controlled and deep. It unsettled him, how much he hated himself at having made her feel *frightened*.

She should feel guilty. *But frightened?*

'She's the reason,' he said quietly, before he could stop himself yet again from revealing the secret he never had with anyone. Not one friend, one mistress in the aftermath of passion, not even a priest. 'The reason for all this.' Harcourt felt Effy tense slightly. 'During the War of the Second Coalition... I don't know how to start...'

Effy could feel the pain and hesitation in his voice.

She knew all too well what it was costing him to reveal this to her. Slowly, she rolled onto her back, and slid her hand onto his. She felt him take a deep breath before he slid his fingers in between her own, and held on tightly.

An anchor, in the here and now, to prevent losing himself in the memory.

'It was only my mother and I. A simple cottage in the French countryside. Just the two of us. We thought we were safe, from the world and the war raging beyond, but how wrong we were. They came one night, and my mother... She thought she could keep them in check. Food, drink, and they would leave in the morning. Soldiers had come and gone before. We should have hidden ourselves, but how could we ever imagine?' Harcourt's voice broke, and Effy held his hand ever tighter. 'The things they did to her... Not even the most twisted demons of Hell would have thought up such torments. In the morning they left. Laughing. I can still hear the sound of the laughter as they rode away. They made me watch, everything. I saw the light go from her eyes, and then, the life.'

Effy's stomach churned. Five men, one woman.

The torture she had endured, and the horrors her son had seen. It made her nauseous.

'I vowed on her grave, her grave that I dug myself, that I would not rest until I saw them punished for what they had done.'

'How old were you,' she whispered after letting Harcourt calm himself for a moment.

The nightmares... God she never would have imagined...

'Fourteen,' he said, swallowing the lump in his throat. The

memories of that night were still crystal clear in his mind, and only Effy's touch kept him sane in that moment. 'I wondered for years why they let me live, until finally I realized. It was all part of the game. But they should have slit my throat. They were careless. Spoke each other's names. Never once did they imagine what they might have made of me that night.'

Harcourt's voice was steel again.

Effy released a breath she had not been aware she was holding, and without another word, raised his arm, and placed it around her shoulder as she snuggled into the crook of his arm, her head against his chest so she could feel his heartbeat racing. She slid her own arm across his chest to hold him tightly, and felt him relax beneath her with a deep sigh, and a low moan.

How petty her own vengeance seemed in the light of his own.

His mother. Vengeance against depraved men who had without doubt hurt so many more since...

In that moment, Effy was acutely aware of the nobility, of the *goodness* hidden beneath all the layers of darkness. Darkness that he had sought out to sooth chase the demons, much as she had sought to do.

How alike we are...

There was no *sorry*, no attempts to talk away his pain, or offer hollow words of comfort.

Only this; her body against his. Her warmth, a shield against the pain of his past. Her embrace, to ground him.

There was no desire, no passion, only gentle care and tenderness, and Harcourt could not help but tighten his grip on her, pull her closer to him, as if he could absorb all that was good and generous and light of hers within himself. He breathed her in, her clean, fresh scent, and felt, for the first time in twenty years, somewhat at peace.

His soul, soothed by the strange creature in his arms. *My twin soul...*

Neither could dispel the feeling, as they fell asleep in each other's arms, that their partnership had evolved into something more, something far more dangerous, which try as they might, they would not be able to deny for much longer.

IX.

Light streamed through the curtains, basking the room in a dusky, half-light, dust swirling in the thick beams of light like the tiniest snowfall. Outside, the animals, indeed the entire world was eerily quiet, as though pausing; waiting.

Effy's eyes fluttered open, then closed again. *Just a little longer...* It had been a long while since she had slept so well; since she had felt so warm and safe. She felt like she was still in a dream, half-awake, half-asleep, her mind still and quiet.

She could feel Harcourt behind her, his arm wrapped tightly against her chest. It felt like his entire being was enveloping her, nestled as she was against him. *Just a little longer...*

Harcourt moaned lazily, his eyes fluttering open and closed much as Effy's had, his mind in that same place between slumber and waking. He breathed in deeply, the delicious essence that was the woman in his arms utterly intoxicating.

His body urged him to bring her in even closer, and so he did. The feel of her, her softness against him exquisite.

And his body responded accordingly.

Dangerous territory...

And yet, the feel of his grip, of his growing hardness beneath her buttocks, it did nothing but stir her own blood. There was a tentativeness. A test. Would she pull away from him? She should.

But try as she might, she couldn't help but relish in her effect on him; even though she knew any warm body at this hour of the morning might have the same effect on him. Effy allowed herself to readjust her hips against his, ever so slightly, but enough to incur a reaction.

Harcourt moaned softly, a purr of pleasure almost, and let himself explore. He should not be doing this, but then, if he didn't, he would regret it.

My wild little fire goddess… He was utterly under her spell. Eyes still closed, intent on savouring each sensation, he moved his hand, slowly. He let it roam over each of Effy's breasts in turn, gently cupping each one, his thumb lazily grazing over her nipples. He felt them harden beneath his touch, felt her arch against him ever so slightly, her responses as slow and deliberate as his own.

Next came her ribs, then he allowed himself to trace the line beneath her breasts, down across her stomach, carefully sliding across onto her hip and thigh. Effy's foot rose to meet his, then explored his ankle, and calf, winding itself around him.

Lowering his head, he nudged a path through her locks to her ear, nibbling gently on the lobe.

Effy couldn't help but exhale sharply, the delicate bite a luscious contrast to the tender caresses of his hand. She let her own hand find its way to his waist, then to his thigh, mirroring his own touch.

When his hand rested on the place between her thighs, she knew the question he was asking. She knew she should resist, but much as she had been unable to refuse succumbing to his potent magnetism in the barouche, she was unable to refuse him now. She wanted to feel his touch more than she wanted to breathe at this very second.

So she answered, hand moving to his buttocks, as taut and as perfectly formed as they had seemed under his breeches. She pulled him in closer, his hardness pressing against the back of her thighs, and she felt his breath as he signed against her cheek.

In one elegant move, his hand was under her night shirt, his fingers finding their way effortlessly to the already slick, wet folds they sought.

Harcourt took his time, skilfully parting her lips, before requesting further entry by subtly rubbing the sensitive nub that guarded it.

Tighter, closer, she pulled him against her, and she relished in the feel of his heartbeat against her own, his heat and strength and power, so controlled, *for her*.

With a gasp, and a slight arching, his fingers entered her, his mouth nibbling on her ear again.

In unison, he began stroking, and caressing, listening to everything her body told him she did or did not like, everything which brought her closer to the edge.

They moved together in rhythm, her buttocks rubbing against his hardness just enough, the sensation taunting and yet potent.

God, she will drive me mad... He wanted her, to be inside her, to drown in her, and yet he knew that would be too far. *Not yet, and this, this is enough... God she knows how to move...*

There was no hesitation, and yet no rush to anything they shared.

Only a desire to relish in the newfound sensations and connection; to relish in the pleasure they knew they were giving the other.

Neither had the desire to take, only to give. There was an intimacy, a trust, a longing to fulfil which neither had felt before.

Effy had given herself before, but not like this.

And Harcourt... Harcourt had never given without the promise of then taking. He had never given selflessly.

And even though he couldn't deny the pleasure he felt as he explored every layer of Effy's core, as he heard her respond, felt her release beneath him, it was unlike anything he had ever felt before.

Together, they moved in unison, touching, caressing, biting, rubbing, teasing, grinding, faster and faster, until together they reached their peaks, with muffled cries and gasps of release.

They lay there, entwined as they had been, their stilted breaths somehow in unison now too, wet and sweaty and sticky and utterly satisfied, clinging to each other and to the dreamlike state they had managed to remain in.

The crow of the rooster outside jolted them back to reality.

Giggling like naughty school children, they disengaged from each other, Effy sliding from bed and out of the bedroom before Harcourt could even open his eyes to watch her leave.

Smiling, he rolled onto his back, and revelled in the heavenly sensations still coursing through his body for a few minutes longer, his heart more at peace than it had been for twenty years.

There were certainly worse ways to wake up.

∞

Effy gasped as she removed her head from the ice-cold bucket of water she had just drawn, chiding herself remorselessly as she quickly washed away the traces of what had just happened. Of the ecstasy. Of the abandon.

Foolish. Careless. Foolish. Goosebumps covered her flesh, and she shivered as she wrung and tossed her hair, leaving it to the spring breeze to dry.

Try as she might, she could not wash away the feel of his touch, the tingling of her skin, the burning, potent desire he had awoken and unleashed.

It's been too long since you've had a man in your bed...

And they had been in such close quarters.

Harcourt was irresistible, and he knew it. He had just proven it.

And now...

Now, you get back to business. No distractions! Resolved, cold and hungry, she stalked back into the cottage, and set about making breakfast.

Harcourt emerged from the bedroom, fresh and clean and fully dressed, and looking so much the handsome incorrigible devil he was. *Why can't you look as plain and unthreatening as any-one else would in that plain country attire?*

Proudly, Effy stalked past him, closing the curtain with a harsh *woosh* so she could make herself decent.

Re-emerging, she found Harcourt waiting for her at the table. He served them as she sat down, a glowing grin of satisfaction on his face that only seemed to make her feel worse.

Harcourt sensed her distance, and searched her eyes for an answer. She was not the first who had abandoned herself to his will, only to regret it later, but that seemed so unlike the Effy he now thought he knew, at least in part.

But when he reached for her hand, she quickly drew it away under pretence of grabbing her coffee.

'Fortescue,' he asked with a frown. 'Look at me, please.'

'What,' she asked coldly, her dark eyes meeting his own with an aloofness and irritation that injured him somewhat.

'We should talk.'

'Should we?'

'What just happened...'

God, why was this so hard? Why was he demanding words?

'Harcourt, I don't need the talk,' she said with a sigh, her carefree manner less than convincing. 'We've been in close quarters, alone, for too long. We've both survived a rather stressful and dangerous situation, and have been forced into very private confessions.'

'*Forced* confessions,' he asked incredulously.

Effy could see the hurt she was inflicting in his darkening and pleading eyes, but it needed to be done, for both their sakes.

No, only for yours. Your heart is the one in trouble. Enough!

'Please, do not misunderstand me,' she said, ever-so-sweetly. 'What happened, was bound to at some point. It is only natural to seek such, release, in conditions such as these. I mean, three weeks ago you wouldn't have even noticed me. Let me reassure you, you are in no danger from me, just as I am in no danger from you. I promise not to fall in love with you.'

Because I already have, fool that I am...

'Well, that certainly is reassuring indeed,' he said, his words as sharp as the edge of a blade. 'Now that we have cleared that up, I suppose we should return to the business at hand.'

'Quite.'

'Quite.'

With a nod, they both disengaged, and finished their break-fast in silence.

After which, they returned to the matters at hand, the planning, the practise, the schooling.

In the days which followed, they found their way back to the cold, companionable silence. They returned to the bitter professionalism they both knew was required of them. They both set aside their feelings, their longing for the other, which, despite their denials, continued to grow. They both avoided each other whenever possible, and retreated to a comfortable distance.

Revenge was a dirty, nasty, dangerous enough business without involving emotions. Effy had saved them, once again, from crossing further into territory that might well cost them their lives.

No matter the hurt they had both suffered, they were safe.

For now.

X.

Three weeks later, early one bright spring Monday afternoon, Harcourt Sinclair and his cousin, the newly baptised Patience Sinclair, arrived back in London. The name, Harcourt's choice, had infuriated Effy, but after him using it for nigh on two weeks straight, she couldn't deny the fact that she responded to it whenever he called.

The choice of the name, the taunting and teasing and coaxing which had come with the suggestion, had signified a shift in their dealings together. From the cold companionship, they had paved a way into a convivial camaraderie, any latent desire or want neatly tucked away beneath a veneer of playfulness.

Looking back, both of them had to admit that the past two weeks had been rather enjoyable, the simple pleasures of country life a welcome respite from the dangers that lay ahead.

Their plans, practices, and schooling, had become almost *fun*, indeed the memory of it made them both smile as their carriage lurched to a stop before the townhouse in Green Park.

It felt odd, entering through the front door, as a guest, and Effy expected at any moment for someone to recognize her, and call her out.

But the servants were indeed all new, bowing and offering their welcome as they took her pelisse, bonnet, and gloves, and showed Harcourt and her to their rooms to settle.

'Your wardrobe arrived yesterday,' the quiet little mouse of a maid, whose position Effy had once had, said with a curtsey as she ushered her into her rooms, across the hall from Harcourt's.

'I'm afraid there is no lady's maid in the house Miss, but should you need help, ring for me and I will do my best to attend to you.'

'Thank you. What is your name, pray,' Effy asked, in her demure, Patience-toned spinster voice.

'Lily, Miss,' the girl said with a curtsey.

'Thank you, Lily. I'm quite used to dressing myself, but I will remember you should I require any assistance.'

Another curtsey, and the girl was gone, slightly disappointed by the look of her at the lack of opportunity to become a lady's maid in all but name.

Effy wandered around the pale cream room, tasteful, classic, and untouched.

How many times had she dusted this room herself? Refreshed the linens though never once any guests had visited. *Other than those who visited Harcourt's bed...* Shuddering at the memory of so many widows, wives, and courtesans passing through, Effy turned away and examined the contents of the wardrobe.

Percy and Harcourt had done well. Rows of expensive silks and linens, in demure and plain colours hung neatly within. Bonnets and accessories, shoes and shawls in matching shades and materials were neatly tucked away.

Effy brushed her hand across the elegant cuts and fine materials, her hand staying on one garment in particular, neatly tucked at the back. She smiled.

One garment; a token, a message he had not been able to resist.

A *risqué*, blood-red ballgown, its perfect cut made to accentuate every curve, but with no adornments. *Rogue...*

A quiet knock pulled her from her admiration and musings.

'Come in,' she called, closing the wardrobe again.

'Mr. Sinclair requests your presence in the library, Miss,' stated Harcourt's new footman, a handsome young chap named George, who seemed intent on showing his age was reflected in no way in his abilities. 'When you're settled, Miss.'

'Thank you, George. Please tell Mr. Sinclair that I shall be down in a moment.'

'Very well, Miss,' he said with a bow before leaving.

With a sigh, Effy left her new room, and made her way to the library, steeling her mind against any doubts, questions, or hesitation.

Everything they had both worked for, everything they both wanted was now within reach.

Wasn't it?

∞

Harcourt stood before the window, just as he had been the first time Effy had met him here, what somehow now seemed like a lifetime ago. George had announced her, much as Rawlings had, and the look in Harcourt's eyes was not so very different from what it had been that day.

Once again he stood before her, lord of the manor, himself once again. The bandage on his hand, and the missing patch of eyebrow the only trace of what had befallen him.

And yet, when he smiled broadly, gesturing to an armchair by the empty grate, she saw a different man altogether before her.

'Everything to your satisfaction, *cousin*,' he asked teasingly, sitting in the chair opposite. Tea had been laid out, but when Effy made to pour, he stopped her. 'Let me.'

'It is a lady's duty to serve tea, *cousin*, you must not forget yourself.'

'There is no one to witness my disregard for the rules of polite Society,' he said, a wicked gleam in his eye. 'Are the clothes to your satisfaction?'

'They are perfect, thank you. Though,' Effy grinned, 'There is a rather unsuitable ball gown that seems to have found its way into my wardrobe.'

'Oh?'

'A beautiful thing, such a shame I shall never have the chance to wear it,' Effy said, a note of warning in her voice.

'We shall see...'

Effy couldn't help but chuckle at his persistence, and smiled as she watched him prepare her tea just as she liked it.

He settled back with his own cup after handing her hers, and they both sipped quietly before he returned to the business at hand.

'Percy has invited himself to dinner this evening,' he said, watching her carefully for any reactions she might then try to hide from him, as he had found her doing all too often of late. He didn't like secretive Effy, he much preferred open, irreverent, determined Fortescue. 'I hope you won't be too tired; I can tell him to call tomorrow instead if you prefer?'

'Why wait? Tonight will be fine. I look forward to making his acquaintance.'

'And he apparently, is eager to make yours,' he said lightly, hoping the note of jealousy was not apparent. *As if she would ever...* 'As is all of London apparently. He has been busy, ensuring we are still welcome in Society, and that your arrival will be well met. His grandmother, you see, has quite the connections.'

'I will be sure to thank him.'

'There is, that is, I have had word from the Runner,' he sighed, all lightness gone. 'No further clues as to the identity of the person seeking my demise.'

'You still think it's Mowbray?'

'We shall see...'

'You mean, we shall see if whoever it is tries again. If they do -'

'Then we will know it isn't him.'

'Don't worry, Fortescue,' he said with a less than reassuring smile. 'We will be careful. And ready, for whatever comes our way.' Effy nodded, less than reassured. *More danger. More chances to lose him.* 'And, regarding the other matter...'

'Nothing?'

'I fear not. Whatever secrets the de Beaumonts may have, they have been very prudent.' Effy laughed mirthlessly and shook her head. *Of course it couldn't be that simple...* 'We will find something, Fortescue. I promise. We will find a way. I was wondering actually, if you might allow me to make some enquiries with

Percy this evening? No mention of you, or your past, of course.'

'Why not?

'We will find a way,' Harcourt said gently, interpreting her lack of enthusiasm as defeat.

Though Effy did feel defeated, she was also less angered, less affected by the news than she should have been.

After everything Harcourt had confessed, Effy had begun to wonder how important her own vengeance was compared to his. She hadn't given up; she had simply relegated the task to the bottom of her present concerns.

'Even if I have to call him out myself.'

'No,' Effy said with a vehemence that took him aback. 'We will find a way, as you say.'

Over my dead body will you provoke a duel Harcourt Sinclair.

Effy's subsequent smile was about as reassuring as his own had been. It wasn't that she didn't appreciate his offer; what woman wouldn't dream of a man so ready to risk life and limb to defend her honour?

The problem was, he would do it out of duty. To respect their deal. And he would be risking so much, *too* much, for her to ever allow it. *No. If it ever comes to that...*

'I have some appointments to attend to, before dinner,' Harcourt said, setting his cup on the table and rising.

'Bolton and Campbell?'

'Indeed.'

'I shall leave you to it then,' Effy smiled, faintly, aware of the dismissal. 'I will see you at dinner, *cousin.*'

With a nod, and a curtsey, Effy left him to his business, and returned to her room, grateful to have some time alone, for the first time in what seemed a very long time indeed.

Her thoughts were muddled, and she desperately needed to recompose herself before continuing their work.

Harcourt watched her go, wondering yet again if he had made a terrible mistake agreeing to this arrangement. Never before had he trusted anyone as he trusted Effy, never before had he considered he might not have to face the task he had appointed himself alone.

But when she had come to him, offered to share the burden, he had felt some of the weight lift from his shoulders.

All the time they had spent planning in the cottage, and now...

He couldn't help but sense something had changed. *Women...*

Yet even as he thought it, he knew that Effy was unlike any other woman he had ever encountered.

Still, when he had offered to call out the viper that had wronged her so, she had seemed terrified. Hesitant. As if her resolve was faltering.

Or perhaps, she was still in love with the snake. Perhaps she feared he would die at his hand much like Almsbury had. Duels were no trifle; he had only just escaped the noose the last time.

Perhaps this had all been for nought, and Effy was not who he thought she was. Only a love-stricken, wounded women after all. The thought of her still in love with that loathsome monster sickened him. *Why should you even care?*

Sighing, Harcourt rubbed his temples.

Tonight. Dinner with Percy. He would see how that went, he resolved. Perhaps she was only tired. It had been a very strange few weeks.

Though he now needed her help, loathe as he was to admit it, he would offer her a way out.

But first, he had to attend to his own business. His absence had endangered the deal that would seal Bolton and Campbell's fate.

Now, he had to focus, and repair matters before it was too late.

XI.

At precisely eight o'clock that evening, after smoothing her skirts and checking her appearance in the large gilded mirror in the hall for perhaps the hundredth time, Effy made her way into the sitting room. Having managed to spend a few hours in solitary contemplation, she felt much restored, and ready to face the day, or rather evening, ahead.

For the occasion, she had chosen a plain chocolate brown silk evening dress, sumptuous and yet demure, to which she had been sure to add a delicate lace fichu. She forewent any adornments, and opted for a severe bun, a single curl on either side to frame her face. This was to be a simple, relaxed, and informal affair after all.

Their guest had already arrived, she had heard the bell and flurry of activity some time ago, and indeed, there he sat across from Harcourt in one of the armchairs by the fire.

Both men looked dashingly handsome, both in nearly matching cream-coloured breeches, cream silk waistcoats, and black, exquisitely tailored jackets, though where Harcourt's necktie was simple, the Viscount's was knotted in a rather complex manner.

She steeled herself; she had not been ready for the sight of Harcourt in evening dress, nor for the butterflies currently taking residence in her stomach. *Are you a woman or a girl?*

Both rose with smiles as she entered, as tall one as the other, though Percy was lither than Harcourt.

Effy curtsied, mindful to keep her eyes downcast and her

smile as demure as possible.

'There you are, Patience,' Harcourt cried triumphantly. 'Let me present my dear friend, his Lordship Viscount Percival Egerton. Percy, my cousin, Patience.'

'A pleasure,' Percy grinned, his eyes studying her intently as he took her hand and kissed it.

His warm hazel eyes were twinkling, and Effy had to admit they were rather unsettling.

Where Harcourt was dark and handsome, Percy was fair, and almost beautiful. His manner was relaxed, and utterly charming, his features so perfect he might belong in a museum.

Effy had no doubt Percy could have any woman he set his mind to, but where Harcourt was very apparently dangerous, Percy's darkness and danger were carefully concealed just beneath the veneer of respectability and perfection.

'I can't think why Sinclair here has kept such a delight from so long from us.'

'You are too kind, sir. Though my cousin has long endeavoured to bring me here, I could not until recently be prevailed upon to do so. But now that I have no family but Harcourt,' she let the last words trail off, repeating the lie they had agreed upon with a somewhat convincing sadness.

'Yes, my condolences for the recent loss of your...?'

'Mother.'

'Yes, your mother, of course. Deepest sympathies.'

Effy nodded gratefully, aware that Percy was not buying into their tale in the least.

Clever fellow. Yet, he seemed amused by the game, and so, she would continue to play it, for now.

Harcourt, who, until now, had been watching them, an inscrutable expression upon his face, looking darker and more dangerous than ever in the firelight, appeared by her side in one swift motion.

He swept her hand onto his arm, and patted it, gazing down at her with the most insincere look of sadness imaginable.

'Shall we to dinner, then,' he said, coddling her as one might an invalid.

With a knowing grin, and a look between the two of them, Percy inclined his head, and let Harcourt lead the way, Effy on his arm.

'He's not buying it,' Effy whispered to Harcourt as they made their way to the dining room.

'No, but then, we don't need him to, really. He will know soon enough the truth of, we just need to entertain him a while longer.'

Harcourt looked over at Effy.

She really was sharp, and insanely clever. Whatever she had done this afternoon seemed to have worked; she was much herself again. He chided himself for the disparaging thoughts he had had.

Looking down at her now, his *cousin*, timid, and unassuming as she had made herself, he could not help but smile; no matter how hard she tried, she could not hide just how beguiling, and unusual she really was. Percy would have been a fool not to notice. As he himself had once been.

The table was laid sparingly, the settings tasteful, but simple. Tiny bowls of roses and impeccably polished silver candelabra were the only decoration amidst the three places that had been set close together at one end of the table.

Harcourt led Effy to the seat at what would be his right, and let his hand linger a little longer at the small of her back than propriety allowed.

Had Percy not been watching them, Effy would have chided him for it, but instead, she allowed herself to enjoy his attentions, however short-lived and inconsequential they may be.

Harcourt settled at the head, and Percy across from her. Within seconds, their glasses were filled, and a variety of dishes had been set before them.

The servants disappeared, leaving them to serve themselves as instructed.

'Hope you don't mind, Percy,' Harcourt drawled. 'As you saw fit to invite yourself like family, I thought we might dine as one.'

'Of course not. I much prefer it to the usual formalities,' Percy chuckled, inclining his head slightly. 'To family, then,' he added, raising his glass, and holding Effy's gaze.

'To family,' the others echoed.

They served themselves, each taking a small selection of the dishes laid out, roast meats and simple vegetables, prepared with care and delicacy.

'So, Miss Sinclair,' Percy said with overt nonchalance but an ever studious and attentive gaze. 'You must tell me more about yourself.'

'I'm afraid there isn't much to tell my lord. I have lived a simple country life, with no adventures nor indeed much excitement to speak of.'

'Percy, please. I really cannot abide all the my-lording.'

'Then, you must call me Patience,' Effy said, lowering her eyes with a humble smile.

'Well, Patience, despite your assurances, I find there is nothing simple about you.'

'You flatter me.'

'Yes, Percy, don't taunt the poor creature, she isn't used to our London ways. She will not understand your humour.'

Effy couldn't help but flinch slightly at the appellation, something Percy did not fail to notice.

He looked between them, and when Effy had met his gaze again, he shot her a wolfish grin. *Clever fellow, but I will not succumb to your charms however you might try.*

'I think Patience understands very well. Besides, I wasn't jesting.'

'What news of London,' Harcourt asked, his jaw slightly clenched.

'Nothing much new, really. You haven't missed much. More engagements, no scandals, other than Hollingham and that actress again, and Mowbray's chit getting engaged to that dreadful Thomas chap. Engagement party's Saturday by the way, I've secured you an invitation. Rather Grandmama has. Other than that, it's all been rather dull, really. Haven't missed much during your *sojourn* in the country.'

Percy's eyes met Effy's again, and held.

He was gauging her; trying to find the truth of her relationship to Harcourt in her reactions. But Effy was too well practised. If demure wouldn't work, hard, cold, defiance might.

After all, she was meant to be a spinster, not an innocent.

'Well, it's good to know that even during the Season one can escape to the country, without fearing to be left behind.'

'Indeed, though, I wouldn't have thought you cared enough about Society, Sinclair, to worry about being out of the loop.'

'Whether or not I care about Society does not change the fact that Society never seems to be uninterested in me,' Harcourt sneered with a raised eyebrow.

'That, is because Society is mainly made up of conniving mothers eager to thrust their daughters onto anyone of fortune,' Percy chuckled. 'Hoping to reform your rakish ways with the love of their good daughters.'

'As if that could ever be possible.'

'Indeed. What do you think, Patience,' Percy asked, returning his challenging gaze to her. 'Is that what you would prescribe for rogues like Harcourt and myself? The love of a good woman?'

'No,' Effy said before she could stop herself.

She knew what she should say, what *Patience* would say, but she couldn't bring herself to.

Besides, she wanted to have a little fun.

'How peculiar. Do elaborate.'

Harcourt shot her a warning glare, but she ignored him.

'I do not believe the love of a good woman would be enough to form the basis of a lasting marriage to men like you,' she said simply, delicately wiping her mouth with a corner of napkin. As if that could counter the scandalousness of her words. 'Understanding, I believe, is essential if one seeks a lasting marriage, and hopes for happiness. Therefore, I would prescribe a good woman, with a touch of the Devil on her soul.'

Percy laughed heartily, never once losing sight of Effy, who simply smiled and looked away.

Touché.

'Oh dear, Sinclair, I do love your *cousin*, she is most refreshing.'

'I'm glad you approve,' he said coldly, his tone suggesting he absolutely did not at this particular moment. 'Though my cousin really should learn to keep her more provoking notions to herself.'

'Come now, Sinclair, don't be such a stick, really. What's gotten into you, you've lost your mirth my good man. Leave the poor girl alone.'

The men's eyes met, and it felt like sparks would fly between them.

Whatever game these two were playing, they seemed to be forgetting their friendship over it.

She shouldn't have let Percy bait her, and now, she would have to fix it.

'Enough,' Effy said simply, leaning back in her chair, resuming her normal self. It was a gamble, but as soon as Percy grinned, glancing at her out of the corner of his eye, she knew it had been a good one. 'If I have to listen to the two of you politely throwing insults and piques at each other all night, I will have to take the butter knife to my own throat.' Harcourt's cutlery dropped to his plate with a clang, and she could feel him staring at her, his eyes cold steel. 'Was my performance really that dreadful?'

'No, your performance was impeccable my dear, *Patience*?'

'Effy.'

'Effy. How, unusual,' Percy said with a slightly condescending smile, settling back into his chair as relaxed as Effy now. 'It's only the circumstances really. Sinclair disappears after an attack on his life, then sends word he is staying with his mistress, and asks for all manner of strange favours? Were you the one who sent me the note when he was attacked, I wonder?'

'Indeed.'

'So *you* are his mistress?'

'I am no man's mistress,' Effy said.

'Perhaps no man has ever made you a worthy offer.'

'Percy!'

'It's fine, Harcourt,' Effy said, with a wave of her hand. This was a new game; one she would have to win if they were to win Percy's help moving forward. 'My affections cannot be bought; only given to those I deem worthy.'

'Rather radical, wouldn't you say?'

'You would not say it of a man.'

'But you are not a man.'

'Indeed, I am not.'

'What are you then?'

They held each other's gaze for a moment, Percy's eyes dark in the fading candlelight, his smile challenging.

Effy smiled broadly, and made to answer, but Harcourt was quicker.

'A very rare creature, and not one for the likes of you,' he said. He and Effy shared a complicit smile, before both turned their attention back to Percy. 'Satisfied now?'

'I meant no offense, Sinclair. Even you must admit it is hard to resist such a lively, unaffected, honest, and rather enticing woman.'

'No offense was taken,' Effy assured him, ignoring the compliments.

'What's this all about then, Sinclair? I can see this dinner has taken a turn, and you two are up to something.'

'Perhaps, we should call for some brandy and cigars.'

'Capital idea.'

∞

If Percy was shocked in any way that Effy remained whilst dinner was cleared, and brandy and cigars were brought out, he made no mention of it. Neither did he make any remarks when Harcourt served her a glass of brandy, though he did seem slightly disappointed when she refused a cigar.

It wasn't that Effy didn't enjoy them, nor that she wouldn't have thoroughly enjoyed one this evening, but she knew that

Harcourt was already none too pleased with her behaviour, his manner was cold and distant, and every time she chanced a glance at him, he scowled.

Worse than that, she wished for nothing more than to somehow win his approval back.

'So, what's this about then Sinclair,' Percy asked, when they had all settled, the gentlemen's legs lazily outstretched before them.

'Another favour, my friend, a rather sensitive matter, really.'

'Do go on.'

'We need your assistance, in tempting Marquess Russell to the table of a rather unusual establishment in Whitechapel.'

'Ah.'

'As I know you sometimes pass time in the company of gentlemen often sought after by the Marquess, I thought...' Harcourt let the words hang as he sipped his brandy.

'Indeed. And this establishment, a gambling hell?'

'Aye.'

'I see,' Percy said thoughtfully, whirling his own drink in his glass, his eyes darting between Harcourt and Effy. 'I suspect, Russell will not be leaving intact?'

'No.'

'I see. Why there? Just could just as well fleece him in any of the more *civilised* gambling hells.'

'That is the catch, I will not be the one fleecing him.'

Percy's eyes narrowed, and Harcourt's lip curled ever so slightly.

His gaze moved to Effy, who cocked her head, and nodded when Percy set his eyes on her.

'Dear God,' Percy laughed. 'You two are mad! Whatever makes you think you can get your *cousin*, into one of those places?'

'I'm already very well-known there, and I believe my reputation will be further incentive for his lordship,' Effy said seductively, sampling the brandy. 'Tell me, have you heard of Black Maria?'

The Viscount's eyes widened, and his jaw dropped.

Effy smiled, and looked to Harcourt, but he seemed intent on ignoring her again. It felt as though he had drawn a wall up between them.

'*You're* Black Maria,' Percy managed to ask dumbfoundedly after a moment. 'Dear God, Sinclair, where the Hell did you find this one.'

'As it happens, she found me,' he said, and Effy thought for a moment she detected a hint of bitterness.

'So, let me get this straight. You want me to lure Russell to Whitechapel, so your *cousin*, the infamous Black Maria, can fleece him? Of what, his fortune?' Harcourt's silence was acquiescence enough. Percy shook his head and took a large gulp of brandy. 'This is a Hell of a favour, you know that right?' Harcourt nodded, his eyes almost pleading. 'Why?'

Silence. Effy downed her brandy, and rose.

'I think, I shall leave you gentlemen now,' she said with a faint smile. 'Percy, a pleasure. I hope we can renew the acquaintance again soon.

With a curtsey and a rustle of silks, she had disappeared.

Percy shook his head, and studied his friend, waiting for an answer.

'I would rather not go into the particulars,' Harcourt said finally. He could not bring himself to tell his tale again, and Percy, friend though he may be, would never look at him the same way again. 'Suffice it to say, Russell did my family great harm some years ago, and I wish to repay the debt.'

'Vengeance? Can't you just call the old man out?'

'Too neat and tidy for the likes of him,' Harcourt spat, and Percy sighed. He had never seen his friend betray anything close to emotion before. 'I understand, if you are not willing.'

'For Heaven's sake, Sinclair, I didn't say I wasn't willing. Just give a man a chance to think.' Percy finished his brandy and nodded when Harcourt offered another. 'You'll do it anyways, won't you?' Harcourt nodded again. 'And get yourself killed in the process. Or worse, *shunned*. I'll help you, Sinclair. I'll regret it for sure, but I'll help you.'

'Thank you,' Harcourt said, raising his glass to toast with Percy.

'I must know, what is she to you, the girl?'

'Just a partner, nothing more,' Harcourt said coolly. *The truth, surely?* 'Which reminds me, any chance you have anything useful on the de Beaumonts?'

'The de Beaumonts? No, why?' Harcourt shrugged. 'I can ask around.'

'Thank you, I owe you.'

'Oh yes, you certainly do,' Percy said with a laugh.

The men toasted again, friends once more.

They talked, and laughed, until finally Percy declared it was well past time he go find trouble elsewhere.

When Percy had left, Harcourt went to find Effy. He had a thing or two to say to her. If he was annoyed before, he was however even more so when he discovered that Effy was nowhere to be found.

Not even the maid who attended to her seemed to know where, when, or how she had disappeared. *Infuriating woman.*

Instead of doing what he knew he should, go to bed and calm himself, he grabbed the bottle of brandy, his glass, sent the servants to bed, and installed himself in her bedroom, to wait for her return.

Sitting there, alone in the darkness save for the fire in the hearth, he nursed his ever-increasing anger with drink.

The evening had been a disaster. Her behaviour had been unacceptable after she had shown so much promise. He had thought everything would be perfect when she had walked into the sitting room, though even he had to admit the plain gown she had chosen, the unaffected way in which she had presented herself, had done nothing to conceal her loveliness and intelligence.

From the start he should have known the woman would be trouble. What *had* he been thinking agreeing to this plan, this *charade*? He had let his guard down, even enjoyed himself, for a moment, enjoyed having her beside him, the touch of her, the scent of her.

And then, like every other woman, she had been foolish, careless, and nearly cost them both everything.

He should have known he would rue the day Effy Fortescue crossed his path.

∞

As she made her way quietly to her rooms via the servants' entrance and stairs, Effy was relieved to find the house silent and still. She knew Harcourt would have something to say about this evening's events in the morning, but she hoped a night's rest would sooth his irritation, if only a little.

It wasn't that she didn't understand his annoyance, but she couldn't continue to live on eggshells with him, waiting for his approval for her every move. They were supposed to be partners. Sharing responsibilities. *Trusting*.

Still, he seemed only able to treat her like some sort of mindless servant, and she, fool that she was, kept continuing to seek, nay *yearn* desperately, for his approval.

With a huff, she slid into her rooms, tossed her cloak, cap, handkerchief and gloves aside, and nearly jumped out of her skin when she spotted the figure lounging in the window seat, lit only by moonlight.

How long had he been here? The fire had long died, and yet he had not stoked it.

'Harcourt, Jesus, Mary and Joseph,' she hissed. 'What the Hell are you doing?'

'I could ask you the same thing,' he growled, his speech measured and thick.

'You're drunk,' Effy spat bitterly, as she made her way to revive the fire. The spring was not that cold, but she now found herself unable to sleep without one. 'You should go to bed, whatever you have to say can wait until morning.'

'No it bloody well can't,' he exclaimed, leaping from his seat.

Even in the darkness, Effy could see his eyes were wild, indeed he seemed a wholly wild thing, hair dishevelled, necktie hanging loosely, no jacket, shirtsleeves rolled messily up.

'I will not let you dictate everything now that you've managed to insinuate yourself into my life!'

'I'm sorry about this evening, Harcourt,' Effy shouted back, heedless of who might hear, thrusting the poker back into its hanging place. 'I know I went against the plan. But plans change! Percy knew very well I was not your cousin, and if we were to have his help -'

'It was not your decision to make!'

'Am I to make any decisions? We are meant to be partners!'

'You're just like all the rest of them, controlling, needing to know everything, but when it comes to your secrets -'

'You need only ask when it comes to my secrets,' Effy screamed, stepping towards him. *Oh how that man makes my blood boil...* 'I've trusted you, from the start, with everything! Just like the rest of them - ha! Would the rest of them have nearly gotten killed trying to rescue you? Spent a week at your bedside tending to you, making sure no further harm would come for you?'

'Where were you tonight, tell me that,' Harcourt spat, moving in on her, a look of disgust contorting his handsome features into something all more frightful and devilish. 'Whoring yourself out, dressed like that?'

Effy froze, her stomach lurching.

True, she was not dressed like a proper lady, but like Black Maria. Black gypsy skirt, black ruffled blouse, black corset.

Harcourt sensed her hurt, and pounced on it like a hungry wolf, prowling towards her, disdainfully fingering the blouse.

He *was* drunk. She could smell the fumes from here. And there was a cruelty in his eyes, an intent to wound in him, that she had never felt before.

Not that she had ever doubted he was capable of such things, but somehow she thought herself immune; or rather, that he would never intentionally hurt her.

'I was renewing old acquaintances, making sure everyone knew Black Maria had returned,' she whispered, with as much strength as she could muster. 'For *you*.'

'What a lovely euphemism,' Harcourt drawled, letting his eyes scan her body in this new, revealing and rather enticing outfit. He knew he had hit a mark, and he knew he did not want to hurt her, but he needed to. To return the wound she had given him, the fear he had felt, the worry at her prolonged absence. 'How many acquaintances tonight, then? Were Percy's attentions not enough for you then?'

'Dear God, Harcourt,' she sneered. 'Are you jealous? Is that what this is? You can't have me, so then, no one else can? Or does it shatter the mask of innocence you have painted on me? *You*, are just like any other man. All you want is some innocent virgin to call your own. To claim.'

'Can't have you,' he challenged, his voice barely above a whisper.

He was so close now, his finger trailing the line of her jaw again.

There was a strange sort of desperation in his eyes now, pure molten heat as they glimmered in the growing firelight.

Effy could feel the tension of his muscles from here, as though a war was raging under his skin.

'I could have you whenever I wished, *if* I wanted you.'

The words cut deeply; he saw that much.

He felt the tension in her body relax ever so slightly, and disappointment flicker in her eyes again.

And for a moment, all he wanted was to beg her forgiveness, drop down to his knees and kiss the hurt he had just caused away. He was ashamed, for the first time in his life, of his deliberate cruelty.

Effy stood as still as a statue, cold as marble, her breathing as controlled as the rest of her. She enveloped his hand in her own, and moved it from her face.

Her touch was ice, and sent a jolt of electricity through him.

'What do you want, Harcourt,' she asked softly, lest her voice break. 'Do you want rid of me? Tell me now and I shall pack my things and be gone.

Silence.

Of course he didn't want that. He wanted her, to stay, to be with him, to be *his*.

The thought of her leaving seared through the rest of the cloud of muddled thoughts and foundationless anger.

'No,' he said gently, taking a step away from her.

'Go to bed, Harcourt,' she advised.

Eyes downcast, he did as bid.

Effy stood standing there until the chime of the clock on the mantel sounded three. Slowly, she undressed, stowing Black Maria away into a box that she then slid under the bed. She donned a nightshirt, and slid into bed.

Sleep was easier to find than she thought it would be. Her anger, hurt and frustration had exhausted her, much more so than her trek across town, back into the hells she had hoped never to see again.

Effy's final thought was that it was her own blind, foolish affection that had blinded her to the truth of the man.

Harcourt had never pretended to be anything other than the cruel, selfish, heartless devil all of London knew him to be. The fact that she had hoped beyond hope that he was somehow anything else, anything more, was her problem.

She would never let herself forget that he was precisely the man everyone knew him to be.

XII.

The blinding light that streamed in when George swung open the curtains in his room was as effective as a bucket of cold water. Though he might need that too, if he was to chase his monumental and splitting headache.

'Morning, sir,' George said in an annoyingly cheerful tone. 'Will you be needing me to help you dress this morning?'

'Yes, I think so,' Harcourt moaned, dragging himself to a sitting position. 'Coffee, first, please.'

'Of course, sir.'

A bow, and George was gone.

Harcourt stumbled to his feet, feeling every drop of the very expensive brandy he had drank a bottle of last night.

He managed to drag himself to the washbasin, and filled it with the fresh, icy-cold water George had just brought in. Without hesitation, he dunked his entire head in, and gasped, feeling it do its worst, and finishing the task of sobering him up. He shook his head, and wiped the droplets off, cursing himself with every breath.

What the Hell did you do? He hadn't meant it, any of it.

Yes, he'd been annoyed, that Effy had seen fit to change their plans, but then, Percy had agreed to help them, and in truth, he might not have had they kept up the game. Loathe as he was to admit it, she had made the right decision.

Of course, he wouldn't have admitted it, he wanted to challenge her, wanted to... *Do what? Make her pay for Percy's interest...*

He had been jealous, especially since she had seemed to reciprocate his interest. *And so, if she had?* He had no claim on her.

And then, the hours had dragged on, and on, and he had drunk more, and the anger had turned into worry, and concern, though why he cared so much if she had been hurt, when he could very well carry on his plan without her, well now, that was something else entirely.

'Coffee, sir,' George said, reappearing and serving him a cup.

'Thank you,' Harcourt croaked, downing it, and pouring another serving himself. 'Is, is my cousin up yet?'

'Aye, sir, won't be long before she goes to breakfast, I think. Lily has just gone to help her dress.'

'Excellent, George, I have something I need you to do. I can dress myself after all,' Harcourt decreed, the coffee hot liquid courage for what he knew he had to do.

Beg.

∞

The bouquet, though not artful, was, in its disarray and sheer size, breath-taking. Effy eyed it carefully, it was hard not to, set down before her, covering half the table as it did. Roses, carnations, hyacinths, tulips, lily of the valley, and even orchids. All the flowers which symbolized an apology.

Though she didn't want to even consider what they had cost, or how long it had taken poor George to collect them all, the gesture was not altogether unappreciated.

It was, entirely unexpected. Effy had spent the morning preparing for another argument, confrontation, or sullenness, *not* for this.

Leaning over in the chair, she glanced down toward the other end of the table, where Harcourt was pretending rather too emphatically to be engrossed in his breakfast.

'This doesn't excuse the fact that you were a cruel boor last night,' she said. Harcourt perked up; he had been waiting for any sign of the thaw. 'But they are beautiful, and I accept your apology.'

'I know my behaviour was unacceptable, and that I was a dreadful cad,' Harcourt sighed. 'I am truly sorry if I hurt you Effy. It won't ever happen again.' Effy nodded, and returned to her food, hidden behind his offering. He wouldn't hurt her, for she wouldn't allow herself to be vulnerable to him again. 'Percy accepted to help, as I'm sure you knew he would. And he will make enquiries regarding the de Beaumonts. In the meantime, I thought perhaps we could attend the Royal Academy's Summer Exhibition this afternoon, and you'll recall we're expected at Brookton House this evening.'

Effy leaned over again, one of her eyebrows raised.

He knew it was a gamble, but then, there weren't many women he knew who didn't like art. And at least, he could *pretend* it would be of use to their plan, though in truth it was only another way for him to apologize.

Harcourt nearly laughed as she remained there, half-suspended and half-hidden behind the bouquet, her eyes narrowing, surveying him carefully.

She looked at home, so delightfully lovely in her anger, and he wondered if this is what it was like to have a wife.

Arguments, flowers, forgiveness.

'Very well,' she said flatly before retreating again.

'The deal is underway again,' he said, trying to fill the silence she seemed intent on torturing him with. 'Everything should be signed and sealed soon.'

'I'm pleased to hear it.'

'Everything… Everything went well, last night? With your establishment of choice?'

'Indeed. I shall return tonight, play a few hands. Would seem odd if Black Maria returned only when the lords arrive, don't you think? Unless you see any objections?'

'No, no, of course not. Fortescue -'

'I should get ready, for our outing.' With an unceremonious scraping of her chair, Effy rose, and plucked one of the stocks of lily of the valley. 'For what it's worth, Harcourt, what I said to Percy last night was the truth. I have never sold myself, no matter how desperate I was. Though I respect the ladies who can do so, I for one, had quite enough experience being treated like property.'

On that note, she left the breakfast room, leaving Harcourt feeling somehow worse, more shameful and contrite then before.

Not entirely forgiven then...

Harcourt sighed, and pushed away his plate of uneaten food. He knew he would regret it later, but for now, he couldn't stomach a bite of it.

At least, she hadn't thrown her plate, or knife, or coffee at him.

At least she hasn't left...

XIII.

Though Effy had never been to one of the grand Society houses, her own debut and Season among the ton having never come to fruition, she thought she at least knew what to expect. Still, she found herself nervously playing with her gloves and brushing her skirts in the carriage, all too aware of the evening's stakes.

All day she had managed to set such thoughts aside, even though the day itself had been as full of promise and opportunity for her and Harcourt as tonight would be.

Their outing to the Royal Academy, where they had been well on display to the *ton*, and some notable figures of the *demi-monde*, had been surprisingly relaxed and soothing.

Every so often, they had stopped, Harcourt introducing his *dear cousin Patience* to this acquaintance or that, and chatted for a brief time, but more often than not they had simply walked the length and breadth of the Academy, enjoying the exhibition.

Art had always had a way of soothing Effy, and though she presumed Harcourt felt no such thing, he seemed intent on finding as much pleasure in their outing as she.

To her great surprise, he had even regaled her with stories of this artist or that, this legend depicted or that, acting as guide and curator. He seemed determined to make Effy forget the previous night's behaviour, and though she could never forget, nor forgive herself for convincing herself he was something he was not, by the end of their expedition, she had entirely forgiven him, and things seemed to have returned to their queer normality.

They had taken tea in a small shop off Piccadilly, then returned to the townhouse for some rest, supper, and of course to prepare for their outing at Brookton House. Effy had selected for the occasion a dark brown round dress of crepe with demi-train and lace trim adorning the bodice, hem, and bell-cap sleeves.

It was elegant, expensive, and along with Patience's now signature simple chignon, it demonstrated her age and position well.

Harcourt had opted for immaculate white breeches, tailcoat, pristine white shirt, embroidered waistcoat and necktie. He had smoothed his hair back, and Effy couldn't deny he was, as always, fiercely handsome.

And so now, here they were, pulling up to the impressive neoclassical, and already bustling entrance of the most coveted and talked about Mayfair residences.

'Do stop fidgeting Fortescue,' Harcourt growled in her ear as they descended from the carriage and Effy yet again smoothed her skirts. 'You look perfect.'

'Cousin Patience is nervous,' she hissed back through a smile as they began to encounter other couples and groups on their way in. 'Cousin Patience has never attended such an event.'

'Well cousin Patience is no nervous wallflower so pull yourself together,' he said. 'Ah, Percy.'

Percy was waiting for them at the entrance, despite their having missed the receiving line, looking as handsome as Harcourt, though more angel than devil in his case, lit by the shimmering candelabras and chandeliers as he was.

Amidst the finery of the entrance, the marble, the gilding, he looked like a handsome prince, and Effy remarked how he stood out from the rest, no matter that he was a master of the house.

How many others, particularly women, seemed to notice as well, though he seemed entirely unaware.

He smiled broadly and strode over to them, kissing Effy's hand and shaking Harcourt's.

'A pleasure to see you again, Patience,' he grinned, making no effort to conceal his examination of her. 'My grandmama will be delighted to make your acquaintance at last.'

'Yes, apologies for our tardiness,' Effy muttered.

'Nonsense, you are perfectly fashionably late, as you can see by the many arrivals timed alongside yours,' Percy assured her. 'Besides, any affair at Brookton House is always busy, and therefore we only keep that darned line going for the first hour.'

'Shall we,' Harcourt said, his hand covering Effy's that lay on his arm.

'Indeed. Best not to keep the old bat waiting,' Percy chuckled. 'You'll need to give her a turn on the dance floor as well Harcourt, you know that's the only reason she indulges you with invitations to everything. And the club.'

'I was going to ask about that,' Effy said, glancing up at Harcourt, whose eyes were set straight ahead.

'Percy's grandmama, a beacon of the perfect Society woman though she may be, loves a good scandal,' he grinned. 'And an assured handsome partner.'

'Besides, my grandmama seems to realize that without an influx of new gentlemen, particularly fortunate ones into our little Society gatherings,' Percy added conspiratorially as he led them through towards the ballroom. 'There will be too many a young lady of good breeding left wanting.'

'Mr. Harcourt Sinclair, and Miss Patience Sinclair.,' announced the master of ceremonies as they reached the door.

Effy stared as they entered the ballroom. If she had thought she had known what to expect, she was mistaken. This, was far, far worse.

Though massive, with towering ceilings, the ballroom was packed. Effy was at once overwhelmed by the scents, sounds and sights. A thousand different perfumes mingled with the smells of men and women.

Colours, textures, voices, music, and the blinding lights of the enormous crystal chandeliers as they bounced and glittered on the gold-gilded mirrors and variety of jewels that adorned every woman.

The heat was stifling, and Effy did not envy any of the women who seemed to have packed on layers and adornments, from turbans to shawls, massive bouffants of crepe frills and multitudes of petticoats. She tightened her grip on Harcourt's arm as they followed Percy through the masses, ignoring the whispers and scowls.

Harcourt nodded to a few people here and there, who responded to varying degrees, concentrating mainly on keeping Effy securely by his side until Percy's grandmother had welcomed her.

He could tell she was overwhelmed, there was a slight flush in her cheeks, and her eyes darted nervously around, but she was bearing it well, the placid, demure smile of cousin Patience affixed on her face.

Finally, they arrived before Percy's grandmother, sat amidst a group of equally discerning dowagers and relics, a jewel amongst them of that there was no doubt.

With strong, angular features, a nose and eyes like a falcon, she sat proudly, watching Harcourt and Effy whilst her grandson proceeded through his own ministrations.

Effy could certainly see where Percy's beauty came from, the woman before them was still breath-taking, though her youthful beauty had morphed into an ageless grace, accented by the simple, yet expertly tailored silk gown, delicate diamond band around her neck, and ruby tiara that brought out the gold eyes so much like Percy's.

'Grandmama, you know Harcourt of course, may I present his cousin, Miss Patience Sinclair,' Percy said, holding his hand out to her. Effy took it, and curtsied, her eyes affixed to the floor. 'Patience, my grandmama, the Dowager Countess of Brookton.'

'So this is the young minister's daughter,' the Dowager said, her voice like ice, yet devoid of judgement. Harcourt's eyes flew to Percy; he smiled and shrugged. He had been embellishing and toying a little on his own it seemed. 'Come to London to reform your cousin, girl?'

'No, my lady,' Patience said with the hint of a smile. 'I don't believe God himself could reform my cousin. Though I do hope my influence will aid his soul in some way.'

'Ha! I like this one, Percy,' the Dowager smiled, her whole face alight. The others around her smiled and chuckled, mirroring their leader's approval. 'You were right to bring her. Very amusing indeed. Now, why is it you have come to London then?'

'My cousin is all the family I have left, my lady,' Effy said sadly, meeting the Countess' gaze. 'And I hoped I might serve as a chaperone, to some young lady in need of companionship. Perhaps I might bring them comfort, and guide them, *with the love of the Lord*,' she added, intently. Percy stifled a laugh, which did not go unnoticed by his grandmother. 'As they seek to find their path in the world, little lost lambs.'

'Minister's daughter, and what is it you said Percival? French aristocracy in the mother's blood?' Percy smiled and bowed, assenting, and ignoring Harcourt and Effy's mutual glares. 'We shall find you a suitable place, and soon,' she added, scowling at Harcourt. 'Lest your cousin manage to exert any undue influence on *you*.'

'I am afraid not the King himself could sway my cousin once she has set her mind on something,' Harcourt countered with a bow.

'Nonetheless, I have decided I like your cousin very much, and will not have you corrupting her,' the Dowager advised. *As if it was possible to corrupt her further, if only you knew*, Harcourt thought. 'Now, I am in the mood to dance, there is a waltz next. Most scandalous. Percy, take Miss Sinclair for a turn, and see that her dance card is full. Then, you can set about finding her a suitable position.'

'Yes, grandmama,' he said smoothly, offering her a hand to rise, then passing her to Harcourt.

'Thank you, my lady,' Effy said with a curtsey as the Dowager passed her and disappeared onto the dance floor with Harcourt.

With a bow and a curtsey, Effy and Percy departed for the dancefloor as well, under the approving yet distant stares of the Dowager's entourage.

'A minister's daughter,' Effy said, raising an eyebrow as Percy twirled her onto the floor with flourish at the first note of the waltz. 'And French aristocracy in my blood? Really, you are lucky I remember some things from Sunday school. And that I speak passably good French.'

'Well, we did need to ensure your suitability. If we are to find you a position, I thought it might add to your charms,' he said cheekily, his eyes wandering.

'Incorrigible,' Effy laughed, letting herself enjoy the moment now. Percy was a masterful dancer, and a clever ally. '*Your* charm will get you into trouble someday.

'Certainly. Though not with you,' he said, his eyes narrowing. 'You are quite immune to me it seems. I wonder, if it is because you are already quite taken with another.' His eyes moved towards Harcourt and his grandmother, who were dancing only a few couples away from them. 'Pity really.'

'One would be as foolish to fall for Harcourt's charm as much as they would be to fall for yours, Percy,' Effy teased.

'I see the lady will not be baited,' he grinned, edging them closer to the edge of the crowd. 'Now, who shall we set upon? Am I to guess that perhaps one of Lady Lydia's bosom friends might be a preferable choice?'

'You are far too clever for your own good, Percy,' Effy said seriously, annoyed that their plans should be so transparent. 'That too, will get you into trouble.'

'But oh so much fun,' he laughed. 'Now, I shall take that as assent. We have a fine selection, then. Miss Mansford,' he said, indicating a rather plain, plump blonde in a mass of pink taffeta by the windows. 'Miss Atterton,' he said, moving Effy so she could spot the tall, gangly brunette in a tasteful blue confection. 'Or my personal favourite, Miss Fitzsimmons,' he continued, nodding at a forlorn, petite girl, looking decidedly bored among a throng of fine-looking gentleman. 'Not the prettiest, but with a dowry of twenty-thousand pounds…'

'It seems Lady Lydia selects her friends carefully.'

'Indeed. Rich, and incapable of matching her beauty,' Percy

admitted. 'Not that it really matters anymore, now that the chit is engaged.'

'I shall defer to your better judgement in this matter Percy,' Effy said with a faint smile, trying to forget Lady Lydia's superiority in many aspects. 'Miss Fitzsimmons it is.'

When they had finished their waltz with a bow and a curtsey, Percy did as he had been instructed, and ensured that Effy's dance card was full.

Clever fellow that he was, he ensured there was a mix of young bucks, married gentlemen, and elderly fathers.

He seemed intent to ensure Effy's comfort and fruition of her plans, doting on her, introducing her, serving her food and drinks despite Effy's assurances that she or Harcourt could manage very well.

Though Harcourt seemed to have taken a step back, dancing with this heiress or that, maintaining his reputation, and insuring he did not halt Effy's progress among the *ton* in any way.

Effy understood his distance, but still, she wished it was him by her side, leading her through the evening. Though she suspected Percy was also using the excuse to avoid being trapped by this eager young lady and her mother, or that.

His popularity was undeniable, and cousin Patience seemed to be giving him the perfect excuse to escape the clutches of the hungry wolves of the marriage mart.

Finally, hours later, Harcourt joined them, announcing it was time they depart.

Percy bade them both good evening, and went off to find some more trouble and amusement, while Harcourt marched Effy out, the stares and whispers they had met upon entry, a far cry from what they had been before.

∞

Safe again in the quiet confines of the carriage, her feet sore from dancing and standing, and her cheeks even more so from all the insincere smiling she had been forced to do, Effy was glad beyond measure to finally be alone again with Harcourt.

The evening had been a success; Miss Fitzsimmons' mother had invited her to tea the following day, to discuss the details of Effy's potential invitation to be her daughter's companion.

'Tonight went well,' Effy said with a smile, breaking the silence Harcourt seemed intent on maintaining. 'Better than we expected. Things are progressing quickly.'

'Yes.'

'Percy was most helpful.'

'Indeed. Did you enjoy yourself,' Harcourt asked lazily, his gaze still affixed at some point out of the window.

'Well enough considering the circumstances. Did you,' Effy asked, a hint of annoyance in her voice, enough to make him finally meet her gaze.

'Well enough,' Harcourt lied.

For in fact, he hadn't enjoyed himself in the least.

Where once he might have enjoyed the endless stream of beautiful women vying for his attentions, or the bawdy chatter with the gentlemen; where once he might have been able to find pleasure and amusement in this sort of gathering, he had found none.

All evening, he had been too busy searching out Effy and Percy, intent on being aware of their every move. All evening, he had watched from afar as she laughed and danced, and quickly became a favourite, among the ladies for her wit and unthreatening position, and among the gentlemen for her beauty and grace.

And Percy... Percy had been the one to show her the way, lead her around, flaunt her, as he quickly and painfully realized he had wanted to do. She was his discovery, his *cousin*, and yet, for the sake of keeping her name and reputation intact, he had been forced to step aside.

He hadn't even dared to ask her to dance once, lest he tarnish what she and *Percy* had achieved, even though that was all he wanted from the moment she had descended the stairs in the townhouse, her dress accentuating her natural beauty and seductiveness without any artifice.

Delicacy, always...

Though he knew it was for a common cause, for *his* cause, he could not help but resent her ability to thrive, and enjoy herself, without him, when it seemed he could do nothing of the sort.

That realization, in turn, had worsened his mood, and now he hated himself for behaving like some maudlin, ungrateful fool.

'Percy said with the rumours of Black Maria's imminent retiring, it should be easy enough to get Russell to the game in the next week or so,' Effy said cheerfully, trying desperately to pull Harcourt from his sulk.

Really, she didn't understand his sudden change of humour. He was acting like a mercurial child, and it annoyed her.

'You are still planning to go to Whitechapel tonight then,' he asked.

'Yes.'

'Would you mind, I mean, if it does no harm to Black Maria, if I accompanied you?'

Harcourt watched as the frown dissipated into a rather enticing smile.

Effy's eyes, which until now had been dark and piercing, softened, and he himself felt lighter for having, at least in appearance, pleased her with his suggestion.

'As you wish,' she said, hiding her excitement rather poorly. 'Black Maria, as it happens, has the reputation of being accompanied sometimes, but only by the most handsome and dangerous rogues. I suppose you will pass muster nonetheless.'

Harcourt cocked his head slightly, then laughed heartily, Effy joining in.

It was impossible not to laugh with him, it was contagious, and so heartening, to be privileged enough to see this other side of him again.

And so, their good humour and bonhomie restored, they returned to the townhouse, to change, set the servants to bed, before returning out into the night.

Percy may have had Patience to himself, but tonight, what remained of it, Harcourt would have Effy.

XIV.

Another ball. An engagement party. And the de Beaumonts would be there, Percy had advised as much. Sarah. Daniel. Seven years since she had seen them. Seven years. Would they recognize her? Would they say anything to out her? God, please no.

The rest of the week since they had arrived back in London had passed in a blur, all seemingly bringing them to this night, this moment, this townhouse in Mayfair. Effy had willed time to stop, to slow, still it would not oblige.

At least she had Harcourt by her side, his strength fortifying her. And Percy would be there, and the Dowager, and Miss Fitzsimmons and her mother. *Lord, I cannot believe I am grateful for their presence…*

The girl was kind, and well-mannered, which had been a delightful surprise to Effy when she had spent the afternoon taking tea with them Wednesday, and then again when they had gone for a carriage ride yesterday morning.

Angelique Fitzsimmons was smart, good conversation, and a lot more sensible than many girls of her age and situation. It would be no great feat to befriend her in truth, and Effy had been both relieved and saddened to hear that she would indeed be allowed to act occasionally as chaperone to the girl in the coming weeks of the Season.

Relieved, for it was as they had willed it to be, and saddened, for she did like the girl, and using her for their own nefarious purposes weighed on her much more than she had expected.

Should have gone for Miss Atterton after all...

It was her mother who was tiresome, ill-mannered, opinionated, and a terrible gossip. Effy hoped that after all perhaps it would be the mother who would let something slip about Lady Lydia, and so Miss Fitzsimmons would have no guilt in the matter.

Still, any company to distract tonight, would be welcome.

Harcourt seemed to sense her nerves, though she was careful not to fidget, as he looked over at her and smiled reassuringly, gently stroking the fingers that lay on his arm. There was kindness, and concern in his eyes, still as dark and inscrutable as always.

The last few days with him had been wonderful; there was no other word for it. They had spent what remained of Tuesday evening in Whitechapel playing cards, laughing, drinking and generally being merry.

Everyone had complimented Black Maria on her new *beau*, and Effy hadn't managed to dispel the pride and glow of her heart as she had enjoyed every second of him by her side. Never mind she knew she was opening herself to hurt again.

It felt, as he touched, teased, languished, and toyed with her throughout the evening, that perhaps, he really was *hers*. No matter the reason, he had leaned into playing the affectionate companion, and she had relished every moment, his eyes and touch making her blood race, and thrilling her much more than her three hundred-pound winnings.

They had repeated their visit Friday evening, and had even more success, very much emboldened by their first. Harcourt seemed intent to enjoy his time with her as much as she did.

After all, revenge *could* be fun.

Now, as he gazed down at her, Effy tried to remind herself of those evenings, full of promise and flirtation, full of laughter and a strange sort of honesty beneath the dissimulation, and literal mask of Black Maria.

The memories, perhaps, would be enough to counter the others now flooding her mind as they entered the townhouse, and the promise of meeting the de Beaumonts loomed ever closer.

It was sumptuously decorated, even beneath the enormous floral arrangements, candles, and ribbons. Crystal chandeliers, enormous paintings, mirrors, and marble. The finest furnishings, and from what Effy could make out of the multitude of guests looming in the foyer at the foot of a rather impressive marble staircase lined with Turkish carpets, it seemed the finest people in London were all in attendance, and dressed once again in their most elegant, eye-catching, best.

'There you are Patience,' squealed a female voice as they passed the threshold. 'Come, come, I've been waiting to introduce you,' Angelique Fitzsimmons said taking Effy's arm before she could protest.

'Angelique, one should not behave with such familiarity at such an occasion,' Effy said in mock disapproval, glancing back at Harcourt.

He did not seem pleased, but he shrugged, and Effy shot him an *I'll be fine* glance.

'Oh I'm just like family here, Lydia is my oldest friend,' she cooed, dragging Effy towards the receiving line. 'Here, His Grace the Duke of Mowbray,' she said, whilst Effy curtsied, eyes downcast. 'Your Grace, Patience Sinclair, and you know her cousin, Harcourt of course.'

Effy could feel Harcourt stiffen, and chided herself for not having been more conscious of how much more painful this might be for him. *Selfish...*

'Of course,' the Duke said coldly, his eyes decidedly fixed on Effy, studying her with disdain. He was a puffed-up old badger, with watery, piggy eyes, and a permanent sneer under his unfashionably bushy moustache. 'A pleasure, I'm sure.'

'And this is the Duchess,' Angelique continued, nonplussed by his behaviour, moving them to face a sour-looking matron with too many frills. 'Patience Sinclair, my new companion, Your Grace. And her cousin, Harcourt, you know.'

'Indeed.'

'And this, this is my dear friend Lydia,' Angelique rattled on, intent on keeping her good humour. 'And her fiancé, the Earl of Doncourt.'

Effy curtsied before the pair, then offered them the brightest smile she could muster.

Lady Lydia was, as she remembered, a beautiful, angelic thing, perfect and smooth in every way, her gown, tasteful and richly decorated, and she smiled back, as sincerely as Effy.

The fiancé was a plain, well-nourished fellow, who seemed bored with the proceedings, and had no interest in any more females. He offered his hand to Harcourt, and Effy heard some congratulations and other non-committal remarks.

She watched Lydia's eyes flit to him greedily, then back to Angelique and herself, disdainfully noting the plainness of Effy's dark blue crepe dress.

'Miss Sinclair, a pleasure,' she drawled. 'I'm so happy *dear* Angelique has found a new friend. Once I am married, I fear I will have too many demands to give her such attention as she requires.'

If Angelique felt the insult, she said nothing.

But Effy was not one to let this little witch injure an exceedingly sweet girl. *Angelic little witch.*

'Yes, I am so grateful for Miss Fitzsimmons' sincere friendship,' Effy said casually. 'It isn't often one finds such young women with such, *unaffected* beauty and kindness.' Effy grinned, as Lydia's eyes darkened. 'All my congratulations on your upcoming nuptials.'

With that, Angelique whisked her away into one of the richly decorated salons, though she did not miss Harcourt's glare, a mix of appreciation and reprimanding.

'Thank you,' Angelique whispered as they made their way towards a group of girls among which Effy recognized Miss Atterton and Miss Mansford, looking only slightly more comfortable in *this* opulent Mayfair house than they had in Brookton House. 'I should chastise you for your words, Lydia is a dear friend, but I appreciate your kindness nonetheless.'

'You do not need to thank me,' Effy smiled. 'I spoke only the truth. Come now, introduce me to your friends, then.'

Angelique squealed again, and led her on.

Effy glanced back, but Harcourt had disappeared, just as he seemingly had at Brookton House. For her protection. Preservation of her reputation.

Yet tonight, with her heart beating out of its chest, and a sickening feeling in her stomach, she wished for nothing more than his reassuring and strengthening closeness.

∞

Harcourt needed some distance. From Effy, and from everyone else. It was unlike him to let his emotions take hold, but between his concern for Effy, for try as she might, she could not hide her apprehension from seeing the objects of her vengeance from him, and the blasted Duke of Mowbray, he could barely think straight. No matter that he was here in very specific, and dangerous business.

He retreated to the quiet, dimly lit, and smoke-filled confines of the gentlemen's salon, where it seemed all the husbands and most of the young gentlemen had retired, all seeking solace, and peace from the chattering hordes of over-excited ladies.

Grabbing a glass of brandy from a servant's tray, he strode to the far window, and watched the endless arrival and departure of coaches on the street below, trying to forget the fact that he was standing in the house of the enemy.

Twenty years. And still the memories of that horrific night flashed before his eyes, as vivid as ever. He wished Effy was here, strong, and silent and reassuring beside him.

But then, perhaps that would only make things worse. The more he got to know her, the more he wanted to know; and the closer he found himself wanting to be.

How liberating it had been to play the enamoured fool, watching her shine and entrance as Black Maria. Though it was only one facet of her, it seemed one of the truest versions.

Free. Seductive. Intelligent. Powerful. He hadn't managed to keep his hands, nor his lips for that matter, to himself, despite the restrictions of her mask. If he was to be her *beau*, he would damn well enjoy every second of it. Though every moment they spent in public after such displays, was torture.

There was no doubt he wanted her, more than he seemed to have ever wanted any other woman. The fact that she seemed intent on keeping him at arm's length, denying them both their desire, for her own was very clear and unmistakable, was the worst of all. If he could have her, then maybe then, things could settle. *Infuriating, damned enchanting minx.*

A clear, cool head, that is what he needed to survive the evening. Not thoughts of Effy, of her warmth, her smile, her dark, inviting eyes, calling him like a siren. Not thoughts of the past. They had a plan. They were here for a reason, no matter how painful it might prove to be, for both of them.

And, he had a plan, something he had not been able to share with her. Surely that was proof she meant nothing to him?

In any case, if she could play cheerful, delightful, and smiling cousin Patience, he could damn well behave himself so they could survive the evening.

'There you are, Sinclair,' called Percy. Harcourt sighed. Not what he needed right this moment. 'I was just telling Russell here about that rather exciting house in Whitechapel.'

Harcourt steeled himself as he turned.

Mowbray was bad enough. *Now Russell too?* Was he to confront every one of his mother's murderers tonight then?

He surveyed the wicked, despicable man at Percy's side with a cold, nonchalant, and appraising glance, one eyebrow raised.

Just as he remembered. Small, wiry, cold, calculating green eyes and a large mouth. Greedy. Sweaty, and sickening. *Delicacy, always.*

'Must you tell all of London, Percy,' Harcourt chided. 'Or shall my secret finds remain secret only if I refuse to tell you from now on?'

'Come now,' Percy grinned. 'You can't keep all the best places, nor all the best partners, to yourself.' Harcourt inclined his head, and lifted his brandy. 'You remember the Marquess? My Lord, Harcourt Sinclair.'

'Ah yes, shipping, isn't it,' the man said disdainfully, offering his hand nonetheless.

'Indeed,' Harcourt said, taking it, though it felt like making a pact with the Devil himself. *No, the Devil would not have clammy palms...* 'My Lord.'

'So, what is this I hear about some excellent games to be had in Whitechapel? Most irregular.'

'Indeed, that is what makes them all the more exciting and thrilling,' Harcourt said, the challenge unmistakeable.

'I've just been telling Russell here that the infamous Black Maria has returned, for one final go before retirement,' Percy added. 'Is she worth it I wonder?'

'There are none like her,' Harcourt said coolly, answering both the asked, and implied questions. 'Quite the challenge, though well worth it.'

'I was thinking of bringing the boys down next week,' Percy said casually, grabbing a glass from one of the footmen passing. 'What do you say Russell? Care to have a go?'

If there was a master to double-entendre, Percy would be it.

The way he said so much, with only a glance, and twitch of the eyebrows, the way he played on people's desires so openly and pointedly, without ever abandoning his cheekiness, it was incredible.

Harcourt saw the doubt, the desire, the temptation flicker through Russell's eyes, and he knew in that moment, the man was his. *God, I owe you, Percy you tinker...*

'Send me card, address and date, and we shall see,' Russell drawled before retreating.

'Ta-da,' Percy smiled, raising his glass to meet Harcourt's. 'Well, that was easier than expected.'

'Thank you, Percy,' Harcourt said quietly, the ill-ease in his stomach somewhat abating now. 'You are a good friend, I don't deserve you.'

'No, you don't. And you don't deserve that *cousin* of yours, either,' he said. 'Which reminds me, where have you abandoned her?'

'She was swept away by Miss Fitzsimmons some time ago.'

'Oh dear. Well, I'm sure she can make it out alive if she needs to,' Percy said, glancing to check no one was within earshot. 'By the way, about the de Beaumonts. Nothing, old chap, I'm afraid. Clean as whistles as far as anyone knows.'

'Damn.'

'Either of you ever going to tell me what this is really about?'

'Trust me when I tell you, it's best if you don't know, Percy.'

'Just be careful, with whatever it is. Someone's already tried to kill you once.'

'Though they have yet to try again...'

'Doesn't mean they won't,' Percy warned.

Harcourt nodded, and Percy dropped it.

He wished he could tell his friend everything, sharing his purpose with Effy had helped him so much, he knew that having another friend on his side would alleviate the burden even more.

But he wasn't lying. It was too risky.

And Percy, unlike he or Effy, had a reputation to uphold. His entire life would be lived in Society, he could not shun nor disregard it as easily as they could. *Besides, the Countess would have my head if I ruined her precious grandson...*

After they finished their drinks, Percy dragged him back out into the main rooms, and led him from group of crinoline and crepe, to group of silk and ribbons. He seemed intent on distracting Harcourt from his thoughts with pretty, flirtatious, and eager women, drinks, and good food.

But for all he tried, Harcourt could not seem to shake the dark thoughts, and longing for one woman in particular.

∞

After the tenth time one of the annoying little blushing chits had asked her about Percy, Effy had had to excuse herself, citing her need for the ladies' withdrawing room, but escaping to the garden instead.

On the way, she had spotted Percy and Harcourt amidst a group of rather excited young ladies, blushing, fanning, and fawning, and though Harcourt had been laughing and, in all appearance, enjoying himself and the attention as much as his friend, it had not escaped Effy's notice that beneath it he seemed in a darker mood than usual.

She wondered if it was Mowbray, or even Russell, she had heard he was present, and she couldn't blame him if he was secretly harbouring desires to burn the house to ash. *I would do it for you if you asked...*

Effy wandered about the more discreet and hidden portions of the garden, which hadn't escaped the lavish decorations that covered the rooms inside.

Ribbons, flowers, torches, intricately carved lanterns and statues vied for attention among the neatly groomed beds and walkways.

Grateful for the escape, fresh air, and solitude, she settled down on a tiny stone bench by some trees, and listened to the echoes of the music and chatter, mingling with the quiet sounds of this small patch of nature at night. A few birds and insects underlined the otherwise peaceful silence of the glorious spring night.

Drawing a deep breath, she felt herself finally relax, the warm breeze heralding summer's imminent arrival, lifting all thoughts of the de Beaumonts who she had gratefully managed to avoid.

Along with thoughts of Harcourt, Percy, Lydia, and the rest of them.

But her peace did not go undisturbed for long.

Whispers, a muffled shout, a figure running through the

shadows at the edge of the back garden, and then, sniffles and stifled sobs.

Sighing, she rose from her perch, and made for the direction of the cries. Even in the shadow of the trees, she could make out Lady Lydia Mowbray's gleaming curls, as she cried rather unbecomingly into a handkerchief.

I would have thought she might be one of those who are pretty when they cry...

'There you are,' cried Angelique from behind her, her delicate heels clicking against the walkway. 'I've been looking everywhere for you!'

Damn. When she turned back, Lydia had disappeared in a rush of silks. Her chance had slipped away.

Or had it?

'Oh Angelique,' Effy cried back, in what amounted to be a stage whisper. She put on her most concerned, matronly look, and held her hands out to Angelique. 'I've just seen Lady Lydia, poor thing, crying in the trees!'

'Oh not again,' Angelique sighed, wrapping Effy's arm in her own, leading them back through the garden. 'Of all nights, too.'

'What do you mean? Is this a common occurrence? Poor thing, she's about to be married, whatever does she have to cry about so?' Perhaps a career in theatre might be open to her, after all, her performance was quite convincing, and from the look on Angelique's face, it seemed to be doing the trick. 'Angelique?'

'I really shouldn't say,' she said, eyes downcast, her expression suggesting she wished to do nothing but.

'We are friends, are we not, Angelique?' The girl nodded, and Effy shot her a reassuring smile. 'You know you can trust me with anything. I do hate to see anyone suffer so...'

'Well,' Angelique said, needing no more prodding, stopping and dropping her voice to a definite whisper. 'You see, Lydia is quite heartbroken. She had her sights set on a young Mr. Hartley, son of a tailor! Of course, her father wouldn't have it, not if he were the last man on earth, but even now Lydia pines so for him! Claims it's true love.'

'You don't believe so then?'

'Perhaps, but that would imply Lydia had a heart to begin with,' Angelique quipped before giggling. 'The worst is that she keeps carrying on with him, in secret!'

'Oh dear...'

'Indeed. She's lucky she's not been caught yet, but honestly, I'm not sure what she's thinking. Doncourt will not have her if there is even the slightest whiff of scandal, and then where will she be? Wouldn't be surprised if her father disowned her and sent her away to the nuns...'

'Poor, poor thing...'

Angelique gave her a look which suggested she believed Lydia to be anything but, and they resumed their walk back to the house.

Percy, it seemed, really was too clever for his own good. He had done well, choosing Miss Fitzsimmons, and it seemed that Effy had done well challenging the affections she bore for Lady Lydia. The girl was all too keen to repay her *friend's* kindness.

Now, to find Harcourt, and escape this loathsome evening and place full of vipers and fallacies...

∞

Careless, foolish, girl. Her inattention, and focus on finding Harcourt once she had managed to extricate herself from Angelique and her friends, feigning a headache, had cost her, very, very dearly.

Of all the people she prayed never to meet in a secluded alcove, away from the prying gazes of the masses, it was *him*. Why had she even come this way? What did she think? That Harcourt would be here, making love to some chit?

Somehow, that option now seemed infinitely preferable to this.

Seven years. He had barely aged. Effy stood frozen in fear, hypnotised like some wild creature as he closed the distance between them. There was no doubt he had recognized her, and there was no way for her to escape, without passing him and making a scene. Her heart beat fast, not as it did with Harcourt, fuzzy, and warm. No, she was cold, and terrorized; a frightened rabbit before a wolf.

Willing herself to stand tall, proud, and intent on not letting him see how much he affected her, Effy waited, watching as he slunk before her, much too close for propriety's sake.

The same emerald green eyes. The same golden hair, expertly groomed and yet careless. The same smile, teasing lips. The same handsome and beguiling face. Smooth, perfect features.

A veneer of warmth, and familiarity as he studied her.

'Well, well, well,' he whispered, his voice sending shivers down her spine. 'Euphemia Fortescue. Or is it Patience Sinclair now?'

'Hello Daniel,' she managed, though she was aware her voice was higher than usual.

She hated that he was so close she could smell him; that same mix of soap, and his own essence, that had clung tight in her nostrils for years, taunting her.

She hated that he was taller than her, so that she had to look up at him, his strong and muscular frame creating a barrier around her. A cage. *Oh, God, Harcourt, please come for me... Please find me...*

She wasn't usually one to wish for a man to save her, but tonight, from *him*, she was.

'Or should I say my Lord? Congratulations on your father's death.'

'I've been looking for you all evening,' he drawled, ignoring her bite, his hand tracing the line of her bodice. Still, she could not move to stop him, though she felt as though she might fall into a fit of sobs if he continued thus. 'I thought I was dreaming when I spotted you earlier. And looking so well.'

'How is your wife, Daniel,' she hissed.

Please, Harcourt...

'Well... How is your, what are they saying Harcourt Sinclair is

124

to you? Your, *cousin*?'

'Bit late to be asking about my well-being, Daniel,' she said, her breathing ragged, a fact which he did not miss, eyeing the rise and fall of her breasts with hunger.

'Haven't you missed me, then?'

Harshly, he grabbed her chin between his thumb and forefinger, and pointedly licked his lips.

A wave of nausea overcame her, and she swayed slightly.

No. No. No.

'Patience.' Harcourt's voice was ice-cold steel, and Effy nearly fell into a faint at the sound of it. *He came, dear God, he came...* 'Time to go, cousin.'

No one it seemed, had been able to tell him where Effy had disappeared to, other than to say she had gone in search of him.

He had had a bad feeling when he had not found her in any of the main rooms, or the gardens, and then, a strange shiver had passed through him. His hackles had raised, and by God if he hadn't known it to be impossible, he would have sworn he had heard her calling for him.

Quite by chance had he found her, and he had known immediately that he had not been wrong in his concern. He could see the terror written on her pale face as the Marquess de Beaumont kept her cornered, his fingers and indeed his entire body holding her captive.

In that moment, he had been very, very close indeed to wringing the man's neck, for his audacity, and all the pain he had, and continued to cause Effy.

He kept his hands clenched, as it would not do well to beat the life out of a peer in the corridor, but if he did not release her in the next seconds, he might do just that, and damn the consequences.

The Marquess turned, and sneered at him, making a show of raising his hands, and stepping aside. Effy did not need further invitation to rush to Harcourt's side, burrowing herself in his arms.

He raised an eyebrow as the Marquess scoffed at her, and made to step for him. *I will kill you...*

'Harcourt, no,' Effy whispered, sliding her arm around his waist, and turning to face *her* enemy. 'He isn't worth it.'

'I'll thank you to never address my cousin again, sir,' Harcourt said, waiting for no reply to turn away, his arm around Effy's shoulders as he ushered her down the corridor towards the foyer.

Without a word, he shepherded her into her cloak, out the door, and into the carriage.

He sat beside her, his arm still around her shoulders, and pulled a blanket onto her legs. *Damn that man!*

'Are you alright?' Effy nodded into his coat. 'You can cry, if you like. I won't think less of you Fortescue.'

'Thank you,' Effy said meekly with a faint smile. 'But I have cried far too many tears for that man already. After all this time... I didn't expect...'

'For him to have such power over you still,' Harcourt said softly.

'Yes. God... I can't, I can't shake it, his hold.'

Effy closed her eyes, and breathed in Harcourt's scent, to dispel Daniel's which still seemed to linger.

Let his warmth and strength wash over her again. *God...* When she had seen him standing there, it was as though Lucifer himself had risen from the depths of Hell to save her. Dark, dangerous, his power so tangible it had felt like the air was electric.

She had even seen a flicker of fear in Daniel's eyes; that had been a gift beyond measure.

'I tried, for so long. Even the lashes couldn't rip away his touch. When I became Black Maria, it was to find something, *anything*, to make me forget, not only Almsbury, but *him*. Passion, pleasure, oblivion. Even opium. I tried it all. But all of it, it only held the demons at bay. I thought, when I learned to live with them, when I realized that none but the touch of love could erase the touch of love, no matter how false it had been, that I had, in some way, conquered his hold. But tonight...'

'You should not have had to face him alone,' Harcourt

growled, feeling guiltier than ever. If only Percy hadn't distracted him for so long, he would have found what he sought much earlier, and... 'I should have been there.'

'You were there, Harcourt, when it mattered most,' she said, willing her tears to disappear back into her body. 'Thank you. I am sorry I know it's foolish. I can't even imagine how you feel, having had to face those men...'

'The first time I saw Mowbray, I had to excuse myself to go retch. I have had to face them too many times before, though it never gets easier,' he admitted. 'And your emotions are not foolish. That man is just as bad as them all in my opinion. You know, I too sought what pleasure and oblivion can offer, I know too well how quickly the demons return. But soon, both of us will be free of them.'

'I hope you're right,' Effy said quietly.

It wasn't long before they arrived back at the townhouse.

Effy finally released him, shivering, although assuring him she would be fine, and disappeared up the stairs.

Harcourt watched her go, his heart and mind raging a silent war inside him. She was most certainly *not fine*. And it cut him to the bone to see her so hurt, yet still willing herself to make nothing of the whole affair.

What she had suffered at Almsbury's hands, she could show and wear proudly on her skin. But what the Marquess had done... How very close he had been to killing that damned spineless viper...

Soon. But in the meantime, Effy, no matter how willing she was to admit it, needed him. He knew it, just as he knew she had called him to her aid. There wasn't much he could offer her, but comfort.

That, he could.

And so, resolved to follow his heart, and not his head, he downed a glass of brandy, dismissed the servants, and gave them Sunday morning off, grabbed the bottle and two glasses, and went to her chambers.

XV.

Foolish, childish, weak woman! God... What had gotten over her? What had possessed her to say so much to Harcourt? She could only imagine what he thought of her now, and none of it was good. She couldn't blame him either, she felt the same way about herself.

Effy sat before her dressing table, staring into the mirror's reflection without seeing anything. She had sent Lily away, rather harshly for which she would apologize in the morning.

But she couldn't bear for anyone to be near her. She had claimed she would manage very well to undress herself, but in however long she had been sitting here, she hadn't managed to remove one single item.

How could he have such a hold on her after so long? She was strong, stronger than this. She didn't love him, and she didn't fear him; and yet, when it mattered most she had frozen in terror, when she had been convinced she could face him and Sarah as though nothing had ever happened. As though their cruelty mattered not one iota.

And then Harcourt had come, and she hadn't been able to stop her mouth from spilling so many truths she had wished to keep to herself. *To preserve some dignity...*

If he had any doubt about her *unworthiness*, she had made it quite clear to him now, speaking of the things she had done to forget what Almsbury, Daniel, Sarah, and Society had done to her.

Harcourt had faced the men responsible for the atrocities

against his mother time and time again, and yet a man had *wronged* her, hurt her, and she stood there like a frightened ninny waiting for a rescuer.

Oh God no, she thought when she heard the knock.

She knew who it was. But she couldn't bear to face him, not now, perhaps not ever again. To see the pity in his eyes.

It hadn't been there when she had most expected it, but now, it was inevitable. *Weak ninny.* She should tell him to go away, that she was fine, but she couldn't will herself to say anything.

Perhaps if she said nothing at all, he would just go.

Of course not, she sighed internally, catching the movement in the mirror as Harcourt slid into her room and came to stand beside her, depositing a bottle and glasses on a table nearby. Still, she could not move, nor speak. If he got any closer however, she might break, and end up a simpering mess on the floor.

Harcourt stared down at the marble statue before him. She had barely even blinked since he'd come in. He could see how hard she was trying to be calm, and still, emotions in check, denied, like he had so many times before.

This was different. He could feel her pain, radiating, and it hurt him, his stomach churning and his heart aching for her.

He glanced down at her hand, posed delicately on the dressing table.

'You're trembling, Fortescue,' he said gently, longing to reach out and hold it.

But he would not give her any excuse to pull away.

'I am not trembling,' Effy retorted bitterly, barely containing the tears threatening to spill all over her cheeks and deepen her shame despite his protestations it would not change his opinion of her. 'I do not tremble. Or quake, or fall into fits of vapours, or any of that nonsense. And certainly not because of a man!'

'You are shaking,' Harcourt said softly, settling onto his haunches beside her.

He could see how tightly she clenched her jaw, struggling to keep her emotions buried.

'I'm cold, nothing more,' she said, clasping her hands together in her lap to prevent them trembling again. 'A chill, that's all.'

'It's nearly summer, Fortescue, and there is a fire.'

There were no more retorts.

She simply closed her eyes, and took a deep breath. Harcourt placed a hand on hers, unable to resist any longer and he felt her stiffen beneath him.

But she did not pull away.

'You said, that you did not believe anything but the touch of love could wash his away,' he said gently. 'That passion, oblivion, could only ease the pain. Let me ease your pain tonight, Fortescue. Let me try and help you forget, if only for a while.'

Silence. Stillness. No refusal. No rejection.

Slowly, he took one hand in his, and brought it to his lips. Fingertips. Knuckles. Palm. Wrist. Forearm, all the way up to the top of glove. Still, she did not move.

Beneath his kisses, he could feel her warmth, feel her absorbing every touch, slowly melting into him.

Her glove fluttered to the floor.

The same, again. Fingertips. Knuckles. Palm. Wrist. Kisses delicately laid at the altar before removing the other glove.

He rose then, laid a kiss on each earlobe, before removing the tiny sapphires dangling there.

The back of her neck; the necklace, gone.

All the while she sat there, seemingly motionless, eyes still closed, but beneath him, he could feel every nerve responding to him, crying out for more.

Taking her hands with the softest of touches in his, he brought her to her feet, and stood her at the end of the bed.

The dress followed the gloves to the floor, as did the chemise, petticoats, drawers, stockings and slippers, all followed with kisses until she stood before him, naked and the most beautiful thing he had ever seen.

Venus. Ishtar. His fiery-angel of destruction, his warrior-goddess. *His.* He inhaled sharply, realizing the beat of his heart was for her. *His.*

Perhaps he could wash it all away for her, for in that moment he understood with a jarring bolt of understanding that he did love her. With all that he was. *My twin soul...*

Harcourt moved to her back, and saw once again the twisted pattern of horror written there. It extended, further than she had shown, onto her buttocks and the back of her thighs. His anger resurfaced, at the thought of all she had endured.

This time, when he touched them, she did not flinch.

Harcourt kissed every single scar, not to erase them, but to mark them as his own. He could not erase them, he would not, for she was right, they made her who she was.

But he could accept them, love them, and protect her from anything that sought to hurt her ever again.

When he had finished, he knelt before her, his goddess of vengeance and love and light, and kissed her in that most intimate of places. Softly, gently at first, once again requesting entry, easing her legs apart, hands on her thighs.

She sighed, and he felt her lean in, opening everything to him, and so he deepened the kiss, his lips and tongue exploring, dipping, teasing, caressing.

Effy threaded her fingers through his hair and tugged, ever so slightly, holding on while he drove her to the brink, and he thought he might go mad with want, need, his own desire pressing hard against his breeches, making itself known. *No, not yet...*

He drank her honey wine until he knew she was just at the edge, her moans and breathing haggard, her nails digging into his shoulder.

Then, he pulled away, and looked up at her.

Her eyes were open now, hooded and dark, and full of the same want and need and desire, but he simply smiled, and rose to his feet before her.

Tauntingly, he divested himself of his own clothes, and relished in her eyes raking across his form, taking in every detail.

Effy watched him undress, hungrily, wanting what he offered more than ever. She had refused herself, knowing her heart might not survive it. But tonight, she needed him.

It didn't matter that he didn't love her; she loved him.

And this one night, would be enough.

She was still dizzy and throbbing from his most intimate kiss, and her skin tingled from every kiss he had so sweetly laid upon it. He had known precisely when to stop, halting her pleasure to increase it.

He knew precisely what he was doing, and his consideration, his care, was more than any other had ever shown her. It meant more to her than any hollow words of comfort could have.

She eyed him as at last the last of his clothes fell to the floor.

The lean, hard muscle. Everywhere. From his broad shoulders, to his ribbed abdomen, and perfectly curved hips. His strong thighs, and the impressive manhood which stood at the ready.

Effy let herself look at him then, in his eyes, and she saw a softness there, which belied everything else about him.

There is something in those eyes I don't recognize...

But before she could make sense of it, he was kissing her, his mouth on hers, as hungry as she was.

If their first kiss had been the appetizer, this was an entire meal. His lips were firm, gentle, and controlled in their frenzy, his tongue actively seeking out hers, inviting her in, dancing with her, and they explored each other as deeply as they could. She could still taste her essence on him, and beneath it, *his.*

Effy could feel his arms, sense them as they held her tight, grounded her, and she gripped onto Harcourt, one hand in his hair, the other on his neck, afraid to let go lest she fall to the floor, like the molten pool of hot liquid that she was.

She could feel his hardness against her, teasing what was to come, but still, she could feel him holding back, giving her everything, denying himself what his own body told her he wanted as desperately as she did.

Slowly, he led her to the bed, never once disengaging for fear she might come to her senses and leave him. Never again would he let her go. She had been forged for him, out of the same fiery depths he himself had been forged. Her flesh moulded to him, he could melt into her, and indeed that is all he longed for.

Harcourt managed to find the edge of the bed, the silk of the light covers brushing against the back of his thighs, and he sat, guiding Effy down with him.

Only then did she disengage from the kiss, standing still ever so close, so that their noses were nearly touching. She gazed down at him, eyes full of hunger, and adoration, and he thought his heart might burst, then and there, if he could not have her.

Effy straddled him, knees tight by his hips, her grip on him loosening no more than his on her. Only to guide him into her did she let him go, guiding his shaft to its home in her core.

Eyes still locked together, she lowered onto him, and with a sigh, returned her hand to his neck.

This. This is love then, Harcourt thought as he found his home within her.

Soft, tender, perfect. His hands moved to her hips, to steady her as they began their new dance. The rise and fall. Together, they found a steady rhythm of entering and departing, her muscles contracting and releasing with divine, tortuous, and exquisite pleasure around him.

Still, their gazes were locked. He could see every strand of hair, every eyelash, feel every breath upon his skin. He could see the flush in her cheeks, the sweat breaking out on her brow, feel her every heartbeat against his chest.

How beautiful and perfect you are my love, Effy thought, peering through the veil to glimpse his soul. Lay open bare before her, crying out to her with every breath, every glint in those burning coal eyes.

Within her, with every stroke, every mounting.

She kissed him then, a kiss full of the love she felt.

Dark, passionate, bare, raw, and undemanding. His kiss could sooth her very soul, repair every broken thing within her.

Harcourt pulled away this time, her touch had seared him, the very depths of him, brought him back to life.

This, this is love, then…

He looked at her, confused, and scared, and she simply smiled, guiding his head to her breasts as if she too felt the same torment, and could not bear the sight of him.

And he was not one to refuse…

Hungrily, he kissed, nibbled, suckled at each breath, until her nipples were hard, and crying out for him. Just as she was.

Harcourt, she whispered, barely audible, as though it was her soul and not her voice that cried out. She was nearly there again, her pulse quick, their rhythm almost frenzied. *Not yet, my love, not yet…*

Without leaving his place inside her, he rolled them over onto her back, and then she cried out. Surprised, the edge, so near.

He took her hands away from his body, locking them above her head. He watched the doubt, the confusion, the willingness pass in her eyes, then deepened his exploration of her core. Thrusting, teasing, reaching every corner of her.

God, how does he know… Effy could barely hold herself back, and still he taunted, changed, just at the last second, but how much more pleasure could she endure. It felt now as though he would break her in two.

She wrapped her legs around him, and opened herself more, arching back to welcome him each time. She wanted to taste him again, to kiss every inch of him as he had her, but no, he wouldn't allow it, staying out of reach, raining kisses on her, until finally, his eyes locked with hers again, and she knew, this time, he would allow her to find that which she sought.

Let me see you, my love, let us go there together… Harcourt saw the understanding, the acceptance in her eyes, as she let him drive her to her completion. He saw her breath catch, her mouth opening, gasping soundlessly, and still she fought to keep her eyes on his.

He felt her shudder, tighten and grasp beneath him, heard the single cry escape as he pushed her beyond it still, finding his own completion with her.

Then, and only then, did he allow her mouth to find his, gasping, needing the kiss as if it would give life, breath.

And so, it did.

Only then, did he falter, his body releasing and forcing him to lay beside her. Still, she did not release him, only followed, wound tightly around him, holding him tight within her.

Their breaths evened, and there was a smile on her lips, a longing in those dark brown eyes as she gazed at him, brushing away his curls with her thumb. He wanted to hold her tight, but he wanted to see her, so he settled his hand on her waist, caressing her as lightly as a feather.

Effy did not want to cry, natural as it would be after finding so shattering a completion as she never had before.

What would he think of her then?

But she couldn't stop the hot tears that escaped, trailing down into her hair. He was so beautiful, *my love*, and how he had loved her. There was no other word. That is what she had felt him give.

No matter that it was an illusion.

'Oh God, Fortescue,' he breathed, pulling her in for a kiss.

Tears. Of what? Pain? Regret? Despair?

He met her lips softly, tenderly, willing them away with his love but he felt her break beneath him, pulling away with a sob.

'Fortescue,' he asked, terrified of what she might say.

'Don't you dare leave me after this,' she said fiercely, clinging onto him.

'Never,' he whispered.

Neither could admit they were not speaking of tonight alone.

Neither could say the words truly on their lips and in their hearts.

Not yet.

Truth. Bare. Raw. Painful. She was his, and he would never let her go. How could she think that of him? Could she fear the loss as much as him?

Could she love *him*?

135

∞

Though she had never felt more sated, and invigorated, more alive and satisfied than she could have ever dreamed possible, Effy's mind would not quieten. She had managed to slip out of bed without waking Harcourt, and padded down to the kitchen to fix them some breakfast, knowing he had given the household their leave for the morning.

If she had remained in bed, she would have tossed and turned, and eventually woken him, and she had hoped a distraction would settle her mind. So far, her expedition had been unsuccessful on that account. She should be exhausted, weary-eyed and dazed; he had loved her, and she him, until the very early hours of the morning.

Indeed, her body was aching, and surprisingly weak, in a very good way, but she could not stop the incessant whirl of thoughts.

Oblivion is what he had promised, and oblivion he had given. Their coupling had been more than mutually satisfactory, as she had long suspected it could be. There was no doubt of the desire, of the heat and passion that lay between them. Why then, had she resisted for so long?

She and Harcourt both had pasts, they were not novices in this game. She had said it herself, it was natural for two such souls, thrust together as they had been, to seek solace in each other's arms. Why then, had she thought it would serve them better to resist their attraction?

Surely, surrendering to temptation was far more likely to satisfy and clear the mind, rather than denying it, as she had said they must to remain focused on their objectives.

The answer struck her as she set the toast on the plates, entirely oblivious to the heat scorching her fingers.

She hadn't *wanted* to succumb.

Because she knew what it would mean to her.

She feared him taking her, then leaving her, as he did all his other conquests. So long as she kept herself from his bed, the inevitable separation at the end of this whole affair would be much easier. *For her.*

After last night, there was no denying she was risking a very broken heart indeed.

Sighing, defeated and unable to find any way to untie herself, she grabbed the tray, and padded back upstairs.

Harcourt was just about to leave the warm, soft, empty comfort of the bed when Effy appeared at the door, a tray of breakfast in hand. She smiled, warming the cockles of his heart, and he relaxed, stretching back into the down pillows like a cat. *God, she looks glorious this morning...* Her healthy, sated glow was as warm as the summer sun.

He had felt oddly distressed when he had woken alone among the crumpled sheets. It had been wonderful enough waking with her beside him when they stayed in the cottage; he could only imagine what it would have been like *this* morning.

But she had left him, as he had always done to the women who had shared his bed, and he felt a strange pang at the thought that after all, last night had only been about oblivion for her. When for him, it had been so much more.

Unexpected. That seemed the word that came to mind whenever he thought of Effy, in any respect. She somehow managed to continually surprise him, not least of all by finding a way to his previously cold, dead, heart. *Love.*

Never, had he expected that would be in his cards. It wasn't for men like him, it had been chased out of his soul by demons, and yet, here he was, like some green boy, madly in love with his *housemaid.*

Or his avenging angel. Or his saviour. Or his cousin. Or Black Maria. Or whatever she was, underneath it all; whoever it was who had shared his bed last night.

For he had no doubt there was no dissimulation as she lay with him; she had allowed him a glimpse of her soul, just as he had allowed her one of his. The question plaguing him now was, *what next?*

She had refused to allow them to succumb to the temptation of their attraction, claiming it would complicate things. And so, it did. He felt more than ever the danger of their endeavour, feared what might happen to her. He couldn't lose her. That would be worse than any fate he could suffer.

Had she known then? Did she somehow suspect that beneath the desire lay feelings which might threaten their cool headedness?

How could she? When he himself had only been forced to face them last night? Unless, she had feelings for him, that she was more aware of? Or had she simply known how he dealt with the fairer sex as a rule, and decided she did not want to suffer the same fate?

Damn. This. This torture, this inability to think of anything else, this is why he had made sure he never entangled his heart in anything before.

Not that he could have in all fairness avoided doing so in this case, he realized as she settled beside him on the bed, setting the tray between them.

A vision as the sun streamed in the windows behind her, making her shine like an ancient goddess.

'Good morning,' she smiled.

'Good morning,' he grinned despite himself. He leaned over the tray, slowly, testing how far she might let him go this morning. *Far enough*, he thought, as she allowed him a kiss. Gentle, passionate, undemanding of anything. He could have sworn she blushed as he pulled away, her long lashes covering her eyes as she fussed with the tray. 'You've been busy. A feast.'

'Well, I was rather hungry,' she said cheekily. 'And I still know my way around the kitchen, so...'

'I'm grateful, I'm famished,' Harcourt said, tucking into some bread and bacon.

'Harcourt,' Effy said hesitantly, playing with a piece of toast. He eyed her warily, suddenly terrified of whatever dismissal she was about to give *him*. 'Thank you. For being there, last night.'

'You don't need to thank me, or rather, I think you found plenty of ways of showing your gratitude last night.' His lips curled slightly as he bit into the bacon, and Effy saw the warm tease linger in his eyes. 'You're not going to become all prudish and womanly and force us to have a conversation about this, are you?'

'You insult me, Harcourt,' she said with mock effrontery. 'I told you once before that you were in no danger from me. What happened last night changes nothing.'

Harcourt's eyes darkened with something akin to disappointment, and his jaw clenched ever so slightly.

Effy wondered for a moment if he was one of those men who were flattered at the thought they could make any woman fall in love with them, particularly once they had seduced them, but then, no. He was a man to avoid entanglements, not to be disappointed at the lack thereof.

Perhaps he thought she meant she would refuse him her bed now. She should, she knew, *one night*, but if her heart was to be broken anyways, she might as well enjoy his company while she could.

'Though, perhaps, it does mean that I was wrong, in insisting we refrain from enjoying each other's comfort.'

Effy raised her eyebrow slightly, and took a rather teasing bite of her bread. Harcourt laughed, heartily, sending tingles through Effy's body. He shook his head and stared at her for a long moment.

He should be relieved to learn that she wanted, nor expected anything. And that she would not deny him the pleasure of her company. Yet somehow he was disappointed that she seemed intent on denying there was more than raw physical attraction between them.

Not that he would be the one to dare broaching *that* subject.

'What do you want, Fortescue,' he asked seriously, studying her, making note of every perfect detail that composed her, to remember it always. 'When this is all over, what do you want for your life?'

'A rather serious and dangerous question, Mr. Sinclair.'

'Indulge me.'

'I don't know,' she said, as though suddenly realizing there would be a life for her beyond their quest. 'My vow, to you, it was, in my mind at least, for life. I suppose I thought I might eventually retire to the cottage, live a quiet life in the country, but now...'

'It seems unlikely? I think you would grow quickly bored of such a life,' he said. 'After all the adventure, the danger, I cannot say I can see you living the quiet rustic life.'

'What about you, Harcourt? Twenty years of seeking revenge, how do you picture your life when that is all over?'

'In truth I have not the faintest idea,' he sighed. 'For one, I never thought it would ever be over. That I would ever succeed. And secondly, well, you know what I am Fortescue. I cannot pretend that I would ever be able to simply begin living a respectable life.'

They sat in silence for a long moment, picking at the food, sipping their coffee.

Neither would admit it, to themselves, or to the other, that although they may not know *what* they wanted for their future, they had a good inkling of *who* they might wish to be in it.

'On the subject of our plans,' Harcourt said, chasing the ghosts of impossible futures away with a sigh. 'I spoke to Percy, about the de Beaumonts. I'm afraid he has had no luck on that front either.'

'I had no real expectations,' she said reassuringly as he watched her carefully. 'I'm fine, Harcourt. I have quite resolved myself to the impossibility of my own vengeance. Truth be told, in the end, I suppose it is only pettiness really. They hurt me, yes, but it is nothing compared to what others have done.'

Harcourt knew she spoke of those *he* sought to ruin, and though in any other case he might have agreed her pursuit was that of a wounded woman seeking retribution, he could not in hers.

He had come to know her too well for that, and if he was honest, it had taken everything in his willpower not to throttle the invertebrate that had injured her last night.

'It isn't pettiness, Fortescue. It is a matter of honour. Never doubt that I understand, nor that I support you.'

Effy smiled faintly. It was a matter of honour. *Mine.*

But she had hoped to find another way to repay the debt she owed the de Beaumonts. Other than the obvious choice in matters of honour. She had thought convincing herself, and Harcourt, that it was nothing worthy of pursuing after all might make it a less likely ending.

Not that she would ever admit it to him. If it had to be done, it would be by her, and her alone.

'Last night, before the incident with Daniel,' Effy said, changing the subject before he made the offer she knew he would again. 'I was coming to find you. It seems we need not look too far to find Lady Lydia's weakness. They are still in contact, and I think with only a little push, we might bring about her ruin.'

'You brilliant, magnificent creature,' Harcourt growled, tossing aside his food to rain kisses on Effy's face.

Giggling, she managed to push aside her half-eaten toast.

He took her again, as if in recompense for her good work. Sweetly, delicately, but with a rough excitement that could not be contained.

They spent the remainder of the morning in bed, satisfying all their appetites. When they could no longer deny that the servants would soon return, and that the *cousins* should not be discovered together, they parted, only to meet again in the study, dressed, to discuss their plans regarding Lady Lydia.

XVI.

I f this was indeed what marriage would be like, Harcourt decided that it might not be quite so dreadful as he had always imagined it to be. It had never been something he thought would suit him, and still, the confines of such an arrangement terrified him. But if a marriage should involve delicious intrigue, delectably depraved evenings, and the company of a clever woman in all things, well, it might not be so terrible a fate after all.

They had set their plans for Lady Lydia in motion, now, it was a question of waiting. As it was with Russell. The deal that would cripple Bolton and Campbell was well underway, and the final *coup de grace* for them all, well that was quite ready as well. Harcourt didn't know why he remained silent to Effy about it; in truth, she hadn't asked, and he didn't feel much like volunteering the information.

For the past week they had led much of what could be believed to be a normal enough life. Effy attended to Miss Fitzsimmons more and more, not only was her friendship and trust necessary, but Harcourt suspected Effy quite liked the chit and enjoyed some female companionship.

It seemed that though Lady Fitzsimmons was not quite ready to engage *Patience* as a full-time companion, she was intent on using her best they could as chaperone for the Season.

Meanwhile he had spent more time at his shipping offices, actually tending to his business which had, for too long, been severely neglected.

When she was not with the Fitzsimmons, Effy was paraded around town, at various balls, exhibitions, parks, and shops, by Harcourt, the Dowager, and even occasionally Percy. Effy became everyone's favourite orphan, and even Harcourt's reputation seemed to have improved thanks largely to the Dowager's doting.

Whatever tinge of jealousy he had felt of his friend's relationship with Effy, had now disappeared, his heart and mind had both somehow conceded that whether or not Percy might have designs, Effy was *his*, and his alone.

Their nights, when Effy had not been playing at Black Maria, alone, much to Harcourt's regret, (apparently the card sharp had a reputation of working her way through men rather quickly), had been spent together. The servants, if they realized anything untoward was happening, said nothing and made no indication of any such knowledge.

No rumours had been heard around town, which meant that Percy had done very well in his household hirings; for secrets to remain secret in London was a rare happening indeed.

They settled into an oddly domestic intimacy, which somehow failed to fall into tedium, or routine. There was still an edge of danger, and excitement to their life together, which fuelled their passion and maintained the exceptional and unconventional edge to their relationship.

Both however, carefully avoided revisiting their feelings, or plans for the future.

Time, it seemed, had halted for them, allowing them to enjoy the other without restraint or expectation. Both knew it would not last long, that soon the realities of what they had set in motion, of their joint purposes, would come calling, but neither seemed eager to face them.

Friday morning, reality arrived in the form of a note from Percy.

Harcourt found himself staring at it, standing at the window of his study, a strange sort of peace within him as he waited for Effy to join him.

'From Percy,' she asked, closing the door quietly behind her.

Harcourt looked lost in thought, cold, distant, and resigned.

Perhaps it was how she herself felt about it, or perhaps he was as altered as he seemed to be. The dangerous power that emanated from him so clearly the first time she had met him here, seemed to have dissipated over the weeks, his air becoming somewhat more subdued, as though a weight pressed upon him, weakening him to some degree.

Not that she could ever doubt his danger, not when he looked at her with those coal black eyes as he did now, strength and resolve pouring from his.

'Russell?'

'Indeed,' Harcourt said with a sigh, his smile belying the intensity of his eyes as he came to her, handing her the note. 'Russell intends to visit Black Maria tonight.'

'Excellent news,' Effy nodded.

Harcourt wondered if she too felt the weight of the world crashing down upon them in that instant, as he did.

He thought he saw her jaw clench, and the light momentarily flee from her up-to-now tender and bright eyes. He ran his thumb against her cheek, inviting her to confide in him, her velvet skin comforting to a degree he never could have imagined. She smiled up at him and leaned into his hand.

Such a simple gesture, and yet so much trust, so much care, so much devotion within it.

'I was beginning to doubt his interest.'

'I never doubted you,' Harcourt grinned devilishly.

'You cannot be there,' she said quietly, but in a tone that offered no debate.

Harcourt felt his throat tighten, and let his hand drop.

He might've known she would say such a thing, but this was his revenge. *His.* He had to be there, needed to be there.

Russell's demise would be his to witness, and if he should take it badly, and come upon Effy…

'Fortescue -'

'Do you trust me?'

Her gaze was unrelenting.

There were many implications to her question; he could see the pulse in her neck quicken, as she waited for him to respond.

'Yes.' He did, more than anyone, from the first; more than he had ever thought he could.

'Then trust me in this. Your hand in this game cannot be seen, nor even suspected. Trust me to be your avenger.'

'I trust you, Fortescue. More than you know. But Russell -'

'Will be well managed. The Proprietors will see to that. As will Percy. I will be safe. Besides, this is not the final act. Just a taste.'

Effy's heart had fluttered when he had all but said it was her safety that concerned him more than her ability to enact his vengeance.

Not that, after the week they had spent, she could really doubt his care for her, if only inasmuch as he saw her as his partner, mistress, property.

She steeled herself against the hope it could be anything more.

'Just a taste,' he whispered, half agreeing, half teasing.

Brushing his fingers over her cheek, he leaned down to kiss her. Tasting, sampling, ever so gently and slowly, his desire for something more than passion. It was a kiss of possession, of marking, of promise, and of trust.

Then, just as Effy felt herself falling into him, he released her, a satisfied glint in his eye as he caught her swaying slightly before recomposing herself.

'I'll be waiting in the carriage,' he said firmly, turning away back to his desk.

Effy nodded, still half stunned, her heartbeat still racing, knowing there would be no further discussion.

He had *compromised*, and as long as he wasn't seen, that would be enough. With a breath, and a smooth of her already perfect skirts, she left.

Though he knew it was for the best, and the more strategic option, Harcourt still couldn't help but feel slightly bitter to be shut out of his own vengeance.

Yes, he trusted Effy.

Yes, he trusted Percy and the Proprietors to keep her safe.

But slowly, it seemed he was being locked out of his own purpose, and if he was honest, it wasn't the fact in itself that bothered him; it was that he actually felt relief and gratitude that Effy was with him, fighting *for* him.

That he was not alone anymore.

He shuddered, eyeing the passers-by beneath the window, laughing, talking, hurrying about their business.

He wondered if a simple life might have suited him once. Or if it might ever again.

He doubted it.

∞

Harcourt felt like a caged animal. Hours he had been here, straight-backed, and as nervous as a wild stallion. He was bouncing his knee, and his knuckles were white from his fingers digging into the leather of the seat. Even his driver and the team seemed calmer than he, silent and steady at their posts.

How much longer can she possibly be? Waiting in the carriage. His idea. And now he regretted it bitterly. At least, if he had stayed at the townhouse, he would have been able to pace the length and breadth of it, or drink himself into a stupor. He didn't even dare leave the carriage and walk the alleys and surrounding streets for fear of being seen. *Recognised.*

Waiting in the carriage.

It had seemed like a good idea at the time. A good *compromise.* He smiled mirthlessly. He had never been the type to compromise. Until Miss Euphemia Fortescue had barrelled into his life and seemingly taken command of it, and him with it. Not only had he let her; he enjoyed it.

Damn the woman. Almost as soon as thought it, he regretted it. She was doing this for him. *But why does she have to take so long?*

He didn't remember her being inside the gaming hell so long when they had visited together.

Perhaps time was just running slower, forced to wait liked some protector awaiting his mistress as he was. *Or perhaps there was trouble.*

No, if there had been, Percy would have fetched him. Unless he and the rest had been taken, or lay unconscious somewhere.

An image of Russell taking his fury out on Effy flashed through his mind and his stomach lurched. *She's fine. She's just being careful. Delicacy, always.*

The door lurched open, and Harcourt jumped out of his skin. He heard Effy's muffled laugh echo from under the handkerchief she wore over her face as she closed the door behind her.

'Did I frighten you, Harcourt,' she mused, dropping the handkerchief, and tossing away her cap, regarding him with a wicked smile and glint in her eyes.

'Startled. Quite the entrance.'

Effy raised an eyebrow and lounged back in the seat.

Harcourt waited with bated breath, but she seemed intent on torturing him even further.

'God's teeth, woman, well?'

Innocently, Effy shrugged, crossing her legs, raising the skirt on her right thigh ever so slowly, ever so tauntingly. She grinned as Harcourt's eyes darkened to the colour of pitch, watching every miniscule movement with deadly intent.

She let her fingers dance in the black folds of her skirt as she moved it ever upwards; until the top of her stocking was exposed, a rather large wad of notes stuffed into the garter.

She ran her tongue over her teeth, a smile of sheer satisfaction on her lips as his eyes widened, and he fell forward onto his knees.

His long, elegant fingers cupped her calf, running upwards towards their goal, sending shivers of delight down to her toes.

'You torturous, wicked, magnificent creature,' he breathed, removing the notes, and kissing the place where they had been.

Cocking her head, she made a little sound of warning.

Harcourt stopped, and raised his eyes to her. *God*, she thought she might burn to ash from the fire within them. Still, she knocked against the side of the carriage, and as it lurched forward, she glanced down towards her other leg.

The woman meant to drive him mad, he was sure of it. She was toying with him; savouring her victory, he could see it in those dark brown eyes, full of desire and need. He could feel it in the warmth of her skin, in the jolts of electricity that seemed to pass between them every time he touched her. *Very well...*

Obliging the lady, he moved just enough, raising his hands in defeat as she crossed her legs, left leg now on top.

Again, she took her time, baiting him, testing his restraint, and her own, as she raised the skirts to the top of her stocking. Another wad of notes, carefully tucked in the garter.

Wicked, wicked, delicious creature. He moaned this time as he took the notes, tossing them behind him, to caress her thigh with his lips. Once his offering had been made, she leaned down, tracing the line of his jaw from ear to chin with her finger. He lifted his gaze, all too aware now of his mounting desire pressing against his breeches. Not even the occasional lurch of the carriage could distract him, or return him to his senses.

There was only her, and he needed her more desperately than ever. Yet, there was a warning in her eyes.

Again, fighting every nerve in his body, he raised his hands, and moved away ever so slightly. She uncrossed her legs, spreading herself before him as she slid herself to the edge of the seat.

But even as he meant to claim her, in any way she wished, as long as she let him bury himself inside her, she stopped him, a hand on his breast.

He was lost, when he saw the pleasure it brought her to feel his heart pounding at his breast, begging her to concede.

Raising an eyebrow, she shifted forward, glancing down at her bosom that even now threatened to spill out of the tight corset. *She is trying to drive me mad...*

Then, he glanced the edging of paper, hidden beside the

mounds of delicate, tender flesh he wanted to drown himself in, and he growled.

His fingers were nearly trembling as he unhooked the top five hooks of her corset, to find another was of notes stuffed there.

That was it, the last of his restraint was gone as he grabbed the pile, threw it beside him, and hungrily pulled down her shirt to reveal her now free breasts.

She allowed him to meet her then, his lips and mouth ravishing her breasts as she clutched his silken curls, pressing him against her. He could hear her ragged breath above him as she arched against him.

This, he knew, was no time for delicacy. Fiercely, he ripped open his breeches, and heard her chuckle teasingly as his erect manhood sprung forth. This was no time for teasing either, for if he did not have her this instant he would die.

Grasping her thighs, he pulled her forward, pushing up the skirts, and finding the hole in her drawers. He rose to meet her then, plunging into her without restraint, without care. Roughly, like a rabid animal, he took her, her cries of pleasure edging him ever onwards.

Effy hadn't known what manner of beast she might awaken when she had started this game but by God, she was not regretting it now. There was a raw, fierce, magnetic, deep lust in his eyes, as he took her. Possessed her. There was no care, only brutal plunder of her innermost self.

Grasping the leather straps on either side of the seat, she arched back even further, wanting him as far and deep inside her as he could. Her legs twirled around each other at his back, as though she could bring him deeper, even as she thought he might break her in two again with his need.

He nibbled roughly on her breasts, gasping for air and grunting, each deep throated acknowledgement of the pleasure she was bringing him, edging on her own.

Until finally, there it was, a thousand stars in the darkness amongst the sweat and stickiness and roughness. She cried out, her knuckles blanching as she clutched the straps.

Harcourt joined her, stilling as every single muscle in his body tensed and released, his seed spilling deep inside her.

Both their breaths were as ragged as he felt his head drop onto her shoulder, her legs slowly releasing him, and her arms encircling his head.

The sudden halt of the carriage brought them to their senses, and the driver must have known what they had been up to for he did not come around to open the door.

Hurriedly, they redressed as efficiently as they could, gathered the piles of notes strewn about the carriage, and descended, heading for the mews behind the townhouse, the smile of satisfied fools plastered on their faces.

The woman really would drive him mad, he thought as they made their way to the servants' entrance. Even in the shadowed moonlight, he could see her glow, and felt his body stirring at the thought of taking her again.

He could lie with her a thousand times, he thought, and still never be sated; never cease to be amazed and surprised by the depths of pleasure they could descend to together.

Yet even now, his body crying out, he decided he wanted a bed to continue his explorations of this unrelenting, beguiling and sinful, delicious creature.

∞

George was waiting for them anxiously at the servants' entrance, his uniform put on so haphazardly it looked as if he had dressed in the dark, which in fact, he had.

If he had any thoughts on Effy's dress, he said nothing, simply rushed up to them as they crossed the threshold.

'I'm sorry, sir,' he squeaked. 'But Viscount Egerton is waiting for you in your study. I tried to say you weren't at home, but he insisted -'

'It's fine, George,' he growled, casting a worried glance at Effy who simply shrugged. 'I'll take care of it. Go to bed.'

The flustered butler bowed, thankful that Harcourt hadn't chastised him any further, and rushed up the servants' stairs.

'Why do you think he's here,' Effy asked, following Harcourt as he marched purposefully towards his study.

'I haven't the faintest idea,' Harcourt said through clenched teeth, his heart racing. But it most certainly could not be good. 'Will you stay?'

'Of course,' Effy said, glad he should wish her with him, hoping she would not need to clean up any bodies nonetheless.

Certainly not Percy's...

Percy, who was leaning nonchalantly on the mantel, a glass of brandy in hand when Harcourt and Effy stormed in quite dramatically.

Effy could feel the tension, unease, and danger emanating from Harcourt again, dark and terrifying in his barely contained anger.

Glancing over at them, Percy raised his glass and emptied it. There was a quiet foreboding in his manner, an odd weariness and exasperation about him.

'Sinclair, Effy, there you are,' he said flatly, as though his presence was entirely normal and acceptable.

'What are you doing here, Percy,' Harcourt growled, trying to remind himself that Percy was his friend.

But the calmness in his manner was decidedly unnerving, and seconds ago Harcourt had been in desperate need of the sensual minx beside him.

Not whatever this was.

'I thought it was time we all had a proper chat,' Percy said with a faint smile, his eyes running over Effy, who was suddenly very aware of how she might look after what happened in the carriage. 'Drink?'

Taking Harcourt's galled silence as acquiescence, Percy lazily poured them glasses of brandy, topping up his own before settling into one of the armchairs, signalling they should join him.

If this was a trap, which it might still very well be, Percy seemed far from concerned, which reassured Harcourt and Effy just enough to comply. Harcourt sat across from his friend, while Effy perched on the arm of his chair.

Percy regarded the picture they presented with a knowing smile, and raised his glass as though to toast.

'What do you want, Percy,' Harcourt asked again, in a less than friendly tone.

'Good God, man, calm down,' Percy drawled. 'I know my arrival is quite improper but then, considering the fact the fact I've just spent the evening with your *cousin* fleecing one of the country's peers, I think we can dispense with formality for a while. I am still your friend, Sinclair, know that much at least.'

'I'm sure he meant no offense, Percy,' Effy offered. 'Your arrival was a surprise, that's all. Is everything alright?'

'Quite,' Percy said with a slight nod at Effy, the expression in his hazel eyes unfathomable. 'But after tonight, I'm afraid I can no longer help you. Not without the truth.'

The words seem to echo in the silent void of the room, the tension between the two men palpable.

Harcourt stiffened, his mind reeling. *Truth.*

The thing Percy wanted, but which he could not give. The truth was painful, and dangerous, and it had been difficult enough to speak of it to Effy. *But to Percy?*

True they had been friends for years, and had trusted each other with many secrets, many glimpses of the darkness in each other's lives. *But this?* He had hoped never to have to tell anyone, and now what, one after the other they were all demanding it?

All of London would know next. Though, if he had thought that might help, he might have considered it. *No.*

If Percy knew, it would be his duty as a peer to put an end to it all. To protect his fellows. To preserve Society from the likes of ambitious *cits* such as Harcourt, clawing to bring them down.

And yet, hadn't he already helped them? Knowing there was more to what Harcourt had asked of him? Knowing the stakes were far greater than he had made it seem?

Harcourt glanced up at Effy, hating it, but knowing he needed her counsel. He searched the dark, fathomless depths of her eyes, the furrowed brow, and the slight curl of the corners of her lips.

'Tell him,' she breathed, knowing what it would cost him.

She laid her hand on his; as before, she would be here for him.

To keep him from the shadows of his past that threatened to drag him down.

Harcourt's eyes darkened, as he nodded, ever so slightly, defeated.

'Trust.'

And so, his heart heavy with grief, suspicion, and fear, Harcourt laid his sad story at the feet of his friend.

Percy said nothing, only listened, sipping his brandy, his eyes flicking between Harcourt, and the place where his and Effy's hands lay.

Effy felt the tension, the pain in Harcourt's touch, heard it in his voice; but he seemed more distant this time, as though recounting it yet again had lessened the dangerous power of the memories. When he had finished, his shoulders dropped, and he sighed.

They sat in silence for a long moment, Percy digesting all he had heard, studying the man before him. They had been friends for years, and he had known there was a devilish fire raging inside the man before him, but this?

This, he never could have imagined. Lessened circumstances, a hard life, yes. But what had been done to him, and to his family, was unimaginable. *A twenty-year quest for revenge.*

Percy could see the toll it had taken on him, the reason behind his distance, the fiercely guarded secrets, the shame, and terror in Harcourt's now pleading eyes, usually so full of certainty and resolve. He understood why the truth had been impossible to share, and what it must have cost him to surrender it now.

He knew too what his duty should be; to whom it should be. He also knew that he had never favoured what *Society* deemed to be right and true, to be just so. He knew that Harcourt was his friend, and that he would stand by him, aid him, in righting a true wrong.

Percy might have loose morals, but he had a code; one as old as the knights of the bygone age of chivalry.

Finishing his brandy, he took a moment to examine the woman at Harcourt's side, who seemed, whether or not they themselves were aware of it, to have changed his friend. Whoever, whatever she was, she seemed to have lessened his burden, and given him the strength to open his heart to others.

Rare creature indeed...

'Thank you, Sinclair,' he said simply, rising. 'I know now the magnitude of what I demanded.' Percy sighed, thinking carefully before he spoke next, Harcourt and Effy waiting with bated breath for any sign he might forsake them now. 'There were rumours, a couple years back. Of cheating. Russell got desperate, and only with the help of some very powerful friends was the accusation forgotten. Push him hard enough, Effy, and I believe he will try to salvage his losses, by any means necessary.'

With a nod, Percy left.

Harcourt and Effy stared ahead in silence, both releasing breaths they weren't aware they were holding.

'Harcourt,' Effy asked gently, not wanting to ask him how he was, for it seemed an impossible question.

'Can you do it,' he said flatly.

'I think so,' she breathed. 'But you know what awaits him if we choose to force him down that path?'

'It will be his choice.'

'Very well.'

Harcourt removed his hand from under hers, leaving her feeling cold, and empty, and strode across the room.

Without a word, Effy left him, knowing she could offer him nothing more. Comfort, he would come find if he wished.

All his life, he had fought the desire to trust in others, for he knew what they could do when they had the power of knowledge. And now, evermore, he was being forced to abandon his guard, lessen his defences, and bring others into his circle.

It hurt, and angered him, and above all, it terrified him more than facing an army of demons alone.

He knew he had been harsh, and cold, and pushed her away even when he wanted nothing more than to bury himself inside her yet again. But she seemed to sense his weaknesses, every one of them, and he could not bear her concern, no more than she would have been able to bear his pity for her scars.

Trust. One simple, tiny *word.*

Which somehow represented so very much more.

Twenty years he had guarded himself against friends, closeness, love. It was part of him, of who he was, and yet now all his points of bearing seemed to be disappearing. His revenge was not his alone anymore.

Any danger which came with it, was not his alone anymore.

And that, was what terrified him above all else.

XVII.

The following weeks were exhausting, for Harcourt and Effy both. Harcourt spent most of his days either confined in his study, or at his shipping offices. When she was not engaged with the Fitzsimmons, accompanying Angelique more and more often, Effy was paraded around town by Percy, or attending to the Dowager, who had also taken a liking to Patience's company. Her evenings were spent in Whitechapel.

Harcourt no longer visited her bed, and though she liked to think he was being considerate, of both their exhausted states which could barely be denied with the dark shadows they were sporting under their eyes, Effy knew in her heart there was more to it.

It had cost him so very much to trust Percy, to open himself, and she knew that this was a retreat of sorts. He was a strong, independent, determined man, who had been forced to release his control of the situation, and Effy understood his need to now protect himself further from the reality of that.

Not that it did anything to assuage the pain of his abandonment.

Serves you right foolish girl... She had let herself fall in love, and she had let herself believe for a moment that his attentions meant more than they had. Yes, he had been kind, and thoughtful, and caring, and he had been by her side when she needed him most.

But that meant nothing more.

Their relationship had taken the turn she knew it would. *A turn in his bed, and then, the end.*

Russell continued his visits to Whitechapel, more and more regularly, more and more intent on being the one to beat Black Maria. It was no longer the allure of the dandies which brought him, it was solely his need to win, and to recoup his losses which amounted to nothing less than what was left of his once considerable fortune.

Effy had let him come close a couple times, narrowing the margins of her victories, to whet his appetite further, and it seemed to be working. By the Friday of the third week, he was very much a desperate man, and Effy sensed that if he were to make a mistake, and attempt to aid his luck, it would be when he returned the following evening.

She had felt it, in his voice, in the cruel, reckless hiss in which he had promised *to end her reign of tyranny*. Though she knew she should say something to Harcourt, she could not bear it. She would wait until it was done.

False hope, an early sense of victory might disturb the fragile peace and stability he had found. Every night he still waited in the carriage for her, but every night when he inquired as to her progress she only repeated a single word: *soon.*

Reckless, however, was not something she could afford to be in the circumstances. Friday evening, once Russell had disappeared in a black cloud of drunken resentment and despair, Effy took aside the Proprietors and told them of her apprehensions. If she was to accuse a peer of cheating, she had to lay the groundwork, and ensure her own safety.

They assured her they would keep their eyes open, as would the extra spotter they would bring in. She was grateful, nonetheless she remained apprehensive. Russell could still get to her if he truly wished it, and well, if she was honest, she was apprehensive about Harcourt.

If everything went according to plan, and she beat Russell, what more purpose would she serve? Things were already in motion with Mowbray's daughter and her tailor's son, and Harcourt had told her the deal to finish Bolton and Campbell was very, very near to being signed.

She had played her part, well enough, but once she struck the final blow, the truth was, he would have no further need of her. Would he dispense of her fully, as easily as he had relinquished her bed?

The thought sent a shudder down her spine. What would she do if he did? *Crawl into a hole and die most likely... Fool!* God what was wrong with her? She had never needed a man to survive before.

And it was her own fault that she had let herself get so attached to Harcourt. Surely, she could dismiss him from her life just as easily as he could her. She was strong. She would survive. She would build a new life for herself. She would have to.

Yet, even as she thought it, she knew she was very sorely mistaken.

The prospect of a life without Harcourt seemed a bland, meaningless, tedious thing she would never be able to bear. *So, you won't... You'll serve him, as you have so far, and you will bear it...*

Yes, she would bear it. Living alongside him with no hope of his affections. So long as he was safe, and happy, so she would live without complaint in the shadows. If he would let her...

But surely, after all they had been through, he couldn't truly object? She could still be of service. Of use. And he still owed her his help...

Not that her own retribution seemed to matter much anymore.

Still, no news of misdeeds, or weaknesses to exploit. The de Beaumonts were untainted, and likely to remain so. There was a way; the only way it seemed to restore her honour. But that would be her task, hers alone if she chose that path.

And if she did, that would mean leaving London, Harcourt, forever. Could she sacrifice that for him? *Anything for him...*

Focus!

The night had come.

Grinning, Effy winked at Angelique whilst her mother's back was turned as she rang the bell for the butler to inform him they were going out and to make preparations.

Even his eyes rounded when the announcement was made, and both Angelique and Effy had to stifle a giggle.

'Thank you,' Angelique whispered conspiratorially into Effy's ear as they made their way through Hyde Park less than an hour later.

'My pleasure,' Effy smiled. 'I thought I might commit some atrocious sin against the Lord if we were forced to stay thus inside all afternoon. Be careful to look suitably tired and forlorn, however. I still cannot believe I managed to convince your mother to allow it. And to come with us.'

It was true, though Effy did not say however that she might have dragged them all to the park if they hadn't come willingly.

She only hoped that it was not for naught, and that little Lady Lydia and her very unsuitable *beau* would oblige them with enough of a spectacle.

Minding their pace, Effy directed them all towards the lake, in soft, cooing, and reassuring tones to ensure Lady Fitzsimmons did not decide to bolt back to the house before it was time. For good measure, Effy sprinkled in some psalms to reassure her the Lord was on the side of them taking the air, and enjoying what *nature* had to offer.

She looks like an overblown camelia, Effy mused, as Lady Fitzsimmons' walking dress, parasol, feather and flower strewn hat and pelisse, all made of the finest silk and linen, puffed about in the summer breeze.

Angelique must have known what Effy was thinking, for she began to giggle, and squeezed Effy's arm.

'Come along, dearest,' Lady Fitzsimmons hissed, hurrying them along. 'We must not tarry here long.'

'Do you not think Miss Angelique is looking so much better my lady,' Effy sighed, bringing her daughter forth for examination. 'Why the colour has returned to her cheeks!'

'Oh yes, yes, quite, indeed,' Lady Fitzsimmons' fluttered, allowing the walk to continue a little further. 'Yes, quite the thing indeed...'

When the lady had turned away once more, Effy rolled her eyes at Angelique and smiled.

So it was for the next half hour as they progressed along the lake, Lady Fitzsimmons stopping to fuss every now and then, and Effy finding a new part of Angelique's anatomy to compliment.

This is more exhausting than a night in Whitechapel, I hope you appreciate my efforts Harcourt Sinclair... Indeed, if he didn't, Effy made a note to remind him she deserved proper recompense for her efforts. Not that it would take much effort to convince him.

Since the night she had finished Russell, he had been more than attentive, making full use of the night's hours she no longer devoted to the gambling hells.

As they neared the Italian gardens, Effy's eyes were sharp and focused ahead. She was sure she spotted some movement in the trees to their right, but she couldn't be sure of who it was, and she couldn't be the one to call them out if they were. That was why the lovely Fitzsimmons ladies were here after all.

It is her; I would recognize those curls anywhere... And the chit wasn't even trying to hide! *Perfect...*

Though Effy did wonder if Lady Lydia Mowbray had any brain at all. To be so easily spotted from the paths, to not even try to hide whilst she enjoyed her lover's kiss?

True, she wouldn't have expected anyone she knew to come along and disturb this little tryst but then again, well, she should have.

Thank goodness they hadn't gotten around to discussing who had invited whom...

'Oh dear! Oh, no, it can't be,' Angelique whispered in wonder, her eyes affixed in the same spot as Effy's. 'Oh dear Lord, mama!'

Couldn't have asked for better pawns, thank you Percy...

Angelique hadn't even needed any coaxing before betraying her dear friend Lydia to her mother.

But then, seeing as how Lydia had treated her in the past

'Then what have I said to disappoint you now, Fortescue. I do hate it when you look at me like that.'

'Like what?'

'Like I have just murdered puppies.'

'As if you ever could do such a heinous thing.'

'Ah, so you do set limits on my terrible tendencies,' he said, his wolfish smile irresistible. 'Well now, why don't we go on a little shopping expedition today? I can buy back your affection, and we can celebrate this new victory properly.'

'Very well, I shall go get ready then,' Effy said graciously, rising and leaving Harcourt to his thoughts.

A dangerous thing to do indeed.

Harcourt sat there for a while, replaying their conversation in his head, wondering what he had managed to say to upset her so.

Had it been his comments on love? Surely not.

He had made it clear that he did not scoff at the idea, how could he, after all; simply that girls like Lydia Mowbray did not have it in them to withstand such a life of hardship as she had now been handed.

Perhaps she was beginning to feel the weight of morality, of her conscience after all. Destroying lives was a messy business, and he had had twenty years to prepare himself. To accept that his soul was well and truly damned if he chose the path of vengeance.

Effy might be the strongest woman he had ever known, but she was still a woman, prone to strong emotions, and saying you were ready to do terrible things was very different indeed to actually doing them.

Why did that not seem likely then?

And why was he according this tiff so much importance? He had said and done far worse to her... *Disappointment...* Somehow every time she looked at him with those darkened, disapproving eyes, he lost his senses and felt like an irresponsible boy again.

Whatever the matter was, he would find it out today. The shopping expedition had been a spur-of-the-moment whim, but thinking on it now, it would do just the trick. He could dote on her, spoil her to her heart's content, and root out the secret behind her mood.

Yes, today will be a good day after all...

XIX.

Having spent most of the day working their way through milliners, dressmakers, haberdashers and tailors across Bond Street and down the arcades, with very little to show for it, Effy had pleaded they visit at least one bookshop before making the journey home.

Despite his efforts, Harcourt hadn't managed to convince her to buy very much at all, his hopes of spoiling her with silks and ribbons having quickly been dashed. She seemed to be enjoying their escapade, but still she held back, from accepting any gifts, nor any counsel or much conversation. *Infuriating woman...*

Not that they could really revisit the details of this morning's little dispute, as it was cousin Patience on his arm today, and not Effy Fortescue.

The fact they kept running into acquaintances here and there, all somehow intent on discussing Lady Lydia Mowbray's disgrace, did nothing to help resolve the matter.

Still, she seemed cheery enough, and he should know having barely taken his eyes off her all day. Dressed in simple, unadorned light brown muslin, she remained, in his eyes, the brightest, most elegant, and stunning creature. A bright, natural, light amongst the fake and frippery surrounding them.

Their outing seemed to have restored some glow to her cheeks, and she seemed much herself, smiling at him brightly and occasionally favouring him with a witty quip or amused comment about this or that passer-by.

He wished life could always be as simple, cheerful, and carefree as it was in this moment. He wished *their* life could be as uncomplicated, unmarred by intrigue, and as delightfully heart-warming as it appeared to be.

Even though somewhere in his heart, he knew they would both miss the intrigue and adventure.

Their life. What a delightful notion.

And so, when Effy had pleaded to visit a bookshop, he had not been able to resist; her eyes bright and warm, tender and mischievous as they were, he might have found a way to give her the moon had she asked.

Besides, perhaps she might finally indulge him and allow him to buy her a gift to restore himself in her good graces, however base a way to do so.

The bookshop she decided on was off Piccadilly. It was large, with open floors and tables laden with all the newest works, wood-panelled walls, and bright green furnishings. Bookshelves lined the walls, and more he knew lay upstairs.

With a quick smile and gleeful shriek, Effy sped off among the books, looking as though she had just found buried treasure. Harcourt laughed to himself, and thought next time he might as well start here if it pleased her so.

She was not the only one so enthralled, it seemed they had arrived at the women's shopping hour. Clucking mothers and their drab little daughters, stern governesses and wild charges mingled among the latest works of Sir Walter Scott, Byron, Lamb, and even Burns. If there were any men who dared venture here as he had, he suspected they had hidden themselves in the higher floors, among the less popular and requested books.

Harcourt wandered around, waiting for Effy to make her choice, perusing this volume and that. He wondered what she would choose. It struck him then, that he really didn't know much about her in truth, not in that sense.

What is her favourite book I wonder? Or poet? Or even her favourite colour? Black, probably, he mused, chuckling to himself only to be eyed disdainfully by a nearby, rather birdlike bluestocking.

Waving an overly contrite apology, he moved away from the

dangerous territory, and glanced up, wondering where Effy had gotten to.

Where indeed? He couldn't see her anywhere, and there was nowhere for her to hide.

He swept upstairs, examining every nook and cranny, only to find sleeping gentlemen and attentive scholars. No Effy.

'Patience,' Harcourt called, his eyes scanning the store as he descended again. 'Patience?'

Groups of young ladies turned, but none of them were Effy.

He whirled around again, but there were no places for her to hide. Panic rising, his stomach churning, he wracked his mind.

She had just been here. He was sure he hadn't heard the bell. Another way out? Why would she run? *She wouldn't…*

Harcourt strode over to the counter, pushing aside a young lady and her mother who looked at him aghast.

They refrained, however, from saying anything when they caught the dangerous, focused look on his face.

'The woman I came in with,' he growled at the terrified shop girl. 'My cousin. Red hair. Where did she go?' The girl's mouth gaped open and closed, her hands and bottom lip trembling. Harcourt pounded his fist on the counter and leaned in, his eyes cutting through her like knives. 'Speak, girl!'

'Th-th-through the back, sir,' the girl whimpered. 'Please, I didn't know, I thought he was her lover -'

Before she could finish, Harcourt ran past her, through the corridors piled with boxes, towards the door which surely opened on an alleyway or mews.

God, no, please…

A man. Come for him, no doubt.

And this was a trap, no doubt.

How much did they know? How many were there?

It didn't matter.

All that mattered, was getting Effy safely out of whatever mess *he* had gotten her into. He had let his guard down, and now, she would pay the price.

Heart pounding, he tried to calm himself as he thrust open the door, hand tightly clenched on the pistol in his pocket. He didn't need to go far, only turn around to see the sight which made his blood ran cold.

His manner, however, suggested cool, calm disinterest; though he would not be able to remain quite so controlled for long.

Effy had prayed he would not follow; that he would know this was a trap, and flee. She had had little choice but to follow the brute, a docker from the smell of him, with the steel tightly pressed against her ribs.

She had thought, perhaps, to escape once she had gained some distance from it, at least enough to scream without it lodging itself in her flesh within seconds.

She had been very wrong.

Four others awaited them in the alley, and she knew screaming would be of no use. Even before they had punched her, in the gut, and square in the face, leaving her winded and with a sore, bloodied cheek. She had tried to defend herself best she could, but they were all tall, insanely strong brutes, who knew well how to keep hold of her and limit her movements.

Her only consolation had been that Harcourt was a very clever man, and that he would know this was a trap, and he would not follow blindly.

He didn't care enough for her to endanger himself, and she had told them as much, for which she had been rewarded with another punch in the jaw.

Dazed, but not without rage, she had rewarded them with spit and blood on their already desperately soiled clothes. How that stupid little shop girl had not realized something was amiss when one had walked into that shop was another wonder.

And yet, despite her protestations, here he was, standing before them, clutching what she knew to be the pistol in his pocket. She saw him calculating the odds.

Five of them. All with daggers and God knew what else.

Against one. With a pistol and two daggers.

Maybe two if he could free Effy, and she could avail of her own blade.

One exit, at Harcourt's back.

Effy saw his eyes darken, even as his body seemed to relax, and he *strolled* towards them. None could mistake the pure rage and danger emanating from him, looking yet again very much the part of a devil, his dark curls and coat billowing around him in the wind.

Harcourt knew the situation was very, very desperate, and if he didn't come up with a clever plan soon, they would both be dead. The odds were not in his favour, even though he could easily tear them all limb from limb for daring to place a blade on Effy's neck as there was now. And for the blows she had obviously received, judging by the trail of blood running down her cheek.

Still, she remained tall, stoic, her eyes watching him for any sign, any clue as to what she should do. He tried his luck, taking one slow step forward.

'That's far enough Mr. Sinclair,' the brute holding her advised, his rancid breath against her cheek.

'Whatever is this now,' Harcourt drawled, in as bored a tone as he could muster. *How could that stupid shop girl think he was her lover?* 'If it's money you want…'

'It's you we want,' the brute laughed. 'I said that's close enough,' he shouted, the blade against Effy's neck digging into her skin.

She felt drops of blood fall to her bosom, and saw Harcourt's lips tighten.

He stopped.

'Now, we know you got some weapons on you, best you be rid of them.'

'Why should I,' Harcourt asked lightly.

The brute behind Effy blinked at him stupidly for a moment, as did the others, who were obviously waiting for him to be disarmed before attempting an attack.

They seemed to have realized the mistake of leaving him with the exit in their attempt to remain somewhat concealed from the nearby busy street and door.

'Why cause if not, the lassie here gets it,' the man holding her said.

Effy might have laughed at his slowness if she hadn't been so tightly held against the knife.

'And? It's me you're here to kill, isn't it,' Harcourt asked, lazily extracting the pistol from his pocket, and waving it about. 'Why should I surrender myself, for that creature?'

Creature. Effy swallowed the lump in her throat as Harcourt eyed her with disdain.

She could feel the hesitation in the man behind her, the blade moving ever so slightly from her neck. She knew what he was doing, she could see the calculation in his eyes, the tension in his muscles beneath the languidly controlled exterior.

She knew what was coming; what Harcourt was about to do. She could not falter. She had to trust him.

And if she was wrong? Well, then she would be dead, and he would run, and live, and then at least it would have been worth it.

'We ain't foolin' Mr. Sinclair,' the man warned. 'You gonna let the lady, your blood die to save your skin?'

'Oh you really are quite off the mark,' Harcourt laughed as if he had just heard the best joke of his life. 'That creature is a *whore,*' he said, raising an eyebrow, his eyes meeting Effy's. *He would not use that word again… I trust you Harcourt. Do it.* 'I paid her to *play* my cousin. She means no more to me than any of you.'

As if making his point, he raised the pistol, and let it move to each one of them in turn.

Effy clenched her skirts in her hand, and stood as very still as she could, trying to look every bit the desperate terrified victim for the spectators. But never once did her eyes leave Harcourt's.

Do it. I trust you. It's the only way. Run.

'You only got one bullet, mate,' one of the others warned, not appreciating the growing difficulty of what was supposed to be an easy job.

'Best I make it count, then,' Harcourt said coolly, taking aim at Effy.

Let it be true...

The would-be-assassins were too stunned to do anything before the shot rang out, echoing loudly in the confines of the alleyway.

Harcourt heard a cry, then watched, as if time slowed, as Effy fell to the ground, limp and lifeless, a patch of growing red over her left breast.

He didn't have time to worry, to pray that his aim had been true.

To pray that she understood, to run to her and apologize and take care of her.

He had time only to drop the pistol, and bolt down the street, mindful to keep his pursuers on his heels until he could get them far, far away from Effy, weaving through the confused and shocked crowd.

Please, God, let my aim have been true. Let her live. I cannot bear it if she dies by my hand...

Either way, the men on his heels were going to pay dearly for having laid their filthy hands on her. For having forced him to what they had.

And hopefully, some might even be willing to talk, about who the Hell was after him.

∞

The rush of adrenaline, the fear of being caught, was the only thing keeping Effy from screaming, moving even the tiniest muscle as she lay face down on the ground, trying to control her breathing so it would seem she wasn't at all while not being sick at the smell and taste of the dirt, blood, and refuse filling her every pore.

Not until she heard the pounding of footsteps, the curses, felt the tip of a boot kick her in the ribs, seemingly to ensure her demise; not until she heard the faint scream of a young woman, did she rise.

Even then, she barely felt the pain.

Shock. It must be. She was numb, and tired, and angry, and fearful, but she knew if she didn't keep her wits about her, she would be lost, even after what Harcourt had just done to save her.

She struggled to her feet, and waved to the girl standing speechless and trembling by the door to calm her. Thankfully, it seemed the girl was also in shock, and hadn't rushed off to find the watch. *Thank God she really isn't a quick one...*

There were no onlookers either; it seemed if anyone had heard the shot, they hadn't ventured to find the source of it.

'I'm fine,' Effy panted, trying to keep her mind straight. 'Calm down, girl!' The girl froze, staring in half awe, half confusion at the terrible sight before her. 'I need you to go find me a cloak,' Effy said, reaching for some coins. 'Quickly!'

If the girl had any thoughts on what Effy should be doing with her injury, she said nothing, only simpered, grabbed the coins, ran inside, and re-emerged minutes later with a simple, but elegant hooded cloak.

Time during which Effy cursed with every despicable expression in her rather large arsenal.

'Good. Now, you say nothing, to anyone, about this,' Effy warned, and the girl nodded, too fearful to object. 'For your troubles,' she said, handing her some more coins.

Throwing on the cloak to hide the spill of blood, Effy grabbed her handkerchief, and pressed it against the wound under it.

There is the pain... Luckily I know pain all too well... Grunting, she steeled herself, and emerged onto the streets.

Percy's. That is where she needed to go.

If there was ever trouble, if she was ever in danger, Harcourt had told her he would find her there. *Please God let him be alive. Let him come back to me...*

At least it wasn't too far. She could hire a hack, but with the masses in this area, she would be quicker on foot. If she could last that long.

Half an hour later, weak, the pain fully present now, throbbing, maddening, her entire body screaming out for her to stop, she arrived on Percy's doorstep.

Only sheer will, the desire to survive, to see Harcourt again, had kept her going, and prevented her from curling into a gutter to let the end come.

Faltering, she struck the knocker against the door, swaying slightly, gripping the rail to steady herself.

Percy's butler, *Thomas is it?*, opened the door, his imperious, majestic manner faltering at the sight before him.

'Percy,' Effy managed. The butler's eyes widened, and he looked as though he might attempt to refuse. 'Please, Percy...'

'Lord, Miss Sinclair, is that you,' he exclaimed, rushing out to steady her. 'I'll fetch his lordship,' he stuttered, helping her inside.

As if her body knew it was where it needed to be, Effy felt it falter, her feet giving way beneath her as she saw the butler disappear up the stairs.

Unable to stand any longer, and unable to make it to any of the chairs nearby, she fell to her knees, the cold marble beneath her somehow welcoming and soothing.

Desperately trying to push away the darkness that threatened to envelop her, Effy pressed her already soaked handkerchief into the wound. The searing pain was enough to cut through the fog of her mind, bringing her reeling back to her surroundings.

Footsteps. *Thank God...*

'Patience,' Percy exclaimed, running towards her. 'Dear God, what happened? Thomas, fetch the doctor, quickly!' Effy felt more than saw the butler rush past her back out onto the street. She looked up at Percy, dazed, trying to focus on his golden eyes as they worked their way across her body. 'What happened, Patience, where's Harcourt?'

'I don't know,' Effy croaked, her resolve failing now too. The pain, the fear for Harcourt, it was all too much. She felt tears welling up. 'Tried to kill us. Harcourt, ran, they followed.'

'Alright, alright,' Percy said, not in the least reassured by any of this. 'Come on, let's get you into the study, I think that's the closest for now. The doctor will be here soon.'

Unable to speak, Effy nodded.

Percy lifted her up into his arms, and she cried out, her shoulder on fire, and her left arm feeling as though it might fall off. Percy rushed to his study, and set her down in a chair.

He gasped when he removed her cloak, and saw what lie underneath.

'Effy,' he said, blanching. 'You've been shot? Oh Lord, no wonder you're so pale. How are you still conscious?'

'Harcourt,' Effy breathed, grateful for the chair.

Already, somehow, she was feeling somewhat better.

Or perhaps it was the light-headedness that seemed now to have overtaken the pain.

'Yes, we will find Harcourt,' Percy promised, pouring two glasses of brandy, downing one before setting the other in Effy's hand. 'Now, tell me what happened, everything.'

'We were in a shop,' Effy said, the warmth of the brandy reviving her. 'This man he put a blade at my back, dragged me outside... There were four others, they wanted Harcourt. They had a knife at my throat... So he shot me. And then I came here. I'm sorry, Percy... He said, if ever there was trouble, to come here...'

'You did right. Wait, Harcourt shot you,' he exclaimed, cocking his head in disbelief.

'It was the only way.'

'Oh dear Lord,' Percy muttered, refilling both their glasses.

The doctor arrived moments later, and was surprisingly glad Percy had already taken to administering strong spirits, considering the situation.

Making it clear there were to be no questions, after his first exclamation seeing the gunshot, and his patient somehow still conscious and somewhat coherent, Percy sat across from the doctor as he began his work on Effy.

There was no mistaking she was in terrible shape, beaten, shot, exhausted, fearful of Harcourt's fate, but by God, the woman before him was nothing short of a marvel.

He watched as she sat still as possible whilst the doctor cleaned and bound her wounds. He saw her wince and clench her teeth when he set about removing the bullet and cleaning that wound, but never once did she cry out.

No wonder Harcourt had taken to her. She was enduring more than most men he knew could without losing their wits or fainting.

By the time he had finished, some colour seemed to have already returned to Effy's cheeks. The doctor prescribed rest, clean bandages every day, liver and other offal, and laudanum. The last, Effy resisted, but Percy took it from the doctor nonetheless as he paid him and set him on his way. They would fetch him back should a fever appear.

Before returning to her side, he sent his valet to Bow Street, to engage a Runner to go after Harcourt. He hoped Harcourt would find his way here soon without help, but he could not just stand by and wait.

Then he asked Cook to prepare some blood stew, and returned to the study.

'I think I've ruined this chair,' Effy moaned, with a faint smile. 'Sorry, Percy.'

'Don't worry,' he chuckled. 'I never liked it.'

'Harcourt -'

'I've sent for a Runner. Cook is preparing you food. I don't suppose you will let me send you to bed?'

'No, not until he is here.'

'Thought not,' Percy said shaking his head.

No matter, he would find a way to force her to get some rest soon.

Whether she liked it or not.

If she died in his care, Harcourt would kill him.

'Thank you,' Effy sighed.

'You are very welcome,' Percy grinned. 'Much more exciting than an afternoon in the park as I had planned, I must say.'

'Chasing after some young ladies I suspect?'

'Aye. Though I feel you were right, I should find a woman with a touch of the Devil on her soul,' he admitted, relaxing back in his chair. 'Harcourt is a lucky man.'

'I'm sure you say that to all the young ladies who get shot and wind up at your door,' Effy mused with a sad smile. 'But I have too much of the Devil on my soul, Percy. Even for Harcourt.'

Percy raised his eyebrows and chuckled. *We shall see*, he seemed to say.

'Did Sinclair ever tell you how we met?' Effy shook her head and grinned, curious, and urging him to continue, if only to distract her from the growing pain. She had to stay awake until Harcourt came. 'I was set upon, one night, foxed as you like I was, stumbling out of some gambling hell. I know, very unlike me,' he chuckled. 'In any case, Sinclair happened to be passing by, took them down, all five of them, quick and relentless. Spared their lives, but only just. Got me home, and well, we became fast friends after that. Owed the man my life after all.' Percy smiled and sighed pensively before continuing. 'I've seen him at his worst, and he at mine. I always knew there was more to him, than he ever let me see. Until you came along that is, and pushed him to trust me. Like it or not, I do believe you two reckless fools were made for each other.'

Cook chose that moment to interrupt, and Effy decided against raising the subject again once she had finished fussing over her, and left them again.

Even though she was not hungry, Effy forced herself to eat. She knew the blood and liver rich stew would do her good, and already she was tiring from all that had happened, and the copious amounts of brandy she had used to sooth her pain.

She forced Percy's remark from her mind, for though she wished he was right, with all her heart, she knew Harcourt all too well to let herself believe him.

Feeling re-invigorated, Percy and she spoke of many things, of his past, his family, his desires and hopes. He seemed intent on keeping her distracted, for which she was grateful, though she could not stop her mind from returning to Harcourt.

Why had he not returned yet? Had he not managed to escape them after all? Had he called the watch? Or tried to dispose of the wretches himself? And then, been overpowered? Killed?

She couldn't bear the thought. He would come back to her. He had to. He was just being cautious. Making sure no one followed here. *Surely...*

Percy seemed to sense her mounting distress as the hours passed, and yet another meal was cleared. Finally, when the sun had set, and the lamplights had been lit, and still no word from Bow Street or Harcourt had come, he handed her another brandy, settling back into his chair with another himself.

Only when her mind clouded, when she felt the droop of her eyelids, and the all-too-familiar drift of her thoughts to a painless void, did she realize what he had done. She should have smelt it, but like a fool she had downed the damn glass.

Percy, you traitor... You slipped me the laudanum...

∞

'Where is she,' Harcourt shouted, waving away the butler's attempts to stall and calm him as he stormed up to the main floor from the servants' quarters. 'Percy! Please for the love of God, where is she? Tell me she's here!'

'Good God, Sinclair,' Percy said, peeking his head out of the study, blinking furiously. He had just managed to find sleep in the chair. 'Calm yourself man! Thomas, it's fine, leave us, dismiss everyone for the evening,' he added as the butler looked at him apologetically.

'Tell me she's here, please, Percy!'

'She's here man, now please, calm yourself,' Percy said in his most reassuring and commanding tone. 'I've only just managed to get her to bed. Had to bloody well slip her laudanum to do so, but the damned girl was in about the same state as you, swearing she'd go back onto the streets to find you!'

'Thank God,' Harcourt choked, his entire body deflating.

Safe. Alive. She was safe. And alive.

If anything had happened to her, because of him, if she had died, by his hand... He dared not imagine what wrath he might unleash unto the world. More than he had already tonight.

Percy eyed his friend, the wild, panicked air, that had somehow faded beneath the wave of relief he had seen wash over him. He had never seen him like this, not in the worst days and nights they had shared.

His clothes were torn, his hair dishevelled, and his hands... Mangled blood and bone. There were cuts on his face, and a slash across his chest. He looked like he had been mauled by a tiger and was about to cry.

Shaking his head, he patted his friend on the shoulder, coming around to lead him to the study.

'No, I need to see her,' Harcourt protested.

'You can see her soon, she needs rest Sinclair,' Percy said. 'You need it too, and you need tending. She's asleep, for now, so clean yourself up and then you may go to her.'

'Thank you,' Harcourt managed as Percy sat him in a chair. 'I am sorry we got you involved in this.'

'Nonsense, I had missed the excitement of, well, whatever this is,' Percy said lightly, fetching the basin of water, the brandy, and bandages the doctor had left for him. 'Here, clean yourself up.'

Harcourt was too tired, and too exhausted to argue, so he simply did as he was told.

He gazed across at Percy who had settled in the chair before him. He too looked worse for wear, and Harcourt could only imagine what it had taken to see to Effy, and keep her here.

Percy had proven himself a loyal, and fierce friend. He had always tried to keep him at arm's length, never able to trust him fully, and yet, he realized, he had trusted Effy to come here, should there be trouble.

He had trusted him in many things over the years, and now, he had trusted him with what he held most precious.

'She told you what happened?'

'You mean, did she tell me you shot her,' Percy asked, a glint of amusement in his eyes. 'Yes. But she didn't really say anything more. Surprised she could talk at all. You would have thought she gets shot every day the way she took it all in her stride...'

'Sadly, I fear she has endured far worse pain.... As to the matter of today, there isn't much else to say,' Harcourt winced, laying a brandy-soaked linen on his knuckles. 'Whoever is after my head seems quite determined. I must admit, I doubt it's Mowbray after all. Though I am no closer to discovering who it might be.'

'The men who set upon you had nothing of interest to share,' Percy asked, raising an eyebrow.

He was no fool, and could well guess how Harcourt had bloodied his hands.

'Sadly not,' Harcourt growled.

Though it had been soothing to dispatch them.

'Very queer business indeed. I know you have enemies a plenty, still, whoever is after you, it seems personal. And they have quite the funds to keep their scent from it all. Unless, this attack is not related to the first, perhaps a retaliation for Russell?'

'No,' Harcourt said, shaking his head. 'We were careful to keep my hand from being seen in that matter.'

'Wise.'

Harcourt nodded.

It could be related to what they had done to Russell, in truth, they had been careful but not fool-proof. And there were Bolton and Campbell to consider as well. Perhaps they knew of his attempts to thwart the deal that would save them...

It was maddening, to be so out of control. Without any ideas as to who he was defending himself against, he would be forced to look over his shoulder until when?

And Effy? What would happen to her? *God, give me strength.*

When he had finished tending to himself best he could, Percy told him the way to Effy's room. He steeled himself for whatever would be waiting for him there, and made a quiet, solemn vow to do all in his power to see her recovered, and safe, always.

The only light was that of the fire. He could see the outline of her, laying on her right side, her hair like rivers of fire across the pillows. Her left arm was in a sling, but otherwise she seemed to be in good health.

Finally, his heartbeat and breath returned to normal.

'Harcourt, is that you,' she mumbled drowsily, her eyes attempting to flicker open.

'It's me, Fortescue,' he said, rushing to her side. He was careful as he slid into the bed beside her, welcoming her as she nestled against him. 'I'm here now.'

'I thought I heard you making a commotion downstairs,' she sighed. 'I wanted to find you, but Percy was sneaky and he laced the brandy with laudanum. But he gave me a ladies' portion, he does not know I have built up quite the tolerance over the years. But you must not tell him, or he will try to give me more...'

Harcourt chuckled softly despite himself, staring down at the wonder in his arms. Shot, drugged, and still she here she was as alive and fiery as ever.

Well, almost. He closed his eyes, breathing her in deeply, allowing himself to thank God for having returned her to him alive.

'I am so so sorry my darling Fortescue,' he whispered.

'You saved us, you have nothing to be sorry for,' she smiled faintly.

His warmth and presence seemed to heal her, even through the haze of the laudanum, reviving her.

'It was the only way -'

'I know.'

'How,' he breathed.

Harcourt had been half terrified she would think he had meant what he had said, and done.

Nothing, nothing had belied her understanding, other than her presence here, and her forgiveness.

'How are you not angry with me? I shot you!'

'I trusted you,' she said simply. 'If I had been wrong, then I would be dead, and that would be fine, for I could not live with the knowledge of having been mistaken.'

Harcourt frowned as he tried to make sense of what she was

telling him, *confessing*, in her own convoluted way.

His heart leapt as he dared to hope the meaning he had untangled was as he thought.

'Fortescue, are you saying you cannot live without me,' he asked, hoping as well that the laudanum would stop her from editing her words.

He felt her nod softly against his chest and he grinned.

'I lied, well, not quite, you see, I had already fallen in love with you by the time I promised I would not.'

Unable to trust himself with words, his heart too full with the knowledge that she, incredible, rare, exceptional woman, loved *him*, he simply kissed her head, his hand gently stroking her back coaxing her to sleep.

He should tell her the truth; that he loved her too, with all of his being, as he never thought possible, but the words remained in his throat. Not like this, for one. *Delicacy, always*.

He would have her be conscious, and fully comprehending when he made his declaration. And then, like wildfire, the dread, the horrible dread of what might happen to her, resurfaced.

Not much longer. Soon, his revenge would be over. The die was cast.

Then, they could devote themselves to hers. He would call out the damn Marquess de Beaumont if he had to, to set her free. To set them both free.

Then, and only then, would he tell of his own feelings, and hopes for what future they might have together.

∞

After two days in bed, having had quite enough of lying about, *recovering*, with Harcourt, Percy, and the entire household fussing over her, Effy had insisted on descending for breakfast, despite the numerous and effusive protestations.

It wasn't that she didn't appreciate everyone's attentions, indeed she had to admit it had felt rather lovely being so attended to, being cared for, even if she knew in Harcourt's case it was driven mainly by guilt.

No matter how many times she assured him he had in fact, saved her life, he insisted on apologizing every time he stepped foot into her room.

It was beginning to be infuriating, and she decided she quite disliked this new guilt-ridden, simpering and attentive Harcourt. He was coddling her, and she would have none of it.

Luckily, she had been spared his sole company, and revisitations of the events after the hazy recollection she had of them the first night, Percy's housekeeper being intent on chaperoning her and ensuring nothing untoward happened under her beloved master's roof. *If only she knew...*

Percy, at least, was insistent on providing good-humour, entertaining Effy with readings, stories, and card games. She was grateful to him for behaving ever so normally, as if she was simply a guest in his home.

Ill perhaps, but no dulcet invalid.

Perhaps his attentions were the reason for Harcourt's ill-humour this morning, for though Effy had thought she had managed to convince him well enough there was no need for jealousy in Percy's case, he had barely spoken a word, or unknotted his brows since she had come down.

'I must to Portsmouth today,' he said finally once they had all finished their breakfast and the servants had been excused. 'I received a note this morning informing me the deal I have been working towards can be signed tomorrow. I should be gone two nights, and return some time Friday.'

'That's excellent news, isn't it,' Effy asked tentatively. He had been working for this for years, surely this couldn't be the reason for his sulking this morning? 'Harcourt?'

As a response she got a look cold enough to freeze her heart.

Harcourt's lips tightened into a tight line, and she saw his jaw clench. *What is the matter with him?*

'Yes, that's excellent news, isn't it Sinclair,' Percy chimed in, sensing Harcourt's mood keenly as well. 'Congratulations, man.'

'Thank you,' Harcourt said stiffly, his gaze shifting to Percy and relaxing ever so slightly. 'May I ask, could Fortescue stay here until I return? I still don't know who is after me, and I won't be able to make firm decisions about what I am to do with her until this business is settled.'

What he is to do with me? The gall of that man…

'Of course, I would have it no other way,' Percy said jovially before Effy could voice her displeasure, which she was sure he, at least, could sense. 'I will keep Effy safe until you return.'

'Thank you,' Harcourt said, rising, the tension in his body palpable. 'Now, if you'll excuse me.'

'Harcourt -'

Before she could either protest or follow, Harcourt had disappeared up to his chambers.

Effy sat frozen for a moment, tears stinging in her eyes, and Percy shot her a look of sympathy and reassurance. *What the Devil has gotten into him?*

Old Effy might have chased him up to his chambers and forced him to speak to her, but new Effy was too tired and hurt to do anything but sit quietly and wait to hear the front door open and close, and hooves racing down the street.

Only then did she excuse herself, *needing rest.*

Once again in her room, Effy lay down on the bed, and silently cried all the tears she had kept inside for years. All those tears she had promised not to shed, not for anyone. Somehow, she knew this was the end.

Harcourt's business was soon to be well and truly finished, and so soon would he be with her. She knew he would insist on helping her with the de Beaumonts, for he felt obligated now, but by God she didn't want his help anymore. Didn't he know none of that mattered to her now?

He would know what to do with her when she returned…

How dare he? Like she was some sort of baggage to be sent wherever he pleased? That is what she was to him. An asset, to be used, and disposed of whenever it suited.

How foolish she had been, believing there was anything else

to what they had shared then fleeting passion and a mutual intent of destruction.

There had been more, to her, but obviously not to him. She had become a hindrance, a risk, and he had felt guilt at having his precious little tool injured, but nothing more.

Well, very well then, she thought when all her tears had been spent, and her heart somehow felt lighter for it. She would not cause him any more trouble.

Tomorrow night, she would settle her own affairs. He would owe her nothing, and besides, she had already decided it would be up to her to follow this course of action should things proceed thus.

Once she had finished with the de Beaumonts, she would leave London, and Harcourt in peace, and never trouble him again.

It might break her heart, but she would survive that too.

Wouldn't she?

∞

Harcourt rode hard to Portsmouth, stopping only to change mounts at posting inns, leaving his own at the first where he paid a hefty sum for it to be looked after properly for the next few days. He could have taken the coach, but he knew the ride would be just the thing to wash away his nerves and worries.

Months, years, he had been waiting for this deal to come to fruition, and now it finally had, and at the worst possible time.

Someone was intent on killing him, and Effy had been injured in the process. He wanted to find the devil after him, but instead he had to leave London, and leave *her*, infuriating, foolish woman that she was.

Every second he spent with her, seeing what he had done, no matter her reassurances that she understood, physically pained him. He had never been so acutely aware of another being's welfare, nor so desperate to make it all better.

And infuriating, disobliging creature that she was, she seemed intent on making nothing of it. He knew well how strong she was, how capable, but did she really have no idea how much her tacit complacency drove him nigh on to insanity?

Did she not know how he lay awake at night, his body and mind demanding to be beside her? Did she not know how worried he was the villains might come after them again, and succeed in taking her from him?

No, for he had been a coward, and said nothing of it all.

Even this morning, he acted like a complete fool himself, cold and irrational and taking his anger at having to leave out on her. It had pained her, and that was yet something else to add to his guilt.

Why couldn't she have just stayed in bed like she should have and let him leave quietly, to return victorious?

Stubborn wench. Even though she would never admit it, and looked outwardly better, as beautiful, and unyielding as ever, he had sensed her exhaustion, and an unnamed sadness beneath the clean and fresh mask she had enveloped herself in.

No wonder, with all she's been put through... He really did only have himself to blame in the end. He had let a *woman* get caught up in his quest for revenge.

Dangerous, dark, immoral, and disgusting business, and his alone, and yet he had encouraged, welcomed her to join him.

What the devil had he been thinking?

Spurring his horse on, he decided he was glad this would all be finished very soon. Then, he could concentrate on finding the villain after him.

Of course, he would have to send Effy away someplace safe, she would protest of course, but he would brook no debate. He would keep her safe until he had disposed of their enemy, and then...

And then, what?

Would she welcome him back into her arms after everything he had done? Could he ask her to? Or would he send her on her way, to live a full, and happy life with some good, proper, gentleman?

Could he?

Yes. If that is what it took to make her happy, he would do it.

He would tear himself from her even though it would mean tearing his heart from his breast. He would give her up. He deserved to suffer.

He would suffer anything, if only she could be happy.

∞

Effy didn't bother being announced, she simply knocked on the study door, and entered, smiling when she noticed the chair she had dared bleed all over had been replaced.

Percy looked up at her from behind his desk at the far end, surprised, and somewhat bemused by her abrupt appearance.

'Effy, you should be in bed,' he chided, looking like a fairy prince, lit as he was by the sun streaming in the massive windows behind him.

'I'm quite recovered Percy,' she said, making her way to him. 'And I cannot stay lying about in that bed one minute longer.'

'Oh dear,' he said gravely, setting aside the papers he had been working on. 'Why do I sense you're about to make trouble?'

'Because you're a pessimist, Percy,' Effy said with a smile. 'I was hoping you might send someone to the townhouse. To collect a ballgown, and my maid, Lily.'

'Did I forget I was to be hosting a ball here tonight,' he mused, raising an eyebrow.

'No. I intend to be at the Fitzsimmons'. I have, after all received an invitation. Miss Angelique has been good to me, it would be a terrible insult to miss her birthday, especially after all that has happened.'

'All of London knows you are *ill*, Effy. What are you up to,' he asked sharply, seeking to divine her secrets, his hazel eyes narrowed on hers.

'Nothing.'

'Then, I'm afraid, I cannot in all conscience let you go,' Percy said firmly. 'You are, despite your protestations, still recovering. Harcourt made me promise to keep you safe, I'm not about to let you go gallivanting about London.'

'Oh, do cease behaving like a mother hen,' Effy quipped. 'Whoever came for Harcourt and I thinks I'm barely holding onto life. We are still no closer to finding out who it is. And if they see me still alive and well, it will throw them. Perhaps I can root them out.'

'And risk your life, again, in the process!'

'Harcourt made you promise to keep me safe from whoever was after us. But even he cannot keep me safe from myself. I will go,' she said, in a tone that told Percy he had lost well before the battle had begun. 'I am not asking you to be party to this, only to send for my gown, and Lily.'

'Fine,' Percy exclaimed harshly. 'But I am going with you, you madwoman.'

'Thank you, Percy,' she said sweetly, before heading for the door. 'Ask Lily to bring the red gown.'

And just like that, she disappeared again.

Percy sighed, raking his fingers through his hair. The woman would be the death of him. Why he had allowed himself to get caught up in this mess, he did not know.

Because it's dreadfully fun, really...

Within the hour, Effy's maid and her gown had arrived. The ladies had shut themselves in her chambers to prepare, while Percy dragged himself to do the same, reminding himself it was a ball, and he should have fun despite the looming threat of death.

Still, it did nothing to assuage the feeling that Effy was up to something else, and soon, they would be in a lot more trouble than fun.

XX.

Celebrating. That is what he should be doing. Jubilant. Triumphant. That is what he should be right now. Instead, he was sulking, nursing a pint of ale in one of Portsmouth's more disreputable inns. Perhaps he should have taken up his new business partners' offer to join them for dinner in one of Portsmouth's finer establishments, but for the life of him he could not shake off his foul mood, and would have made for terrible company.

At least he was clever enough to recognize that, he mused wryly. At least he hadn't endangered the deal whilst the ink was not yet dry by spending an evening subjecting his new partners to his temper and frustration.

Are you happy? That is what Effy would ask him if she were here.

He certainly should be. Between signing that deal, and finally dropping off the letters that would seal all his opponents' fates at the head offices of the newspaper yesterday, he should be dancing a jig and ordering rounds for the entire city.

But the knot in the pit of his stomach would not come undone.

Everything was going perfectly according to plan. Only it wasn't. Effy had been injured. Someone was out for his head. And he had a feeling of dread, a chill down his spine, that he couldn't shake.

Perhaps it was simply that he had never expected to get this far, not really. Twenty years, and finally it would all soon be over.

In truth, he never thought he would live to see the day. Yet he had, despite it all.

Perhaps it was all just the immutable worry for Effy. His *true* partner in all this. *Ha! True partner indeed.* Yet he hadn't told her about the letters.

Why not? He had been of a mind to, before she had gotten shot.

Before I shot her...

And he knew well enough that even despite the injury, he could have told her about them. About what they meant, and what would happen once their contents were divulged to the world.

Why hadn't he then?

At first, he had kept part of the plan from her because he didn't want to trust her with everything. And then... Things had become complicated. And more recently, well, if he was honest, he knew what their revelation would mean. *More enemies.*

Even before his decision on the road here, he had known, somewhere deep in his heart, that he would have to let her go. He could not ask her to take more risks for him. *Because* of him.

Besides, she will find out soon enough...

Knocking back the remainder of his ale, he surveyed the premises, and the collection of the dregs of humanity before him, debating whether he would spend the evening here in his cups, or return to his hotel, and sleep off his mood. Sleep away this unrelenting feeling of dread.

For once in his life, he decided on the latter. He wanted to ride off early in the morning, leave this all behind, and get back to Effy as quickly as he could.

With a growl of resignation, he rose, and stalked out of the inn.

The fresh night air, laden with notes of dead fish and refuse, along with the noise of the nearby port, hit him like a wave, and he swayed slightly in the doorway.

He hadn't had that much to drink, but the combined effect was enough to sober him, and restore his focus and resolution.

'Penny, sir,' came a croak from behind him. 'Penny for an old weary soldier?'

Harcourt turned sharply, eyebrow raised, to survey the beggar, wondering if for once he might be charitable.

Both he and the beggar froze as their eyes met, and Harcourt's mouth curled into a satisfied, terrifying sneer.

'Well, tonight really is my lucky night,' he drawled, slowly closing in on the beggar as he tried to scramble away. 'Not so fast, Rawlings, you cockroach.'

Rawlings hadn't even made it to his feet by the time Harcourt's fingers were curled around his neck.

Screaming and crying like a baby, he was dragged into the dark shadows of the alley by the inn, and thrown up against the wall. If there were any witnesses, they did not dare even offer the scene a second glance.

Harcourt surveyed the despicable wretch before him. Emaciated, terrified, he looked like a starved rabbit caught in the jaws of a wolf.

Oh but you are, he mused, his fingers tightening until Rawlings blue face was visible even in the dark, dank gloom of the alleyway.

'Please, sir,' he rasped, clawing at Harcourt's hand with dirtied, sweaty little fingers.

'I have some questions for you, Rawlings,' Harcourt hissed, loosening his grasp just enough so the man could talk. Breathing was a regrettable addition. 'Who hired you to betray me?'

'I… I don't know sir,' he whined, tears making strange markings on his face as they streamed through the layer of dirt thereupon. 'I swear, it was some brute, came sniffing around, gave me five pounds, and a promise of keeping my post…'

'Ah, see, now I don't believe you. And I know your type, Rawlings,' Harcourt snarled, lifting the man even higher from the ground so his toes were squirming. 'After five years of service, you would have made sure you had someone worth betraying me behind that offer. Tell me who it was, and I will, perhaps, spare whatever is left of your miserable life.'

'I can't, sir! She'll kill me!'

Surprise flared in Harcourt's eyes, like fireworks in the black as pitch nothingness they were.

Rawlings knew he was lost, and it took only seconds before he betrayed the name.

I should have bloody well guessed, Harcourt thought as he threw Rawlings down like the rubbish he was, only just managing to keep his temper under control enough to spare his life.

Besides, he didn't have time. He needed to get back to London without losing another minute. This was far worse than he imagined.

Effy, Percy, they were both in danger. The Lady had missed him twice now; if she was desperate enough to come after him in the first place, she would be more so now, and the fear of discovery would not keep anyone safe.

I know I have lost your favour, Lord, but please, get me back in time. Get me back to her before it is too late. I will finish this.

Anyone who spotted Harcourt Sinclair that night on the London Road, truly would have thought it was the Devil himself who had come thundering up from Hell.

XXI.

he red one. He should have known then that he would be right about the trouble. Though Percy knew Effy belonged to Harcourt, it didn't stop his mouth growing dry, nor something stirring in his breeches. Clearing his throat, he checked himself, and extended an arm to the goddess descending the stairs.

The dress was unlike any *Patience* had ever worn. Indeed, not many women of the *ton* would risk being seen in a dress that seemed more suited to a courtesan of the *demi-monde.* Effy was definitely up to something if she was wearing this.

It fit her generous curves to perfection, hugging and emphasising every asset the women possessed. It was unadorned, the cut and fit enough in itself, the rich, blood-red silk flowing with her every move.

It seemed to set her skin and hair on fire, giving her the air of Venus herself. Long black gloves, and two tiny emeralds were all the additions she had chosen. Her hair had been swept up into a loose gathering on her head, perfect curls framing her face and trailing on her neck. Not even the sling she deigned to sport marred the perfect image.

Effy grinned as Lily set her evening coat about her shoulders, and Percy couldn't help himself but smile, every care and worry seemingly melting away under her spell. *Damn the woman.*

Percy shook his head, and offered his arm again, to lead her through the door, grabbing his hat, gloves, and stick from Thomas as he did.

'Why do I have the sinking feeling that Miss Patience Sinclair has in fact, died,' Percy said as they settled into the carriage. 'And that Effy Fortescue is up to something?'

'You're a pessimist, Percy,' Effy smiled, feigning innocence.

'And you are a stunning, seductive siren,' Percy said seriously.

'It was the only ballgown I had left, couldn't very well wear something I've been seen in before. Not my fault Harcourt has a twisted sense of humour.'

Percy grunted unbelievingly, returning his gaze to the busy streets, his hat twirling in his hands.

Much too clever for your own good, Percy, Effy thought, watching him. She knew she should tell him the truth, even Harcourt had bared his deepest secrets to the man before her.

But try as she might, she couldn't bring herself to.

Percy had been good to her, even when Society would have demanded he turn a blind eye. She couldn't let him get involved in this. Already, he was coming, which, though she suspected he would, she had hoped beyond hope to dissuade him from.

Already, there would be talk. After all, she would be arriving with him, looking like this, after having spent the last few days in his home.

It couldn't be helped. This was her last chance. Harcourt was away. And though it pained her to think Percy's name would be marred with rumours after tonight, he would recover, and it would be nothing compared to what Harcourt would suffer if she didn't put an end to her business before he returned.

A matter of honour.

Hers, and hers alone.

There was no other way, she had tried. So it would come to this.

Please God, give me strength.

And let Daniel de Beaumont be too much of a coward to deny the challenge.

∞

'If you were hoping to provoke a scandal arriving dressed like that on the arm of my grandson, you have achieved your purpose,' the Dowager scowled, eyeing Effy from head to toe. 'Quite scandalous indeed.'

'I assure you, my lady, it was not my intention,' Effy said truthfully. 'I begged your grandson to let me come alone, and well, the dress... I'm afraid I had no other new ones, and my cousin bought this to tease me.'

'Oh don't fret so, child,' the Dowager said, pursing her lips, and lowering her voice. 'I love a good scandal. I am quite well aware that your attentions lie elsewhere, though my grandson could do well with someone like you. You're a clever girl, and not at all what you seem, do not think I have not noticed.'

'Thank you, my lady,' Effy said quietly.

Something caught her eye, and she faced the Dowager squarely, placing a hand on hers.

The Dowager was more intrigued than shocked, and cocked her head inquiringly.

'I am grateful, my lady. For all the kindness you and your family have shown me. I wish I had known you in another life. And I am sorry for any disrepute that might befall you or your grandson's name after tonight. Know, that it was never my intention.'

Before the Dowager could protest or reply, Effy had disappeared into the crowd, her eyes firmly fixed on her quarry.

She felt a pang at the thought she might injure the Dowager, or Percy, or even Angelique. But honour must be restored.

The blood debt needed to be paid.

∞

The Marquess and Marchioness de Beaumont were, to Effy's great satisfaction, enjoying the pleasure of their own company when she found them. Tucked into a small alcove by the window, they were surveying the room, no doubt whispering snide comments about those within, judging by the conspiratorial glances, whispers, and laughter.

Sarah was just as unchanged as Daniel, her perfect golden curls swept up and complemented with sprigs of roses. Her green eyes, so much like Daniel's, yet less vivid, shone out with malice and contempt. She had gained some frown lines, and a stiffer back than Effy recalled, but underneath the semi-opaque green silk and lace evening gown, she was still very much the deceptive harpy she had always been.

Plastering her most bland, Society-appropriate smile on her face, Effy strode towards them, lending herself the air of greeting long-lost friends for any onlookers.

No more fear, no more doubt.

Harcourt had given her strength; the courage to do what she must. *I love Harcourt Sinclair, and never again will you hold power over me Daniel you reptile.*

The looks of mingled shock and disgust that flashed on the Marquess and Marchioness' faces sent shivers of delight through Effy. She watched them both examine her, from head to toe, appreciation in Daniel's eyes, and sheer jealousy in Sarah's.

Worth a bloody fortune…

'My Lord, my Lady,' Effy said cheerfully for all to hear as she stopped before them. 'How lovely to see you both again. It has been too long.'

'Indeed,' Daniel managed after gaping for a moment. Sarah snapped open her fan, fluttering it as though it might drive away whatever terrible scent caught her nose. 'Miss *Sinclair*, a pleasure.'

'*Sinclair*,' Sarah scoffed, her voice dropping to a whisper. 'Good God, Effy, you didn't marry that *cit* Harcourt Sinclair, did you?'

'No, my dear,' Daniel said before Effy could. *He didn't tell her about meeting me at Mowbray's ill-fated engagement party then…* 'This is Mr. Sinclair's *cousin*.'

'*Cousin*,' Sarah asked incredulously, but if she wondered how her husband knew, she made no mention. 'Dear God, what sort of farce is this? Oh, I see,' Sarah drawled, recovering, her eyes cold as flint as a sneer curled her lips. 'You have become that rake's mistress, and he thinks he can parade you around London, in good Society with that rather ridiculous subterfuge.'

Sarah laughed and draped her arm over Daniel's possessively.

'I am not Harcourt Sinclair's mistress,' Effy said coolly.

Not strictly the truth, but then, she needed him to say it.

And he was being too quiet. *Come on Daniel, I know you want to…*

'That dress suggests otherwise, *Effy*,' Sarah sniped. 'Though I must say, I applaud your resourcefulness. I thought you would have the decency to find a gutter to go die in after that business with Lord Almsbury.' Effy's lips tightened but she said nothing. 'I might have known you would find a way to use your body to survive, as you always did.'

'Your husband taught me well what price I could fetch if I was ever so inclined,' Effy said, pointedly inclining her head to the Marquess.

Say it.

'Yes. It seems that even after all these years, my dear,' Daniel sneered, Sarah's arm still possessively draped on his. 'You are still nothing but a whore.'

There it was. The word she had been waiting for.

A satisfied smile on her face, without any hesitation, Effy pulled off her glove, wincing slightly as it caught on the edge of her sling, and before he could fully realize her intent, she struck his cheek with it.

It might well have been a gauntlet of pure steel for the reaction she got. His and Sarah's eyes widened in shock, his hand flying to his cheek in disbelief, speechless. Effy's heart was pounding, but she could not stop. Not now while she had the advantage.

People were beginning to pay attention.

Sorry to ruin your birthday Angelique…

'I call you out, my lord,' she said, her voice pure ice. 'I demand restitution for your insult.'

Daniel recovered quicker than his wife.

His eyes darkened, and his lips curled into a dangerous sneer. He studied her for a moment, before laughing, aware now of their growing audience.

'You cannot be serious,' he scoffed. 'A woman cannot call out a gentleman.'

'There are no rules to forbid it. I'll remind you the French seem to find no issue with such cases,' Effy said, raising an eyebrow. 'Do you fear then, to face me on the field of honour?'

'No gentleman would ever face a lady,' he retorted, his confidence returning.

Still, there was worry in Sarah's eyes as she scanned the faces of the crowd surrounding them, as they waited with bated breath for the outcome of this extraordinary event.

'Besides, my dear, no one would ever stand second to you. Quite impossible, you see.'

'I will stand second to the lady,' came Percy's cool voice from just beside her. She dared not even turn to face him. 'Unless, that is, you still *presume* to refuse the challenge?'

Effy watched the thoughts run before Daniel's eyes as they flicked between her and Percy, and the crowd around them.

He was in an impossible position, and she saw the disgust flash on his face, before it was replaced by his usual, casual mask.

'Very well then, I shall have my second attend to yours.'

'We require a name,' Percy reminded him.

'Thompson. I will send him along.'

'Excellent.'

The crowd gasped in unison as the de Beaumonts marched through it, attempting their utmost to appear composed, when in fact it was quite apparent just how ruffled they were.

Effy caught a few shocked faces, disapproving looks, even some admiring ones, and nods of approval as she turned to face Percy, letting go of the breath she had been holding.

Under his cool, relaxed exterior, she could sense his anger, his hazel eyes flashing fire, and his lips tightly drawn.

Extending his arm, he wrapped hers into it, and swept them through the ballroom out towards the balcony, ensuring they were alone before releasing her.

'Thank you,' she whispered, feeling very much a child about to be reprimanded. 'I did not mean for you to get involved in this.'

'Yes well, you might have thought to find someone to act as your second then, and prepared this little escapade a bit better.' Percy sighed, raking his fingers through his hair. 'I did know you were up to something.'

'I am sorry Percy.'

'Harcourt will murder me when he finds out.'

'He must not learn of this, Percy, you must promise me,' she pleaded.

'That's why you did this, isn't it?'

'We made a bargain, his help for mine,' she sighed. Percy had just staked his reputation and standing in Society for her. She owed him the truth, at least. 'Once the deal in Portsmouth has been signed, his *business*, will be over. He will see to it that mine is as well. I could not risk it. Harcourt has a life beyond this mess, here, I can't endanger that. Besides. It is my honour which demands restoration. He need not know; it will be over before he is even back in the city.'

'You're mad, you know that right? You will be finished after this.' Percy sighed, shaking his head.

'I know.'

'You're not going to kill him, are you?'

'No. I intend for him to live with the shame of having been beaten by a woman.'

'Any idea what he will choose for weapons?'

'Swords. Even he will not dare shoot at a woman in public.'

'And you are competent? Your wound, it still isn't healed.'

'I am competent enough. My father's master at arms taught me well.'

'You really have more than just the touch of the Devil on your soul,' he chuckled softly. Effy relaxed, allowing herself to smile. 'I should have known, with that hair of yours.'

'Oh Percy, thank you,' she exclaimed, lightly kissing him on the cheek. 'Do not think I am not aware of what this may do to your reputation.'

'Nonsense,' he grinned, and Effy would have sworn he blushed. 'The ladies will not be able to resist me after this.'

'As if they could before.'

'Be forewarned,' he said, leading her back to the ballroom. 'If Harcourt does murder me, I will come back to haunt you for the rest of your life. Or if grandmama does for that matter.'

Effy laughed, her heart lighter even though death, dishonour, or maiming, might very possibly be waiting for her in the morning.

'Noted. By the way, I think I might have to borrow some of your clothes, Percy...'

They did not linger at the party, merely made their presence known again before departing.

Both could tell the entire room, indeed, probably the entire city knew of what she had done, and though some might admire her for it, they would not remain in her company.

It didn't matter. Her honour was worth more than anything they could say of her.

Just so long as Harcourt stuck to his plans, and didn't hear of it, at least until she was gone from his life, she could handle the rest.

Though she would never have believed it possible, she was happy to have Percy by her side for it. A friend. To stand beside her, to believe in her. A reassuring presence that would give her strength in what was to come.

For although she had once been a very skilled swordsman, it had been many years since she had practiced. *Let's hope it comes back as easily as riding a horse...*

XXII.

It was still twilight when the carriage pulled up at Battersea Fields. Yet even in the gloom, even through the haze of the mist of morning, the throngs of people come to witness the duel were clearly visible.

Effy drew a deep breath and said a silent prayer for courage. She had done without the sling this morning, but her arm ached like the very devil, and there was still very much a weakness in it.

She could feel Percy's intent gaze on her, his nerves probably worse than her own if the incessant drumming of his fingers on the window was anything to go by.

Finally, when she had steeled herself enough in the quiet solitude of the moment, she tugged on her gloves, smoothed her hair, and smiled at Percy.

He shook his head, then descended, and offered his arm. He placed his other hand on hers, and Effy wasn't sure if she was trying to reassure her, or himself.

'I will be fine, Percy,' she said softly.

'I know,' he lied.

Percy led her across the fields to the appointed place, and Effy thought that if anything were to happen, it would in fact be a rather glorious day to die.

Dawn was coming, bright, dreamlike pinks, purples, and oranges rising from the horizon, spreading across the landscape like coloured water.

Though she tried to pay them no attention as Percy set her

in her place before leaving her to discuss the matter with Daniel's second, Effy did recognize some familiar faces amongst the crowd.

People she had encountered over the past few weeks, who awaited the upcoming historic and shocking event eagerly. Some tried to offer encouraging nods, while others whispered disgustedly in each other's ears. She wondered fleetingly what the odds were.

Then she returned her attention to the matter at hand, enjoying the fresh, clean air, and the magnificent sunrise the angels seemed to have gifted her for this special occasion.

Across the field, she could see Daniel, sporting breeches, and a crisp white linen shirt, same as her, his legs and feet bare. He stretched languidly, preparing himself.

She inclined her head to him, enjoying the look of utter displeasure and apprehension. Sarah, was nowhere to be seen. *Shame...*

Effy removed her own stockings and boots, well, Percy's, and set about warming her muscles, paying particular attention to her left arm, trying to ignore the incessant fire that seemed to burn down through it to her fingertips.

The field she noted, was quite dewy, more so than she would have hoped. No matter. She had faced worse odds.

Percy was striding towards her, looking none too pleased, but maintaining his usual composure.

He did look quite like a fairy, or sprite, rising from the fading mist, his hair catching in the flame-like light of dawn.

'You were right,' he said, sidling in next to her, ignoring their audience. 'Foils. First blood. I have informed the second of your injury, I hope you don't mind, I didn't think you would want to risk losing on a technicality, and besides de Beaumont had already seen the sling...'

'Quite right,' Effy said nonchalantly, hoping Daniel would have the sense to behave like a gentleman and respect the rules. 'Thank you, Percy.'

'We could still -'

'No, Percy.'

'Be careful,' he sighed, shaking his head again. 'It's wet.'

'Thank you, Percy,' Effy smiled, before kissing him on the cheek.

There was rush of murmurs in the crowd, and Effy was sure Percy blushed.

'Now your reputation truly is ruined. Now, let's finish this.'

Together they marched to the middle of the field, where Daniel and his second met them.

Whilst the spots were marked, Effy made sure she never once let her eyes stray from Daniel's emerald gaze. *I am not afraid. I will not cower. I will beat you.*

Perhaps it was a trick of the light, her own wish or imagination, but Effy thought she detected fear in those once enchanting, now sickening green eyes. She smiled, and went to her appointed place.

The silence was thick with anticipation and dread.

Effy checked her breathing, her stance, the weight and feel of the foil in her hand. She waited, blood rushing through her, pounding and deafening.

Until she saw the flutter of the handkerchief.

'*Allez*,' Percy said, a note of resignation beneath the strong, unmistakable command.

Daniel launched forward, attacking without restraint or hesitation.

Effy was ready, parrying each attack deftly, forcing him to strain to remain within her guard.

The crowd's gasps and commentary were somewhat reassuring, pacing the fight and allowing Effy's mind to abandon any thoughts which might take her from this place, this purpose.

Though it had probably only been minutes, it seemed to Effy it had been hours. Time stilled, the world waiting. Only the rising dawn, the growing light and heat signs of it passing.

Not quite as easily remembered as riding, she thought, using every trick in her arsenal to parry and retreat, to advance and attack occasionally without risking a nick from Daniel's blade.

Her body was not used to this sort of exertion anymore, and the field was in fact slippery, her toes clutching the grass and mud the only thing keeping her from falling to his mercy.

It did not help that it took a concentrated effort to keep her injured arm out of reach, without using it for balance.

But he is tiring too, she thought, reviving her own sore, aching body. His breathing was harsher, ragged, and beads of sweat were streaming from his brow.

Even so, Effy knew he was the better swordsman. More style, more grace, more ease. *And years of practice...*

Daniel lunged again, fury and need in his eyes. He wanted to finish it; it seemed to annoy him that it was taking so long to beat a woman.

Particularly, *this* woman.

Very well... A turn, a parry, and she let him get close, almost too close, the blade mere inches from her sword arm.

It spurred him on, but he was leaning, not supporting himself, and when Effy parried another attack, slipping aside, he fell forwards onto the ground.

The crowd gasped, cheered, and laughed as Effy held fast, returning to a neutral position, waiting for him to return to his feet.

The look in his eyes was deadly as he rounded on her, but he raised his hand towards the seconds.

'*En garde*,' Effy said, resuming that very position.

'You really think you can win, don't you, my dear,' Daniel sneered.

'Oh, I know I can, Daniel,' she mocked, knowing he was losing control now. Her own breathing, laboured as it might be, was still even, her nerves steel. This was her day. 'And I shall. And you shall live with shame far greater than any you might have wished upon me.'

Daniel let out a terrifying cry as he lunged again, catching her foil in a twist, and reeling her in as she tried to parry.

Grabbing hold of her hilt, he smashed it upwards, catching her left eye, a glint of satisfaction in his own as the crowd gasped and whispered *foul*.

'De Beaumont,' Percy screamed, running towards them along with Thompson. 'Desist this instant!'

Sneering, Daniel disengaged.

The damage had been done. Effy was dazed, and she could feel a nasty gash above her eye.

Blood began trickling into her eye, essentially blinding her. *Viper!*

'Effy, are you alright? We can -'

'No, Percy,' Effy hissed, her eyes still fixed on Daniel's. 'I will not win like this.' She felt more than saw Percy nod, and lead Thompson away. *'En garde.'*

Looking back on that day, Effy would recognize that moment as the moment Daniel lost. She saw the defeat in his eyes, and the fear again.

The crowd must have known too, for the only sound was that of a latecomer joining the party and being hushed.

It was over within minutes after that. Effy attacked this time, relentless, stronger, with more fire in her than ever. She had tired Daniel, and he had no strength nor mind left to sufficiently parry, her movements were too quick, too precise, while his own were sloppy, and slow.

She saw the pain flicker across his face as her blade ever so gracefully, ever so lightly, grazed his arm.

Time slowed as she retreated, watching his eyes leave her to fall on his torn sleeve, and the slight trickle of blood now forming there.

'Enough,' Percy cried, rushing towards them before Daniel could do anything else ungentlemanly. 'First blood has been spilt.'

Daniel's jaw clenched, and he lowered his blade.

Percy looked to Thompson, and he nodded.

'Has honour been satisfied?'

'Yes,' Effy said, her mind and body numb.

'Very well, then this matter is over,' Percy declared.

Effy did not move.

Not as the crowd half cheered, half groaned, underscored by the clink of money changing hands.

Not as Percy disarmed them both, handing the swords to Thompson.

Not even as Daniel left the field, sorrow, disgust, and shame in his eyes.

Done. Seven years... It's done... Effy took a breath, and felt tears sting her eyes.

If not for the rush of blood still flowing through her, concealing the aches and pains, the exhaustion, both physical and mental, she would have fallen to the ground.

Thank you, God...

'Here,' Percy said, placing his handkerchief in her hand. 'Are you alright?' Effy nodded and winced as she dabbed the cut above her eye. 'Masterfully done, Effy.'

'Thank you,' she said faintly, the sharp new pain bringing her back to the time and place.

'Let's get you home before - oh bloody Hell...'

Effy saw the panic on Percy's face, and followed his gaze, her heart pounding again. *It can't be... He's in Portsmouth...*

Or not. Among the crowd now milling away, in a mixture of despondency and excitement, towering above the others, was Harcourt Sinclair, his face, thunder.

Effy's stomach lurched, and she could sense Percy's had too.

Yet, even as she stared, waiting for the storm to come, Effy noticed that there wasn't the mix of disapproval and anger she might have expected.

Terrifying a sight he might present on first impressions, but on second glance Harcourt looked apprehensive, and almost, *afraid?*

∞

Arriving back at Percy's, his nerves a mess, so afraid he was of arriving too late to warn them of the danger, Harcourt had been surprised to discover that neither the man himself, nor Effy were in. *It's not even dawn...*

On edge as he was, he lost his temper quite quickly with Thomas, who within seconds of his scowling, shouting, and near blows, had finally relented their whereabouts.

If he had been angry before, now, he was in a rage.

Cursing Effy, Percy, their ancestors, the whole of London, the scoundrel de Beaumont, and anyone he could think of, he had borrowed one of Percy's mounts and ridden off in a fury towards Battersea Fields.

What was she thinking? A duel?

How that had even come about, been allowed, he did not know. *And Percy as your second you madwoman, I'll wring both your necks if you survive this...*

Safe. He had told the man to keep her safe.

And now she was duelling peers at dawn? *Can't leave you for one day...* Why they Hell had she done such a reckless, dangerous, scandalous thing? Why hadn't she waited for his return? He had promised to help her, to do anything to help her restore her honour...

Oh for the love of... He heard it as soon as he asked himself the question. He had promised to do anything, and she knew he would probably call the damn Marquess out, and so *she* had done it, to protect him.

She would argue it was *her* honour, and she was right, but he knew that in the end, it was to save him from killing the man on the field.

Devious little vixen, he thought, galloping towards the meeting place.

By the time he finally did arrive, his mount and he were both breathless, not that it mattered. All that mattered, was getting to her.

The duel was already well underway when he arrived, and he wrestled his way through the crowd to get a better vantage point, hushing and grumbling welcoming him.

He knew he could not let her see him lest he distract her and cause her to make a mistake, so he held back, still able to see it all above the heads around him.

God she's magnificent...

Never before, and never again, had he seen such a breath-taking sight.

A warrior goddess, descended from the Heavens to reap her vengeance...

His heart was in his mouth as he watched her, his fists clenched, praying she would survive, unhurt. *Please God let her win...*

Onwards she attacked, lunging, parrying, relentless in her advance. De Beaumont was tiring, he knew she must have tired him well before.

Good, Fortescue, delicacy, always...

It truly did take his breath away, watching her, as cunning and fearless as any man, and the corners of his lips curled as he admired her form, dressed as she was in men's clothing, her copper hair glinting in the sun as she moved, seemingly effortlessly.

So caught up in the sight before him, it wasn't until it was well too late that he noticed the figure close behind him, and felt the press of a pistol at his back.

Harcourt stiffened, alert but powerless. The crowd was too thick, and he could not risk making a scene lest he distract Effy, who seemed to be very close to winning.

'Don't even think about it,' hissed a voice in his ear, unheard by any but he. 'Be a good boy, now.'

Even despite the circumstances, Harcourt felt his breath return, and his heartbeat return to normal when Effy won.

He smiled, proud, and relieved, that she at least, would live through the day. That's all that mattered to him anymore. *Her.*

He wasn't entirely sure what the devil at his back had planned, but he had hoped at least it wouldn't involve either Percy, or Effy. That somehow, they would disappear from the field, unaware of his arrival, so he could finish this once and for all.

Damn you Percy and your eagle eyes, he thought however when his friend spotted him, and he saw Effy turn.

She was holding a handkerchief to her eye, and he wondered for a moment what the Hell de Beaumont had dared to do.

You were right, Fortescue, I would have murdered him...

Harcourt wanted to scream, wanted to tell them both to leave, but he knew it would serve no purpose. Effy would never run, and having seen what she could do, he doubted strongly Percy could ever manhandle her off the field.

Besides, she knows...

He saw Effy search his eyes, saw her see something there of his fear. He saw her eyes move to the figure beside him, and the understanding wash over her.

Leave, run, please God, make her run...

'Lady Almsbury,' she called in nothing short of a shout.

Harcourt groaned.

Foolish, foolish woman... He felt the figure behind him stiffen, the pistol lodging further into his back as she tried to hide her purpose from the eyes of those who had stopped in their departure from the field.

'Lady Almsbury!'

More stopped and turned, surprised and whispering.

Could it be true? Could it be her? With Sinclair?

Effy was striding towards them now, Percy on her heels, a confused but intent look on his face.

Harcourt noticed Effy checking they had an audience, before closing the distance.

'Why it is you my lady,' she shouted again though she was not even a foot away from them. 'Everyone in London thought you retired in Switzerland. What a pleasure.'

Effy's eyes belied her.

She looked up at him, concern, and panic in her dark, murderous eyes. She had altogether a frightful appearance, her hair a wild mane, the wound above her eye oozing blood even now.

My beautiful avenging angel...

'Harcourt, are you well, cousin,' she said coldly, her hand on his. 'Why cousin, come here now, I must greet Lady Almsbury properly.'

Don't, he wanted to scream, but he was not quick enough.

Already she had pulled him to her side to face the Lady intent on taking his life. *Masterful but foolish.*

'It is you,' Percy exclaimed, with more cheer than both knew he felt.

The pistol was clearly visible now, aimed at it was at Harcourt's gut, and he quickly understood.

'Why my lady, is that a pistol,' he asked, as loudly as Effy had been.

Gasps. Screams. Whispers.

The crowd was growing again, halting in their retreat, and there was a panicked, desperate look of pure, molten hatred in Lady Almsbury's eyes now.

A cornered animal. *Nothing more dangerous...*

'Back you meddling fools,' she screamed in a voice not of this world. 'I will have this devil's life before noon!'

Higher she aimed the pistol, hand trembling, backing away from their reach, a mad, harrowed witch.

Her hood had fallen, and Harcourt could see her now in all her stretched, emaciated, demented glory.

'I was going to kill that bitch of yours, but then you appeared and now it shall be as it should be!'

Harcourt waved down the onlookers who tried to approach, signalling them to stop.

'Back all of you! I will have his life!'

'Like Hell you will you twisted, disgusting, wretch,' Effy screamed, stepping before Harcourt. 'Don't touch me Harcourt,' she snarled as he made to move her away. 'You too Percy, this is between her and I now.'

'*You,*' the fallen baroness hissed, recognizing Effy at last. 'It can't be!'

'Oh but it is, *my lady,*' Effy growled back, Harcourt's power and strength fuelling her as he stood at her back. No one would take him from her. 'Surprised to see me? Been a while, too long I think.'

'Step aside, girl,' Lady Almsbury ordered, recovering some of her courage. 'That devil killed my husband, and I will have his life!'

'You will not! Your husband was the devil, not Harcourt. He did a service to this world when he wiped him from the face of it!'

'You know nothing!'

'I know,' Effy said, her voice as clear and sharp as broken ice. 'That you have now tried to killed Harcourt Sinclair three times. And that you, madam, are a coward. And very soon, all of London will know what you have done.'

'Ha! You think they will condemn me? For seeking justice?'

'Justice was done the day your despicable, disgusting, worm of a husband died,' Effy said, a smile forming on her lips. Almsbury's blood went cold, and she froze. 'What the Hell, I have no reputation left to save,' she said lightly.

Enjoy the view gentlemen...

Effy tore off the shirt, her breasts bound, but the scars on her back unmistakable. She heard Percy gasp, and felt Harcourt reach out, but before he could, she stepped forward and twirled, so that all their little audience could see.

'See, see what the *honourable* Baron Almsbury did to me!'

Again, gasps, whispers, and shudders passed through the crowd. Effy dared not look at either Harcourt or Percy lest she lose what she had won.

She kept her eyes on the woman before her, willing her to desist.

'Relent, madam. You are finished,' Percy said finally, stepping forward. 'Lower your weapon. All of London will indeed know what has passed here, but arrangements can be made for you to leave England with whatever you may have left.'

They all watched, breath held, waiting, silent and still.

Lady Almsbury clutched the pistol tighter, willing herself to shoot, but then finally, she relaxed, and lowered the pistol. Everyone breathed again, one collective sigh of relief.

In one swift movement, Percy had the pistol in his own pocket, and was steering the defeated baroness away into the small crowd of onlookers.

Some joined him, others stared in wonder, unsure of what exactly had passed.

'You utter madwoman, I should have you committed,' Harcourt growled, putting his coat on Effy's shoulders, and turning her to face him. 'First you fight a duel, and then you step in front of another pistol. Once should have sufficed you! Am I never to be allowed to play the hero and save you then?'

'Oh, but you already have.'

Effy looked up him and smiled, passing her right arm through the coat, and tightening it around her.

How resplendent he was, the rising sun at his back. His hair was a mess, his black eyes full of concern, a shadow of a beard appearing on his cheeks, and his necktie was undone.

But he was safe. *Alive. Still. Forever now.*

'You're early,' she said simply, enjoying watching his frown merge into disbelief.

'That's all you have to say for yourself,' he scolded.

'How was Portsmouth,' she asked innocently.

'Oh dear God...'

Laughing in the face of death my angel... How like you...

All of a sudden his heart exploded, with relief, with love, with admiration for the woman who had just, yet again, saved his up-to-now miserable life.

He swept her into his arms and kissed her, fiercely, passionately, punishingly. He scolded her and loved her, hated her for frightening him so, and thanked her, his lips hot, his whole body aflame with searing passion and desire and need.

Every single one of Effy's fears, doubts, all her pain and worry melted away with Harcourt's kiss. She had been so angry, so scared, for so long, and now it was over.

Her honour had been restored, and even though her life in London was truly over, she was glad of it. Harcourt's vengeance had been enacted, and the dark cloud that had hung over them since he had first been attacked now lifted.

God, how I love you...

Yet even as she thought it, she realized the truth of their situation.

It was over.

All of it. His Vengeance. Hers.

Them. He would continue his life here, and she would…

Well, she wasn't sure what she would do, but the pang in her heart told her it would be without him.

Suddenly, the most painful, the most terrible, unthinkable, the most heart-breaking reality she had ever had to face was at last before her as she had known it would be one day.

Stifling a sob, Effy pulled away sharply, before she could no longer do so. She dared not look at him, lest she fall to pieces and lose whatever dignity she still had.

Stepping back, she glanced towards the road.

'I wonder where Percy's gotten to,' she said flatly.

'I'm sure he'll stop by when he's taken care of the deadly baroness,' Harcourt said wistfully.

Why won't you look at me woman?

He had to tell her, the truth of what he felt, all of it. Already he could sense she was pulling away again. *No. Not now that we can finally live freely you stubborn wench.*

His resolution to send her away had vanished along with Lady Almsbury. *Free.*

'So, what now, Fortescue,' Harcourt asked, casually as he could, straightening his necktie.

Effy managed to return her gaze to him, steeling herself.

He looked years younger, lighter, happier. *Good, you can be happy now my love…*

'I do have a cottage waiting for me in the country,' Effy suggested, all too aware the idea was nonsense.

'A quiet country life? I think not,' Harcourt laughed. 'After today you've proven that could never be your fate.'

'I know,' Effy conceded, her heart tightening. She knew what she wanted, but she also knew that she had made quite certain that was impossible. 'The Continent perhaps. Black Maria speaks French, and Italian, and I think she would learn German rather quickly.'

'You seem to be forgetting your vow Fortescue,' he said seriously. 'I think you'll find, your life had been pledged to me.'

Oh dear God, surely not?

How could she return to the way things were before? Slinking back in the shadows whilst he lived his life, removed from her and yet so near?

No. Her stomach tightened, and she shook her head.

'I can't,' she choked, her strength finally failing. 'I know I made a vow, but, well, I thought... And you see, I am a very strong woman, but I can't...'

'Can't what, Fortescue,' he growled, before her again, his arms on hers, a dark, dangerous look in his eyes. She looked up to him, pleading. 'Dear God, Fortescue, you're trembling.'

'I don't tremble, and certainly not because of a man, not even you Harcourt Sinclair,' she exclaimed, and he saw the tears welling up in her eyes.

He had only meant to torture her a little, but this?

He pulled her against fiercely.

'Don't, please -'

'You foolish woman, hush. I only meant to jest,' he said, hoping she was reassured enough to let him finish, pulling her back away to face him. 'You're not going anywhere without me, I love you you stubborn, reckless, dangerous, surprising creature.'

'But, but,' Effy stuttered, blinking at him furiously, overwhelmed by his words, and unable to fully comprehend them. 'No. You, you can't. You have a life here, it is not over for you. But I cannot stay, not after this. I can't let you throw it all away -'

'Oh, do cease your nonsense, by God woman, I thought you different,' Harcourt chided, his grip tightening ever so slightly as if he feared she might bolt at any moment. Which, he suspected she might by the panic in her eyes. 'You aren't *letting* me do anything. You will not be rid of me, my love. You are my twin soul, and I will not be parted from you.'

Effy was dizzy, her heart pounding as though it wanted to leap from her chest, her lungs functioning no longer, and her head swirling.

She had just fought a duel, Harcourt had nearly died, so it was entirely understandable. The shock of it all was fading, and yet she knew it was his words that were causing her body to suddenly fail, her usual strength and countenance vanished.

Harcourt Sinclair, deadly rogue, master of revenge, loves. Me.

Of all the impossible things.

Harcourt waited, watching, letting her process what he saw she could barely. If he hadn't already been sure of her feelings, a braver man than he would have cowered and run with her blatant refusal to accept his truth.

He watched the confusion, the disbelief, all pass through her eyes, half hidden as they were beneath the strands of copper that flew elegantly across her face in the summer breeze.

He watched that perfect mouth he knew so well open and close as she struggled to find words. Then, finally, he saw those rich chocolate eyes focus on his eyes, searching for any dissemblance.

But there was none to be found.

When Harcourt smiled, that reassuring wolfish smile that was his, Effy sighed, and melted. *Harcourt loves me. As I love him. Dear God.* Shaking her head, she grabbed hold of his waistcoat, and pulled him in close.

The world did not exist for them as their lips touched again, the love both had denied, believing it their fate to be denied it, searing through them.

There was nothing gentle about this kiss, so different from any they had yet shared. It was a kiss of desperation, of the dire need to possess and mark, and ravish.

They knew each other, or thought they had until that moment, their lips and tongues melding into one as they sought deeper truths, forging a bond that could never be broken.

Harcourt's hands steadied her, steadied them both as she wrapped her arm around his neck, pulling him further into herself. It was as if they sought to stop time, to fill it with all they had refused and denied, drinking each other's essence and soul with a thirst that could never be slated, not in a thousand years.

How long they remained there was anyone's guess. Finally, drawing long breaths, they parted, still clutching each other lest they fall to the ground.

They smiled, both hearts full with the love they saw in each other's eyes.

'Shall I take you home now, Fortescue,' Harcourt asked, his voice promising to finish what they had begun here, on the field of honour which had restored both of theirs.

'Yes,' Effy agreed, not caring that tears now streamed down her cheeks freely.

Home. Something she had long lost hope for. *Home.* A new dream.

Caring little for what anyone who might glimpse them had to say, Harcourt threw his arm over her shoulders, and led her away.

When they arrived home, they made no show of appearance, simply rushed upstairs to love each other, which took some care and planning considering Effy's condition.

They remained in their chambers all day; not even hunger was able to draw them out until well after the servants had gone to bed.

∞

The morning after Battersea Fields, Harcourt and Effy sat politely at the breakfast table. Harcourt was reading the paper and Effy had settled on a book. To the untrained eye, they were the picture of absolute normalcy and good behaviour. Though, there was not one single person in the house who was fooled by the picture.

The servants of course said nothing, but their mix of admiration, disapproval, and shock, could not be hidden, no matter how well trained they were. Their unease was also palpable, not because of the unusualness of the household they worked in, but because of the uncertainty they felt regarding their own futures.

Grinning, Harcourt slid the paper across to Effy. Eyes narrowed, she took it, perusing the front page. *Peers caught in despicable spying plot.* Mowbray, Bolton, Campbell, Russell, Almsbury; all named there as traitors to the Crown.

He watched as shock, understanding, and finally appreciation flickered across her face. She gazed up at him, the hint of a smile at the corner of her lips.

Harcourt shrugged, raising his eyebrows; he felt glad that he managed to surprise *her* for once.

'Apologies, the news of your rather extraordinary duel was relegated to the back pages.'

'You sneaky devil,' she chuckled. 'This, this is what you were keeping from me then?'

'I was not keeping it from you, *per se*,' Harcourt grinned. 'It was more a case of you did not ask, so I did not tell…'

'How,' Effy asked, dumbfounded. 'I mean… How did you know? How did you find proof?'

'I told you, they spoke very freely that night,' Harcourt said, shadows in his eyes. *Some wounds can never truly heal…* 'As for the proof, I found some very interesting letters whilst we were at Mowbray's party. I knew such a man would be careful to ensure his safety against the others, it was merely a case of finding a way into the house…'

'They will not survive this, those that are left that is,' Effy sighed, shaking her head, dropping the paper back to the table.

She studied Harcourt for a moment, wondering, well, many things.

'Harcourt, why all the rest? This, alone, would have finished them.'

'I wanted to strip it all away from them,' he said quietly. 'Every single thing they held precious. Make them suffer, make them fear. This, this was merely the *coup de grace*. Besides, I couldn't be certain they wouldn't find a way to keep the scandal quiet.'

'I understand. Are you alright, Harcourt,' she asked gently. Despite all the time they had spent together; she had never been able to bring herself to ask. 'I mean, really.'

'I will be.'

Effy nodded.

Honesty. She preferred that to empty lies and reassuring half-truths. In time, he would be. They both would be.

Together, they would find their light.

'Excuse me, sir,' George said tentatively from the door. 'Viscount Egerton is here for you.'

'Excellent, send him in George,' Harcourt waved.

'Yes, sir.'

George bowed and left.

Effy glanced over at Harcourt, and he smiled reassuringly. Moments later, George returned, announced Percy, then disappeared again.

'Percy, what a pleasant surprise,' Harcourt said, rising, offering his hand. 'You look tired, man. Coffee? Breakfast?'

'Please,' Percy said, settling himself across from Effy. He did look tired, dark shadows under his eyes, and a certain carelessness in the details of his dress which gave him a hint of dishevelment. 'I hope you don't mind -'

'Nonsense,' Harcourt said, serving him. If Percy found it in any way odd, he said nothing, only nodded graciously, sipping his coffee as though it was the elixir of life. 'You are always welcome.'

They sat in silence for a few moments whilst Percy demolished his plate and finished two servings of coffee.

There was no tension, but Harcourt and Effy both seemed to know Percy's visit was not one of pleasant courtesy.

'Thank you for that, Harcourt,' Percy sighed, leaning back in his chair, seemingly refreshed and more himself. 'I confess I have been rather busy and preoccupied the past few, well, hours.'

'Because of our mess,' Effy offered graciously. 'I am sorry we got you so involved, Percy. Truly.'

'Tush, I am not,' he said, raising his hand. 'It's all been rather exciting really. A Season to never be forgotten,' he chuckled. 'However, there are some things I thought you two should be aware of.'

Harcourt nodded, and Percy proceeded.

'Lady Almsbury has fled to America, with whatever was left of her disposable fortune, which wasn't very much considering most of it was spent keeping her in hiding and hiring the brutes that came after you. I dare say after what's come out this morning, she will never be seen nor heard from again. She was already, quite close to the edge by the time I got her onto a ship. Doubtful she will even make the journey.'

''Tis more than she deserves,' Effy spat.

Harcourt covered her hand in his, and Percy nodded.

'Effy... I, like many others, heard the rumours, but I never,' Percy said intently, begging for forgiveness. 'Please know, I would never have imagined, and stood by.'

'I know, Percy.'

'I am sorry, for what happened to you.' Effy nodded and Percy continued. 'The rest of the news I'm sure you know, or at least guessed. Society is in an uproar, between the spying, which I assume was you Sinclair, the duel, Russell's disappearance, and well, Lady Almsbury... Quite a mess really. I'm not sure if you were hoping to stay in London, I doubt it, but well, in the event you were I thought you should know you would not be welcome. Many have suffered from those you tore down, and you have more enemies than ever. I'm afraid even my dear grandmama would be obliged to cut you.'

'Thank you for your concern, Percy,' Harcourt said with a slightly reassuring, rather wolfish smile. 'But we intend to quit London as soon as we are able.'

'The Continent?'

'Indeed.'

'Excellent, well, I'm sure you will both be very happy, and get into inordinate amounts of mischief.'

'Hear, hear.'

'Well, I should be off, I'm sure you two have, *plenty* to occupy yourselves,' Percy said, a mischievous glint in his eye as he rose. 'I will see you again before you leave.'

'Of course,' Effy said, rising with Harcourt.

'Ah yes, I'd almost forgotten,' Percy said, reaching into his pocket. 'From Miss Fitzsimmons, she rather almost attacked me this morning as I set off, said this was for you.'

'Oh, thank you,' Effy said, surprised, taking the letter.

What Miss Fitzsimmons might have to say to her now was a mystery.

'Thank you for everything Percy,' Harcourt said, shaking Percy's hand. 'You've been a tremendous friend, and please know, should you ever be in need...'

'Oh yes, of course, don't worry, your debt will be called on soon enough.'

'Goodbye Percy,' Effy smiled, taking his hand.

Percy shook it, and they both beamed at each other; she had well and truly won his respect and friendship.

A wink, a nod, a bow, and he was gone. Harcourt stared at the closed door, bemused, and stunned by his good fortune for a moment, then turned back to Effy.

Frowning, she too wore a bemused smile as she perused the contents of the letter Percy had given her.

He waited, and when she had finished, she gazed up at him, the bemused smile even brighter.

'Miss Fitzsimmons congratulates me on my success at Battersea Fields,' Effy said, a chuckle beneath her words. 'She says she hopes we remain friends despite all that has passed, and thanks me for my kindness in the past weeks. She looks forward to renewing the acquaintance in the near future.'

'Well, who would have guessed that little chit knew her mind so well after all,' Harcourt mused, pulling Effy into an embrace.

'I confess I am glad she does not hate me,' Effy sighed, enjoying the feel of Harcourt all around her. *Home.* 'I always did quite like her really.'

'I don't think anyone who has met you could ever hate you. Try as I might, I never could,' he chuckled.

'You're bias though.'

'Fortescue... You don't... You don't regret getting involved with me,' he asked, suddenly serious. 'With all this revenge business?'

'Don't be daft, Harcourt.'

'Well, it isn't really a ladies affair, really, and wouldn't you have preferred, I don't know, a good, proper, respectable gentleman who didn't ask you to lie, gamble, get shot and disgrace your name?'

'You forget, my love,' Effy said, gazing up at him. 'I am not a lady.'

'Yes, that is true,' he murmured, his smile wolfish and hungry. 'I could never have loved a lady. Now, shall we go pack?'

Effy nodded and reached up to kiss his jaw.

In a second, she was in his arms and being carried up the stairs to his bedroom. She knew there would be no packing, not at least for a few hours.

Who would have guessed, she thought. *The indomitable rake fell in love with his housemaid, and I with him. What a strange turn of events.*

And yet, she knew it could never have been any other way.

The strangeness is what made it so real, and honest, and perfect.

EPILOGUE

The warm summer breeze that wafted through the lines of cypress and olive trees did nothing to cool Effy as she lounged on the white marble terrace. Her thin linen dress still clung to her, even in the shade of the looming mansion behind her. Perhaps later she would cool off in the hidden pools at the end of the lush, magnificent garden. Once the rest of the household had gone to bed.

Italian summers were a far cry from the English ones she had known her entire life, and though they had already been here a month, she still had not grown accustomed to the heat.

The seaside next, I think...

'There you are darling,' came Harcourt's voice from behind her. 'Thought I might find you here.'

Harcourt swept down, kissing her thoroughly before sprawling out on the chair beside her.

He stretched out languidly; Italy seemed to suit him. He had no problems with the heat, indeed he seemed to relish in remaining far too long beneath its harsh rays.

His skin had darkened to a rich, lush golden hue, and his hair had lightened, ever so slightly.

Italy had transformed him into a Roman god of old.

'I've been trying to find some way to cool down,' Effy said, fluttering her fan as if to punctuate her point. 'How much longer must we endure this?'

'Ready to move on so soon, my love? I thought you liked Italy, particularly after that terrible winter spent in the Swiss Alps.'

'At least in the winter I could find ways to warm myself,' she sighed, throwing him a suggestive glance. 'Black Maria will wilt if she is forced to withstand this heat much longer. Can we perhaps find somewhere by the sea next?'

'Whatever you wish,' Harcourt sighed, taking her hand, and laying a kiss in her palm. 'Though we will have to be sure to bring along some of this fine Tuscan wine…'

'Who shall we be next, then,' Effy grinned, laying her head back, closing her eyes and enjoying his touch.

Still, it held as much thrill as the first time.

A year together already, and none of their passion had faded.

'Lovers? Cousins again? I quite miss Patience…'

'We could be husband and wife for a change.'

'Are you asking me to marry you again, Harcourt,' Effy sighed.

'If I am, will you refuse me again?'

'If I refuse you again, will you keep asking?'

'Sadly, yes,' Harcourt mused, turning to gaze at Effy.

Despite the fact she despised the heat and Italian summer, it still suited her.

Romantic, laid-back, passionate Italy seemed to make her more beautiful by the day.

'I do hope one day to make an honest woman of you.'

'With whom to live a dishonest life? Ha!'

They both chuckled, and Harcourt laid his head back against the chairs, enjoying the warmth, the feel of the breeze, the touch of her hand beneath his fingers.

A year, almost to the day, since they had left London and the scandal they had created behind. Since they had begun their lavish Gypsy-like tour of France, Switzerland, and now Italy.

A year, since dashing all propriety, Harcourt and Effy had dined with the servants, and told them of their plans to leave. Since they had invited any who wished to join them on their adventure.

They had promised the shocked, and wary servants that there would be danger. There would be scandal, there would be no wedding, but there would be wine, and good times, and excitement, and love.

George and Lily had come along, the rest had stayed with the house when it had been sold.

A year, since Harcourt had passed the reins of his business onto Percy, who had been seeking some means of making use of his life. A year since the friends had parted, though Percy promised to visit them, wherever they might find themselves, soon.

A year, since Black Maria had wreaked havoc on the Continent, her reputation and fortune, and skill, growing every day.

A year, of adventures, and danger, and love.

A year, since he had begun asking Effy every day to marry him. He didn't quite know what had possessed him the first time, he wasn't the type, and Effy seemed quite content to live their little life of sin.

Perhaps it had been waking next to her the day before they left, her copper curls shining in the morning light, strands delicately laid across her body. Seeing the wound he had given her, so close to her heart.

A year of refusals.

Effy seemed reluctant to tie herself to him so conventionally, and though he did not fear she could ever leave him, lest her heart be torn from her breast, same as his, it had now become part of the game. He would ask, she would refuse.

Though one day, he mused, she might say yes. And then, he wouldn't quite be sure where he would be.

Perhaps if she ever got with child.

Then, for the sake of the babe, she might relent. Though it wasn't in their plans, and they had always been careful, he wondered if someday they might change their mind, or who knew, an accident perhaps.

He was growing increasingly fond of the idea of being a father, particularly if it was Effy who would bear his child.

A year, since their passion had grown, since their love had grown, blooming more every day, like an immortal fire.

A year, of continual surprises; the wonders of his woman it seemed, knew no bounds.

Particularly when she was looking as gorgeously inviting as this, he couldn't resist.

Gracefully, he rolled off his chair, and slid onto hers, rolling her onto him.

She made a startled cry, mock fighting him, until she settled on his lap.

'Wicked, wicked, man,' she cried, kissing him lightly with every protest. 'I was just beginning to cool down, now you have made it impossible!'

Brushing some stray tendrils from her cheeks, he took her face in his hands and brought her lips to his.

God, how could she not tire of this? This delicious, handsome man who loved her so? His lips knew her too well, still they explored deeply, intent on silencing any more resistance.

Harcourt pulled away, and she saw the satisfied, cheeky glint in his eyes, and he licked his lips, enjoying every last bit of her taste on him.

'You know, there are some delectably fresh pools at the end of the garden,' he said huskily. 'Perhaps a swim might cool you down?'

'Really, what if we are caught?'

Harcourt's eyebrow raised.

The one which still retained the scar from what seemed a lifetime ago. She sighed, passing her finger over it, thanking whatever powers responsible for bringing him to her. *My avenging angel. My twin soul.*

Relenting, she shrugged, and let Harcourt carry her away, all the way to the end of the gardens, to the cool fresh pools hidden within walls of hedges and vines, giggling as he rained kisses upon her.

They loved each other there, for the rest of the afternoon, until they could no longer resist the temptation of dinner and wine. They had time.

All the time in the world, all their lives, to love one another, whenever, however they wished. And so they would.

They would not reject the gift life had brought them, after

they had suffered so much darkness, sorrow, and pain.
Neither had ever thought they would ever dream again.
And yet, here they were, living one.

AUTHOR'S NOTE

Harcourt and Effy are very dear to me, and I hope you've enjoyed their story as much as I did writing it. I admit having always had a fondness for villains, and it is with that in mind that I began this series. I wanted to give my 'villain' a proper love story for the ages, as well as a counterpart who could be a true match for him in every way.

Going in, I knew these would be two people who had survived great trauma, and I have sought to represent their wounds and scars with respect, sensitivity, and care. To allow them to show, and share, and feel. To allow them to heal; though not magically, nor entirely. Healing is a process, and I do not believe one which has a definite end, so I found it important to represent it as such.

As a note, I do not condone vengeance as a way to deal with such trauma as these two have; that was born mainly of my great love for Edmond Dantes. Talking, and sharing, with others, and professionals is of course essential. If you or someone you know is a survivor of any trauma, please know that there are a number of charities across the world who can help.

On a more historical note, I knew before writing their story that it would end with a duel, fought by the lady, for her own honour. Though there are no records of duels fought by women in the UK, that I could find at least, there are of course many famous ones from the Continent.

Women challenging men, or other women, for reasons as serious and as ridiculous as any duel fought on British soil. My favourite, and probably, the most famous of these ladies, is Julie D'Aubigny. If you haven't heard of her, I urge you to delve into her tale.

Although there may be no official record of women fighting duels in the UK, I personally like to think that some did. Somehow, somewhere, and that the records were simply never made, or lost.

For we all know, that women who take control of their own story, their own destiny, have existed for as long as humanity itself.

ABOUT THE AUTHOR

Lotte R. James

 Lotte James trained as an actor and theatre director, but spent most of her life working day jobs crunching numbers whilst dreaming up stories of love and adventure. She's thrilled to finally be writing those stories, and when she's not scribbling on tiny pieces of paper, she can usually be found wandering the countryside for inspiration, or nestling with coffee and a book.

Be sure to keep in touch on Twitter @lottejamesbooks!

BOOKS IN THIS SERIES

Vixens & Villains

The Viscount & The Lighterman's Daughter

They've hidden their true selves - but can they find each other?

Viscount Percy Egerton nearly lost everything in the wake of his friend Harcourt Sinclair's scandal. Not even taking over a shipping company and playing night-time vigilante has helped him find what he wants most; himself. But when the daughter of one of his workers bursts into his life, he'll soon find everything he ever wished for is within his grasp, if only he has the courage to reach out...

When Meg Lowell is dismissed and forced to return home to Sailortown, she is desperate to find the means to survive, and keep her family from destitution. Clever, and hardworking, she has no fear, that is until she meets Percy, and he threatens her with the most dangerous thing of all; love.

Redemption, adventure, secrets, desire, and love in the docklands of Regency London.

The Bodyguard & The Miss

Their pasts are full of secrets – but will the dark truth set them free?

Angelique Fitzsimmons is not the girl all of Society believes her to be. Only a select few friends know of her scandalous and adventurous self, but not even they know of the terror lurking in her heart. Neither can they ever, which is why she runs away without a word. Only, she wasn't counting on the unsettling guard sent after her...

Will Hardy is nothing if not a man of his word. A year he has endured guarding Miss Fitzsimmons from no one but her reckless self; and so he must again when the spoiled chit decides to run away. But soon, he realizes there is more to her than he thought, and if only he can learn to open himself, they will both be able to find what neither was looking for to begin with. Love.

Redemption, adventure, secrets, desire, and love across Regency Britain.

BOOKS BY THIS AUTHOR

Rosemary & Pansies

When Flynn Carter is offered a job in Coombe's Cross, she can hardly refuse. Not even if that means working on Hamlet with temperamental director Clive Reid or movie-star heartthrob Jake Thornton. Her tough exterior seemed impenetrable armour enough until she met Jake...

No matter that he is here to save his career from scandal and ruin, his ego it seems hasn't suffered one bit...

But, they must learn to work together if they are to save the show, their careers, and whatever this is that is growing between them...

A sweeping and sweet low-heat contemporary love-story set in the magical world of theatre!

Printed in Great Britain
by Amazon

11338382R00141